A LIFE INCOMPLETE

A LIFE INCOMPLETE

NANAK SINGH

Translated from the Punjabi by
Navdeep Suri

HARPERPERENNIAL

HARPERPERENNIAL

First published in India in 2012 by Harper Perennial
An imprint of HarperCollins *Publishers*
4th Floor, Tower A, Building No. 10, Phase II,
DLF Cyber City, Gurugram, Haryana -122002
www.harpercollins.co.in

This edition published in India in 2019 by Harper Perennial

2 4 6 8 10 9 7 5 3 1

P-ISBN: 978-93-5302-490-1
E-ISBN: 978-93-5302-659-2

Typeset in 10.5/14 Scala at
SÜRYA

Printed and bound in India by
Manipal Technologies Limited, Manipal

More Fact than Foreword

I like to escape to the verdant hills to put the finishing touches to my novels. In keeping with this annual pilgrimage to the Himalayan foothills, I reached Dalhousie on 15 September 1940, carrying with me the manuscript of my latest novel *Jeevan Sangram*. But the solitude that I craved proved elusive. Just too many people, too much noise. This was not the Dalhousie of yore.

Within a couple of days, a feeling of restlessness enveloped me and I decided that there was no point in staying on. On 20 September, I hired a porter who could carry my modest belongings and we started walking with no particular destination in mind, simply a vague notion that we would drop anchor when we reached a quiet, scenic spot. I wanted to spend four or five days in a place like that so that I could gather my thoughts and perhaps scribble a few pages.

I started the descent from Dalhousie along the lush green banks of the Raavi as it hurtled through the valleys. Inappropriately nicknamed Skinny, the porter was a burly, loquacious fellow and a native of these hills. Over the next four days, we happily traversed vast meadows, climbed narrow trails and chatted about anything that came to mind. My hill mate had a vast repertoire of local folk songs to keep me entertained. His favourite, clearly, was one titled '*The Brahmin's boy*' which he sang with a particular verve.

Looking back, I don't think I've ever enjoyed myself as much as I did during those four days. True, my legs and knees often got bruised over the steep climbs and slippery descents. True also that the soles of my shoes pretty much gave way. But the sheer joy and abandon of those days will forever linger in my consciousness.

On the fifth day, we crossed the Raavi to enter Chamba district, rested for the night and resumed our journey the following morning. Skinny belonged to Chamba and his simple songs seemed to acquire an extra note or two as he approached his birthplace. We took a narrow track that afforded magnificent views of mountains covered with foliage and adorned by a multitude of flowers. Looking down, we could see a string of crystalline streams snaking their way across the slopes. Labouring under the substantial load that he was carrying uphill, Skinny was now sweating profusely. But unmindful of his exertion, he continued to sing the local melody:

Lost is the damsel's mind
In the brooks of Chamba
Yea in the brooks of Chamba
It rains and she finds joy
In the arms of her lover boy
Yea, lost is the damsel's mind.
And the Prince of Chamba
He wants special tribute
A look, a glance
From the damsel's eyes so cute
O lost is that damsel's mind.

Lost in the melody of his favourite song, he appeared oblivious of the fact that the ascent was becoming precarious. His foot slipped only for a brief second but this was enough for the weight on his back to unbalance him completely. I saw him as he toppled over and tumbled a good ten or twelve yards down the slope. It must have been his lucky day because a rock protruding across our path broke his fall and stopped him from plunging into the unknown depths of the ravine where he would have vanished without a trace.

Reaching out to him, I removed the load from his back and saw that apart from several nasty bruises, he also appeared to have fractured his right arm midway between the shoulder and elbow. The poor fellow was in severe pain and to make matters worse, we were in a remote area with not a soul in sight. I pulled out the tincture iodine that I always carry in my baggage and applied it to his cuts and bruises. Using a small towel, I also bandaged his fractured arm and helped him lie down in a soft area near a bush before setting off to look for help. I hadn't walked for long before I chanced upon two local boys who seemed to be coming up the hill in our direction. Telling them about our accident, I offered them a generous reward if they could help us out of our predicament.

The boys spoke of an exceptionally pious soul who lived in a cottage some two and a half miles away. The saint was deeply respected for his knowledge of both Western and traditional medicines which he dispensed free of charge to anyone in need. That would be the place for our patient, the boys said.

One of the boys picked up my baggage, while the other gave a hand to Skinny as we set off for the saint's abode. The path was difficult and it took us over two hours to get there. As we walked, the boys spoke in hushed tones about the saint. 'His selfless devotion is just out of this world...he goes around to the homes of the poorest to treat them...day and night, he tirelessly visits the sick and the destitute, offering treatment to some, solace to others...' And so on.

Upon reaching the cottage, we set our patient under an ancient tree. I gave a generous tip to the boys for their efforts and, after bidding them farewell, paused to take in the surroundings. It was like a small corner of paradise itself. The romance of the verdant hills and valleys around me was enhanced by the beauty of the saint's simple abode.

His cottage was not particularly large. But clad in vines and creepers and set amidst a variety of fruit trees, it seemed blessed with a very special charm. 'What a lovely setting to complete my novel,' I thought as soon as I set my eyes on this place.

Before entering his cottage, I had visualized the saint as the usual mendicant with matted hair and saffron robes. To my surprise, he appeared a perfectly regular sort of person, around fifty years old and possibly belonging to the Sikh faith. Dressed in a simple, khadi attire, a hint of grey in his flowing beard, it was his eyes that gave a sense of the extraordinary. They were sparkling, alive and vibrant even as they radiated that rare tranquillity which very few attain. He was surrounded by a largish group of patients, a crowd that was perhaps larger than usual because of a recent outbreak of malaria in the district. I greeted him with folded hands and he responded, not with the gesture of blessings so typical of saints and holy men but with a polite 'Sat Sri Akal' that reflected his Sikh background.

Turning to my patient, he gently cleaned his injuries, bandaged his arm and arranged for him to lie down on a bed.

He then opened the door of an adjoining room and asked me to relax while he completed his work. The room was full of shelves and cupboards lined with all manner of medicines – the kind of stuff one would be lucky to find in a reasonably well-stocked city clinic. How did he manage to assemble all of it in such a remote location? I wondered.

After spending the entire day amidst his patients, the saint walked into the room just as I had finished eating my dinner. Sitting down in front of me, he looked closely at my face and asked, 'Are you Nanak Singh?'

'Yes,' I replied. 'How did you recognize me?'

'All your earlier books carried your photograph,' he replied. He added that he had read quite a few of my works.

He paused for a while before saying, 'I've really been looking forward to the opportunity of meeting a writer like you. I am fortunate that you have come here because I want to tell you my own tale. I believe that once you have heard me out, you will probably have enough material for a new novel.'

What does a blind man want but two eyes? Instead of putting together a story from my own imagination, I was being offered one on a platter. Readily accepting his proposal, I sat down to listen to his narrative. It took well over three hours for him to complete his fascinating story and when he finished, both of us had tears in our eyes. He then got up and took me across to the first room. Opening a cupboard, he handed me a small wooden box and said, 'Here! That's the rest of the material for your novel.'

Opening the box, I saw an old notebook, its cover on the verge of separation from the rest of the body. Every page, every available space of the notebook had been used to write. Even the insides of the covers were filled with jottings from top to bottom. It looked like pages from someone's diary, each section clearly marked with the year, month and date. The writing was in neat, clearly legible Punjabi script and it seemed to have a certain feminine touch.

The box also had a small photo, of a young lad, perhaps fourteen or fifteen years old. The photo was in a terrible condition, as if someone had torn it into small pieces and then tried to put it together like some sort of jigsaw puzzle. The effort had succeeded only in part because it looked like a couple of small pieces were still missing. In addition to the photo, the box also contained a few letters, a plain kerchief and a paper that looked like someone's will. A closer look at the document revealed that a gentleman by the name of Ganga Vishan had decided to bequeath a fortune of some twenty-five thousand rupees to his son-in-law. It was dated February 1923.

Reflecting on the contents of the box and the three-hour-long narrative of that noble soul, I instantly knew that I had enough material for a full-fledged novel. After handing over the box to me, he approached the bottom shelf of his cupboard and pulled out a small sketch, a portrait. 'I made this,' he said. 'Although it does pertain to your future novel, I can't part with it. Some of my most precious memories are embedded in it.' Sighing deeply, he closed his eyes, possibly to hide the fact that they had again become moist.

The portrait carried the title 'Adh Khidya Phul'.

That portrait and the story behind it also had a profound impact on me and, as I started to absorb everything I had heard, my mind drifted to another set of events that I had myself experienced. The vicissitudes of life over the last few years had temporarily erased those pages from my mind's diary but that day those painful memories were revived. A similar flower had blossomed in my life too, at a time when I had just about crossed over from childhood into youth. But it had withered away before it could bloom fully.

The powerful effect of that noble soul's narrative, and the revival of my own distant memories, persuaded me to set aside my nearly complete manuscript of *Jeevan Sangram* and I started to work on a new novel which I tentatively titled *Adh Khidya Phul*.

The title of the portrait was not the only inspiration behind the name of this novel. Some eighteen years ago, I had started to write a similar story. This was in 1922, when I had been imprisoned by the colonial authorities for participating in the Guru ka Bagh agitations that sought to free the management of Sikh shrines from British cronies and restore their traditional independence. Some 1500 of us were incarcerated in Borstal Jail in Lahore for persisting in our campaign. While in prison, I ran into a prisoner who had been recently transferred from Gurgaon Jail. He had been imprisoned for his involvement in the Satyagraha that had been launched by the Indian National Congress. He was carrying a set of novels by the legendary Munshi Premchand. Reading his absorbing works provided me the motivation that I too could start putting my thoughts on paper and perhaps strive to become a novelist. I contrived a simplistic sort of structure and started writing my first novel, which I called *Adh Khidya Phul*. But in a search carried out by the prison authorities, my manuscript was confiscated and I could never again lay my hands on it. The abrupt loss of my first effort also nipped my literary ambitions in the bud and it was years before I could pick up the threads again.

And as I started to write this new novel with that old title, I also started to remember the storyline of my first effort. I spent around three weeks in that hermitage to write this novel, which draws less on imagination and more on actual events.

NANAK SINGH
Amritsar, 1940

1

May 1922. It is around midnight and pitch dark. Not a leaf stirs. And the occasional puff of breeze that has lost its way and entered the confines of the prison, too, is scalding, like the heart of a jilted lover.

The forbidding walls of Borstal Jail hold thousands of prisoners within their grim perimeter. Many of them languish in hundreds of tiny funereal cells. Burglars, dacoits, fraudsters and murderers are the denizens of this township, locked up in its cages, reaping the punishment for their crimes. Of late, however, a new kind of inhabitant has come to occupy this parish. Innocent of any wrongdoing, the fresh arrivals have cheerfully stepped into the ogre's den as reward for their unflinching commitment to their country and to their religion. Numbering in their thousands, they are the activists of the Guru ka Bagh campaign.

Ward No. 3 is the temporary abode of these valiant patriots and defenders of the faith. Sentenced for terms ranging from six months to two and a half years, they spend interminably long, sleepless nights and count the days. Hot, humid and stuffy, the night is nothing short of hell for the prisoners. Most people would be sleeping soundly in the comfort of their beds at this time. But only a person who has spent a precious part of his life in captivity can understand how long a prisoner's night can be. The searing heat and buzzing mosquitoes are of course a nuisance even if you are sleeping out in the open. For the unfortunate prisoners lying on coarse blankets in cramped, ten-square-foot cells, however, the tortures of these summer nights are of a different magnitude.

Around 8 in the evening, the prisoners are rounded up into their cells, which are then closed with large padlocks. They say that after a day's hard labour even a bed of nails can look inviting. It may hold true for those who can go to bed and wake up according to their free will, whose hearts are not being constantly pierced by the barbed arrows of forced separation from their loved ones, for those who are outside the depressing confines of the prison. The prisoner's sleep, however, is quite different; he lies on the hard floor of his cell, painstakingly counting every day, week and month since his separation from friends and family, measuring how many have gone by and how many remain. When he closes his eyes, he sees the day's hard labour in the prison compound, hears the constant grind of the flour mill, the screeching and whirring of the oil seeds crusher on which he has toiled countless hours. The body is uncomfortable and the soul restless. Eyes ache from the unending wait for that moment when the sleep fairy will come and gently carry him away in its lap.

It is around midnight, the time when guards start their third shift for the night, when the prisoners can fly on the wings of the sleep fairy, leaving the confines of their gloomy cells to visit their loved ones, to fleetingly embrace them. When sons hug their mothers and try to quench the pain of separation, husbands join their spouses and become oblivious of their hardship and suffering, and sisters are dumbstruck as they listen to their brothers' plight in prison.

For the guards, it is the time of the night when prisoners appear to be sound asleep. With one exception, however. The occupant of Cell No. 13 is a young man of around twenty-five. Hands gripping the iron bars of his cell, he is peering intently into the impenetrable darkness of the night outside.

The young Sikh is light skinned and of a slender build, with a short auburn beard on his handsome face. His restless gaze suggests a certain fickleness of mind, raising doubts about the courage of the heart beating under his firm chest. Of course, it is probably easier to guess the dimensions of the pearl without opening the oyster than it is to figure out what the human heart is capable of. Only the rarest of souls are blessed with the ability to discern the contents of a letter without even opening the envelope and it should come as no surprise if an ordinary mortal fails in this task.

The courtyard outside is dark and deserted but the prisoner's intense concentration suggests that he sees something. He is clad only in baggy shorts and a short-sleeved tunic with regulation prison stripes, and his hands frequently leave the iron bars to itch a rash, to shoo away a mosquito buzzing around his ears or to extract his revenge by swatting at one camping on his neck and merrily feasting on his blood. Visibly restless and uncomfortable, he seeks escape from the mosquitoes by backing away from the bars and wrapping himself in the blanket. But this only takes him from the frying pan into the fire. Within minutes, the effect of the blanket on a hot and muggy night has him sweating and feeling suffocated. Casting aside the blanket, he moves around in the cell for a while before resuming his vigil at the bars.

A large mulberry tree stands a short distance away in the courtyard. With not a leaf stirring in the still of the night, it vaguely resembles a shapeless mound. Gazing intently at it, a thought crosses the prisoner's mind, 'Isn't this tree a prisoner like me, standing for years at the same place, waiting for liberation from its endless captivity?' He looks at the dark form of the tree with sadness and trepidation. Hearing the sound of a sparrow emanate from the direction of the tree, he thinks, 'Perhaps this unfortunate one is also missing the companion who left their nest after a squabble and hasn't yet returned.' The bird's cry sounds to him like the wailing of a young bride who has been separated from her husband.

He sees a young maiden of around twenty, bright eyes brimming with tears as she pines for her lover. Juxtaposed to this image, another scene flashes in his mind's eye. This one shows a newly married girl of about eighteen, silky eyelashes hiding a dreamy-eyed expression as she thinks of her husband and of the joys that marriage has brought her. Long hair cascade all the way to her slender waist, her arms – adorned with the red bangles of the newly wed – look like they are straining to embrace her loved one. In a flicker, however, his mind shifts to another image – this one as disturbing as it is heart-rending. The comely face is now ablaze with anger; those loving eyes smoulder like embers, and flames of jealousy leap from every pore of her delicate frame. Her words are like deadly arrows aimed straight at the hapless young man who faces her. 'I've seen the true colours of your love...who would have thought that you would turn out to be such a fraud...nectar on your lips and poison in your heart...go and marry her if you want...oh, my fate...couldn't the nurse have given me poison the day I was born and spared me this misery...I must be accursed...'

His face a picture of torment, he responds, 'Don't accuse me like that, for god's sake...I am innocent...It is true that I have loved her, but it was purely platonic...I'll leave this place for ever if you continue to riddle my heart with your accusations...I swear I'll never see your face again.'

The sparrow again starts to chirp in the willow tree and this time it seems to be taunting him, 'Go if you want to...your threats don't scare me...trying to mask your guilt with these ploys, aren't you?'

A train passes by in the distance, its clatter more audible in the still of the night than it would have been during the day. The young man sees himself in the train as it speeds into the night, leaving his beloved far behind. The train is heading for Lahore and Amritsar and, as the lights of Peshawar dwindle in the distance, he feels the light of his own life dimming. His heart pounds louder than the rhythmic chug of the steam engine.

A voice from the watch tower calls, 'Number 3! Akali Barracks! All okay.' To his ears, however, the words echo the sacred war cry of the Sikhs, 'Bole so Nihal; Sat Sri Akal'. Buoyed by its repeated chants, the Akali armies seem to be marching ahead towards their goal.

This view from behind the bars is a familiar one, something that he has become accustomed to during his six months in the prison. Always the same outstretched arms of his beloved, the pulsating breasts, the pining eyes and the cascading tresses. He senses himself bridging the distance between them, getting close enough to touch her, to quell the pangs of separation, to satisfy his unquenchable thirst for her. But somewhere in the neighbourhood, the gongs of a large clock strike loud into the still night, instantly shattering his reverie, leaving him lost and disoriented. The clock strikes another four times before falling silent, satisfied that the listener is reeling under its impact.

His dream has vanished. Even the chirping sparrow in the tree has become quiet, silenced perhaps by the deafening toll of the bell. A few minutes later, he hears the sound of measured, heavy footsteps heading in his direction.

It is the sentry on his beat, patrolling the ward at regular intervals from four to seven in the morning. He wears the conventional khaki uniform, a red stripe running through his matching turban, a large bunch of keys perched on his shoulder. He stops in front of Cell No. 13, grasps one of the bars and says, 'Hello there, Kuldeep Singh! All well? Didn't sleep much, did you?'

'No, Ahmed Khan,' the prisoner replies, looking at him affectionately. 'One, this oppressive heat; two, the wretched mosquitoes perforating the body wherever they can. How does one sleep under these circumstances?'

'And three?' the sentry enquires with a mischievous glint in his eye. 'Why don't you just admit that it is the lovely one with the red bangles who is not letting you sleep? But don't you worry too much. Another five or seven days and you'll be free – the entire lot of you. I've been working in these prisons for over a decade now and the pattern is clear. Two kinds of prisoners find it hard to sleep; the ones that are condemned to be hanged and the ones whose release is imminent.'

Ahmed Khan belongs to the Frontier province, the same part of the country where Kuldeep Singh too was born and brought up. Within the confines of a prison, the relationship between a jailor and a prisoner is not unlike the one between a wolf and a lamb. But that is hardly the case with these two. Hailing from the same province, they have established a nodding acquaintance which is now rapidly growing into a genuine friendship.

A prisoner could be doing time in jail for a criminal offence or for his political leanings, but a mention of the word 'release' has a very special sweetness about it. Only the prisoner knows how it can lift the spirits and light up the heart. Kuldeep has heard rumours over the last few days that the authorities were planning to release those arrested during the Guru ka Bagh agitations. The rumours become more tangible when the warden taunts them by saying, 'Go on...enjoy these coarse chapattis while you can...in a few days they will become no more than a distant memory.'

But hearing from Ahmed Khan that their release could be imminent makes his sleepless eyes close involuntarily. Feeling inebriated with a new sense of anticipation that is only heightened by the sentry's smiling reference to his lovely red-bangled one, his arms ache to reach out and bring her into his embrace.

'So what are you thinking?' the sentry enquires, slipping his arm between the bars to grasp the prisoner's arm. 'Or would you like me to take a shot at delving into your mind?'

'Go ahead,' Kuldeep replies, peering through the dim light to discern the teasing smile in his friend's eyes.

'Ok, here's what your mind is saying:

If only I were a bird
Flying to soothe my lover
To make our peace
And bring her closer
I swear by God,
Not a moment to lose
Nor a day's delay
And another night of separation

'Have I guessed right?' he asks. 'Although I have to say that she is the one who should be soothing you.'

'No, Ahmed Khan,' Kuldeep sighs. 'I am the one who will have to do the appeasing. The greater blame lies with me for having acted in such haste. Sure, she got into a huff and told me to go away. But does that mean that I should have actually walked out on her like this?'

'But if an innocent man is accused in this fashion...?' the sentry asks, a furrow creasing his gentle countenance.

'Of course her accusation was false, Ahmed Khan,' Kuldeep interjects. 'But I too was at fault. I know that my love for Saroj was platonic but surely I should have been more sensitive about my wife's feelings. A wife wouldn't put up with her husband if she feels that he cares more for his sister or mother than he does for her. And in this case, Saroj isn't even distantly related to me. So the suspicions that our relationship aroused in Satwant's mind are perfectly understandable. If I had handled the situation calmly and responded with greater maturity, things wouldn't have gotten out of hand. I am the one who got into a huff and rushed off.'

He sighs again as a long-dormant memory springs unexpectedly from the distant past and fleetingly overlaps with his thoughts of Satwant.

This wonderful part of the human body that we call our heart has so many different chambers, so many layers that we are often unaware of what lies beneath the surface. But every now and then the subconscious triggers a chain reaction that lifts the lid off one of the chambers to reveal something from the long-forgotten past. Kuldeep's experience is similar.

'But listen, my friend,' the sentry says teasingly, 'you pine for your wife day and night. How come she has never come to visit you? Even the most distant of relatives has the courtesy to pay a visit every month or two to a family member who is in jail.'

Ahmed Khan's friendly barb is like a thorny bush scraping against Kuldeep's bare torso. Hiding his pain and embarrassment, he mumbles, 'You do not know, Ahmed Khan. Would she not have visited me if she had been able to? Unfortunately, her condition did not permit her to come.'

Nodding in sympathy, the sentry says, 'So be it. Let us also talk about something else. You don't sleep all night. What's the matter? Are you trying to kill yourself?'

'Look here,' he points to his chest and says, 'Satwant lives inside my heart. So there is no question of my dying.' His face has an ethereal bliss as his thoughts again focus on his beloved.

'Oh sure! And is that why your face has shrunk to the size of a snail!' The sentry smiles affectionately at him. 'You've already lost at least twelve pounds. Now, if you continue to spend sleepless nights you are going to shrivel up and start resembling a shrimp. You'll get home and she won't even recognize you.'

Kuldeep embraces the warmth cloaked in Ahmed Khan's jests and replies, 'Don't you worry, my friend. All signs of weakness will vanish the moment I catch a glimpse of Satwant. Give me a fortnight after my release and I am willing to wager that it is you who won't be able to recognize me.' Pausing for a moment, he says more seriously, 'I must confess, my dear friend, that I am becoming rather fond of you. So make sure you don't act like a policeman when it comes to our friendship.'

'The five fingers are never the same,' Ahmed Khan says as

his hand moves through the bars to clasp Kuldeep's. 'Insha Allah, our friendship will be the envy of those around us.'

'Alas!' Kuldeep sighs. 'Wouldn't it have been wonderful if we had belonged to the same faith?'

'Don't you talk like a fool!' Ahmed Khan admonishes even as he tightens his grip on Kuldeep's hand. 'Does love have any religion?'

'Really?' Kuldeep exclaims with unconcealed excitement. 'Will you stand by this friendship?'

'Insha Allah Ta'la.' Ahmed extends his arm through the bars and thumps Kuldeep's back. 'If God keeps me alive, I swear that I will make our friendship an example for the world to marvel.'

Kuldeep's eyes well with emotion and a couple of teardrops gently descend down his cheeks as his friend continues, 'Kuldeep, God Almighty is my witness when I say that I've come to love you more than my own brother. I just can't fathom this magic spell that you've cast on me.'

'Didn't you say,' Kuldeep murmurs as he feels the warmth of Ahmed's embrace through the bars, 'that you will take a month off and come to Peshawar?'

'I'd like to, if I can get my leave sanctioned.'

'Satwant will be absolutely delighted to meet you,' Kuldeep muses as he savours the prospect of a visit by his friend. 'Just think of the kind of respect that she will have for you once I tell her of all that you have done for me. We've been married for two and a half years now and I have to say that a great virtue of Satwant's is her unfailing courtesy towards my friends.'

'Of course I will come,' Ahmed responds with barely disguised pleasure. 'But for now, you are the one who has to accept your sister-in-law's hospitality.'

'Well!' Kuldeep smiles. 'Do you think I am going to force myself on my bhabhi uninvited? Shouldn't you get her permission first? Surely you don't want me walking into your home, only to find her taking refuge behind her veil and retreating into a corner!'

'Don't you worry about that! We bade goodbye to the burkha quite a while back. And as far as getting her permission is concerned, she is the one who has been after me, insisting that you have to come home.'

'Is that so? What does she say?' Kuldeep enquires, noticing his friend's eyes shine with affection.

'She has declared that if my friend leaves town without meeting her, I won't deserve to see her face for the rest of my life.'

'Amazing! I don't meet her and your marriage goes into the dustbin? For you, that must be worse than getting a life sentence. I guess that I just have to meet her before I go. But did she really say this or is it all part of your wonderful imagination?'

'The proof of the pudding lies in the eating, doesn't it?' Ahmed Khan retorts resolutely.

The clock strikes six, nudging Ahmed Khan to move on. 'A whole hour has gone by while we were chatting,' he observes as he reluctantly tears himself away.

Kuldeep is suddenly overcome with sleep. As a cool early-morning breeze wafts into the cell, he drifts into his paradise with Satwant as soon as his head touches the low earthen platform that serves as his bed.

2

The smallish house of about one and a half floors is located near the tonga stand that serves the needs of passengers using the Peshawar Sadar railway station. It is a modest dwelling, reflecting the middle-class status of its residents. At one time, this used to be a sparsely populated neighbourhood, with no more than ten or fifteen similar dwellings spread around in no particular pattern. The hay market was situated to the right of these houses, while the Frontier High School lay to the left. The horse carriages of the tonga stand were scattered along the road in front of the houses, while a smaller lane behind them led to Nathiha village. The passage of years, however, has wrought such changes in the neighbourhood that if one of its earlier residents wandered into the area today, he would struggle to find a single familiar building. Those modest dwellings have been replaced by an impressive housing development called Sahib Ganj because the prime investor is one Dr Sahib Singh. The hay market has also vanished, making way for the palatial bungalows of the great Khans. Spanking new four-storey buildings have come up where the tonga repair shacks used to conduct their daily business.

The house has three rooms in all, two on the ground floor and one upstairs. It has been rented by Sadhu Singh. He and his wife occupy the two rooms on the ground floor, leaving the room on the upper floor for his son and daughter-in-law. During the last six months, the room upstairs has housed just one occupant, their daughter-in-law.

Sadhu Singh is a frail, slightly built man of around fifty.

Over the years, a combination of acute asthma and an addiction to opium has reduced his slender frame to a mere skeleton. He works as a trader of gur and sugar in the Pipal Market area of the town. The work is seasonal, lasting no more than three or four months of the year. He does precious little for the remaining months but the handsome earnings during the busy season are more than adequate to last the whole year.

Despite his attachment to opium, Sadhu Singh is regarded as a noble, god-fearing soul with deeply traditional views. He has risen above the common traits of deceit or deception. His religious beliefs, too, seem shorn of partisanship. For Sikhs coming to his door to collect funds for a guru's festival, he readily parts with a rupee and a quarter with folded hands. And Hindus raising money to commemorate the Goddess Kali also know that he will give them whatever he can muster. His wrist displays the steel bracelet that symbolizes his commitment to the Sikh faith, and around his neck he wears the sacred Hindu thread. During troubled times, he goes to the neighbourhood gurudwara and pays for a special recitation of the Sikh scriptures from the Guru Granth Sahib. But it is Shankar, the Brahmin priest at the temple, whom he seeks during the shradh period when he has to propitiate the family's departed elders. His daily routine includes recitation of the Japuji Sahib and also the eighteenth chapter from the Gita. He has just one offspring, Kuldeep Singh, who participated in the Guru ka Bagh agitation and has been in prison for the last six months. A prison sentence in defence of your faith – for Sadhu Singh this is more a matter of pride than a source of anxiety about his son's welfare. If anything, it is Kuldeep's altercation with his wife and his decision to leave their home without informing anyone that bother him a lot more.

He is married to Gian Kaur, a woman who bears no resemblance to the knowledge or enlightenment that her name suggests. Short and heavily built, she appears some five or seven years younger than her husband. Like him, she also professes complete devotion to her religious scriptures but it is her volatile temper that really sets them apart. It is either the hapless Sadhu Singh himself or their daughter-in-law, or usually the maidservant Radhia who are the principal targets of her venomous rage. Gian Kaur is also a devout disciple of the patron saint of Hoti and is seldom seen without the rosary that she obtained from his shrine. But the beads of the rosary do little to dilute her anger and she seems completely untouched by the humility and spirituality for which the sage is renowned.

Gian Kaur's daughter-in-law has been virtually bedridden since the day Kuldeep left their home. There is no dearth of theories about Satwant Kaur's sudden and somewhat mysterious illness, with two schools of thought predominating in the neighbourhood. The first believes that it is nothing but pangs of separation following her husband's abrupt departure that have pushed her into this state, while the other firmly ascribes it to the mistreatment that she suffers at the hands of her mother-in-law. Or, perhaps, there is a grain of truth in both!

There is little doubt that ever since her son's departure two dominant themes have emerged in Gian Kaur's vocabulary. Her chants of 'Waheguru, Waheguru' seem to resonate louder than usual as her fingers maintain their incessant rhythm over the beads of the rosary. Punctuating her praise of the wondrous god are the curses that she intermittently hurls in the direction of her daughter-in-law, with some of the choicest abuse reserved for the ones who gave birth to her and brought her into this world.

Kuldeep had already been away for four months when Satwant gave birth to a son. Her health progressively deteriorated and, within the family, there is now a firm belief that she is suffering from the dreaded tuberculosis. With this in mind, a wet nurse hailing from one of the poorer states of eastern India has been hired to tend to the baby. The child has been removed from Satwant's room and all contact with the mother is forbidden even as the poor thing longs to nurse him.

Radhia, who joined the household to double up as maid and wet nurse, is married to a horse keeper named Ganga Ram. Herself a mother of four, she often comes to work with a daughter in tow, who is no more than a year and a half old, leaving behind at home her three older children. It was tough going in the beginning. Radhia lived in the Lal Kurti market which is some distance away. Returning to her home after sundown and then rising early to cook for her own family meant that she was inevitably late in arriving at Sadhu Singh's place. Meanwhile, Satwant's famished child wailed at the top of his voice, creating an air of panic and consternation for everyone around him. A resolution to this daily crisis was urgently needed, and Sadhu Singh showed the wisdom of his years by renting a modest dwelling very close to his own place to accommodate Radhia's family.

Not that Radhia is exactly an angel. Dishonest, cunning and insolent, she is a tough woman to handle. Gian Kaur cannot stand Radhia's proclivity to pinch whatever she can from the kitchen. The lethal mixture of Radhia's attitude and Gian Kaur's temperament has become the cause of daily warfare between mistress and maid.

Radhia's complexion is dark as coal and the absence of three or four front teeth has left a gaping hole in her mouth. She has small eyes, a rotund belly and a slight limp that does little to impede her hurried gait. When suckling Satwant's child, the foremost thought in her mind is to prevent him from taking too much, lest it leaves too little for her own daughter. Gian Kaur gives her at least a litre of milk every morning, yet fails to silence her daily refrain, 'Oh! What am I to do? There's hardly any milk in my breast. I am sure my daughter is going to starve. Such exploitation! If I get nothing to eat or drink, where will the milk come from?'

Her behaviour is a nuisance for everyone in the house. Gian Kaur has caught her stealing on more than one occasion. Nothing major, mind you. Just the occasional handful of sugar whisked away from the jar to disappear into a neat little bundle in a corner of her sari. Or an attack on the cream accumulated on the surface of freshly boiled milk, a swift move that lifts a handful of cream from the milk pan and delivers it straight into the gaping mouth of her daughter. Or a bowl or tumbler tucked under her armpit as she leaves for the day. Or a few annas pinched each time she goes to buy something from the market. Not that her petty thieving brings any visible prosperity to her house. Her husband is an inveterate alcoholic, and a slacker to boot. He has seldom retained a job for more than a few days, his attachment to liquor ensuring that he gets into an ugly fight with his employers and speedily returns to his good-for-nothing status. Whatever Radhia brings home, through honest toil or through her pilfering, sinks into the same bottomless pit.

Despite all her evident shortcomings, Gian Kaur finds it difficult to get rid of Radhia. She is constantly on the lookout for a better alternative and has quietly put out the word that she is looking for someone reliable. But a decent wet nurse is hard to find and the mistress reluctantly swallows her pride and does what she can to placate the maid and retain her services.

The last couple of days have been particularly difficult. Radhia has been acting strangely and has even refused to come to work, leaving poor Sadhu Singh no option but to visit her place and make a special appeal to her husband. The trouble, apparently, started the previous day when she was feeding Satwant's boy. She was trying to pull him away from her breast and he continued to cling to it. Infuriated, she slapped the child just as Gian Kaur was passing by and all hell broke loose.

Radhia, of course, has her own grievances. Despite her efforts to give the lion's share of her milk to her own daughter, it is the boy who is growing healthier. Her girl, in contrast, is getting weaker by the day, often suffering from an upset stomach and diarrhoea. Radhia's overfeeding of her daughter and plying her with any cream that she can lay her hands on have ironically become the principal cause of her ill health. Plagued by jealousy, she dreams of swapping the dark skin and weakness of her girl with the boy's fair skin and robust health.

3

At first sight, the upper floor of Sadhu Singh's house looks like a completely unnecessary appendage. Scarcely can a sound be heard emerging from it, nor can any activity be discerned. There is seldom any visitor to the room. Like a shroud, a deathly silence envelops the space. But if one can pierce this veneer and look inside, there is much that he might find in this apparently deserted room.

A flight of stairs leads from the common area in the ground floor to a doorway at the top. A darkish doorframe supports a set of two doors that open inwards into the room. Perhaps intentionally, the hinges have been placed in a way that the doors close on their own, shutting out the world to the occupant of the sombre room that lies on one side. The cries of pain emitting periodically from the occupant seem to float up to the doors and crash right back into the room. And if a muffled groan occasionally manages to escape the confines of the doors to arrive in the living area downstairs, it is received with studied disinterest. The listeners, it appears, have tuned their ears to subconsciously block out this unwanted sound.

A gentle push on the doors is enough to allow the visitor to enter. Like the shutter of a mousetrap, however, they close the moment you step into this space. A small toilet with a single door stands in the right corner of the room. This door, too, has a mind of its own and it insists on swinging open even after you think you have closed it firmly.

A three-panelled door on the left leads to the room. The panels on the left and right are mostly closed, while the one in the centre tends to remain open. Something brushes against your head as you enter the room. It is a dried twig from the auspicious acacia tree, tied with a red string to the top of the door frame. Most of the leaves have withered and fallen away, perhaps knocked off their perch by some heartless gust of wind. How long will the last few drops of sap keep this dying twig alive? When will a noble hand appear to pull down this unnecessary adornment and cast it away? The lower ends of the doorframe bear large, oily stains. Over time, the accumulation of dust has turned them into ugly patches of grime. Had the room witnessed an auspicious moment, when oil had been symbolically poured at the corners of the doorstep to welcome a new arrival? Will some gracious spirit come to scrape off these unwanted memories?

Enter the room and you see a window in front. Shutters ajar, it opens into the street below. Nestling against the wall right below the window is a plain-looking cot. It is woven from coarse twine and the ropes holding it together have clearly frayed and broken at several places. A few knots here and there are evidence of attempts to reunite the broken bits.

A crumpled brown sheet and a plain cotton mat provide the occupant of the bed some protection against the rough fibres of its twine. Sobs of grief punctuate the low moans of pain emanating from the huddled frame of the patient. The room has a rather bare look about it. A couple of medicine bottles, a small cup and a mug with a thin spout sit haphazardly on a small table near the foot of the bed. Giving them company are seven or eight little paper wraps containing an assortment of medication, some looking visibly damp from contact with water or other liquids spilt on the table. A black steel trunk rests near the corner of the window and perched on it is a smaller, beige-coloured relative with small motifs. An upturned glass tumbler, possibly one that had contained milk, is the centre of attention for an army of brown ants marching in a single file to a spot near the head of the bed. Perhaps the contents of the inverted tumbler have already been polished off, because more ants appear to be making the trek back from the tumbler than those heading towards it. It is tough to determine if the ones returning have enjoyed a meal or are coming back disappointed.

From the patient's ashen face it looks like all lifeblood has drained out of her body. A set of red bangles adorns her skeletal wrists, lurching along with every movement of her arms. Every time she straightens her arm above her head, the bangles chase each other up her elbow and all the way to her upper arm. A hint of a smile flickering on her pale lips, she looks wistfully at the antics of her bangles and lets out a deep sigh. Her expression is reminiscent of the farmer seeing his ripe crop decimated by an untimely hailstorm and murmuring, 'O God! Such is your design!' She is reminded, perhaps, of the day before her wedding. Her friends had struggled to slide the bangles over her hands so that they could reach her wrists. They seemed too small for her and a few drops of blood had emerged from fresh scratches to mingle with the crimson shade of the bangles. Tears of pain had welled in her eyes but the promise of imminent companionship and conjugal bliss embodied in the bangles was enough to mask momentary discomfort. Much like her smile now conceals her dejection and despair.

Her head rests on a pillow with a scruffy, stained cover. The usual dirt and dust have mixed with the oil from her hair to give it a particularly discoloured appearance. The central portion of the pillow cover is worn out and frayed from constant rubbing against her head. A greenish sheet covers her frail body, extending all the way up to her bosom. One bare arm lies by her side, while the other rests gently on her chest. Her gently heaving bosom, so empty, can be discerned under her kameez. Empty, because of the gaping void left by her unfulfilled aspirations, by pangs of separation, by the relentless assault of remorse and guilt, and by the incessant taunts and insults that she has to endure. Ever since her husband's incarceration, she too has been sentenced to confinement in this room. Kuldeep's parents have visited him in prison on at least three occasions without giving him the slightest idea of his wife's debilitating illness. They are aware, of course, of their son's infatuation with his wife. How will he deal with news of her condition? Will he be able to handle the shock? Kuldeep's mother knows that if she loses her daughter-in-law, she will probably find a better substitute without too much difficulty. But what if something happens to her son?

Satwant, on her part, is constantly tormented by thoughts of the poison-tipped barbs that her tongue had fired at her husband. 'Go if you want to,' she had thundered. She had spoken in anger, not knowing that her words would inflict such a deep wound on her husband's tender heart. She knows that she had erred and she wants to seek his forgiveness, even by prostrating herself before his feet. But Kuldeep had left, and his feet had never returned to her doorstep. And Satwant, plagued by her own guilt, had established a lasting friendship with the sickbed.

Kuldeep's departure left Satwant on a funeral pyre of remorse and repentance. To make matters worse, her mother in-law constantly showers the choicest of invectives on her: 'Oh you damned witch...devourer of your brothers...you have squandered my most precious asset...may everything you cherish be reduced to ashes...may everything that you touch remain barren...' But Satwant has had to take these in her stride, for she herself had told her mother-in-law about her altercation with Kuldeep and his consequent departure. In any case, how can she complain about anything that Gian Kaur says when she uses far worse epithets to curse herself and her actions?

How long will this two-and-a-half-year-long imprisonment last so that her husband can return home? Will he want to return home even after his release from prison? Satwant grapples incessantly with these thoughts as she struggles to keep her emaciated frame going from one day to another. Childbirth had produced a host of attendant ailments that were taking a steady toll on her frail body. She feels the implacable hand of death advancing towards her. She might have tried to resist its march if she had been allowed to nourish that lovely little symbol of her happy times with her husband. But Gian Kaur's decision to forbid the child's entry into her room has sapped her strength to fight and she can sense her life ebbing day by despairing day. The burning desire to meet her child, the pangs of separation from her husband, the fear of death itself – all get progressively dimmed. She is like the gambler who has been losing heavily and now, having placed his last bet and lost that as well, finds himself penniless and curiously at peace.

She has not seen her mother-in-law for over a week. Her father-in-law does make the effort to drop in once in a while and also takes care to ensure that she has the requisite food and medicine. It is left to Radhia to come a couple of times every day to give her some milk or help her with her medication. Not that she does this willingly or out of concern for the patient. Bustling into the room with a scowl on her face and a barely concealed grumble on her lips, she does the bare essentials and leaves, in keeping, no doubt, with categorical instructions from her mistress that she is not to spend a minute longer than is necessary in the room.

Satwant finds it hard to get much sleep these days. She spends most nights in that uncertain state between sleep and wakefulness, dozing momentarily only to find herself stirring within a few minutes. The din from the busy street invades her room through the open window and creates an incessant buzz around her. There is no respite from the shrill calls of the tongawallahs who clearly think that a higher decibel level is their best hope of attracting the potential customer. 'Just one more passenger for the town. And you, Bibi! Where are you headed? Towards Dabgari Gate? Come, I'll take you there for two annas. No? Okay, how about six paise?'

Or it is the piercing whistle of the constable from the neighbouring police station as he screams, 'Hey you tongawallah! Look where you are going! Are you blind?'

Sometimes it is the man from the hay market urging the constable to buy a bale of fresh grass.

On other occasions it was the vendors shouting to sell 'hot chapattis and kababs' and 'fresh ice cream from pure milk'.

At times the irritating nasal twang of the seller offering dried lentils and crisp murmura.

Or the particularly annoying chants of the one who sits right below her window, selling 'potatoes and chick peas; hot and spicy'.

Or the parrot that twitters all day from its small cage near the naan bai's tandoor next door, imitations of random sounds punctuated by ear-splitting screeches. Or the naan bai's little helper inviting customers to sample his fresh-from-the-oven naan.

It is the early part of the evening and Satwant has raised the pillow to prop herself up against the wall, having listened all day to the cacophony from the street below. Like every day, the same dissonant notes of the same jarring voices. Her eyes rove around the room feebly, as though searching for something. Feeling somewhat more unwell than usual, she raises her arm to examine the back of her hand. The pale skin is almost translucent, revealing an entire spider web of veins and joints. Rubbing her hand against her face, all she feels is one set of bones against another. She doesn't need a mirror to tell her that her bedraggled skeleton could scare anyone away. She cringes in fear, trying to withdraw from herself.

A pair of pigeons flies in through the window and perch themselves in a niche in the facing wall. Nestled comfortably, they coo and caress with their slender necks, playfully kiss and nibble each other with their beaks. But it isn't long before their mood changes and the gentle nibbling is replaced by angry pecks. The male soon flies away in a huff while the female stays, waiting perhaps for her partner to return. She sits like that for a long time before giving up and flying off disconsolately.

A deep current has swept Satwant off in its powerful flow and, when she comes out of her trance and blinks, she hears the sombre notes of the beggar in the street below, as he sings soulfully in Raga Malkauns:

Alas! With my lover I had a fight
It's left me repenting, crying
And sleepless night after night

Scenes from that fateful day six months ago flash before Satwant's eyes. The throbbing pain of separation and the heartache of remorse are like fiery embers residing deep inside her – dormant but not quite extinguished. A shiver goes through her spine as she hears the gentle reproach of the beggar's song, afraid that it will fan the flames she is wrestling to contain. Tears stream down her cheeks as the voice below continues:

Writhing in agony, alone
Like a fish outside its water, gasping

Eyes half-closed, Satwant's mind views a rapidly moving set of images. Desires that have been reduced to ashes seem to show signs of life. Every pore in her body, every particle in the room resonates with the lament, 'Alas! With my lover I had a fight; it's left me repenting, crying'.

She continues in this state for quite some time, drifting back into the present only when Radhia enters the room to give her her medicine.

4

'Have a sip of this, Bahu,' Radhia says, addressing her as the daughter-in-law of the house. She pours some medicine into the cup and extends her arm towards her. Satwant raises her pillow a bit higher to prop herself up and take the cup. She holds it in her hand for a while as she looks at it with a vacant expression. Then, perhaps because her feeble arm has tired of holding it, she gingerly sets it down.

With barely concealed irritation, Radhia mutters, 'Come on, Bahu. Gulp it down. I have other things to do, you know. And it's also time for the little fellow's feed.'

The reference to the child jolts Satwant into consciousness.

She picks up the cup to drink her medicine before turning towards the maid.

'Radhia,' she pleads, 'will you please do me a big favour?'

Having heard her on many similar occasions, Radhia has a pretty good idea of what to expect. Without waiting for Radhia to respond, Satwant continues, 'I haven't seen my child for so many days. Will you please bring him around today whenever you get the chance?'

Raising her hands to her ears, Radhia responds, 'That won't be possible, Bahu. You know that the mistress will box my ears if she learns about it.'

Satwant realizes that the avaricious maid is unlikely to help unless she is compensated. Having anticipated this situation, she reaches under her pillow to pull out a two-anna coin and says, 'Here! Try to bring him over when you see the mistress busy with her prayers, will you?'

Radhia grabs the coin and briefly bares her gaping teeth to reveal the semblance of a smile as she flees from the room.

A little while later, Satwant finds herself holding her son against her breast, feeling his chubby limbs and peering into his smiling eyes. Radhia stands by the windowsill and concentrates on the altercation between a tongawallah and his passenger as it unfolds on the street below.

Satwant's eyes brim with tears. She feels her empty bosom quiver with the release of milk. The Lord alone knows how she has longed to nurse her child against her breast since the day he was born...a longing that, till this day, has remained unfulfilled. Today, she can no longer control herself. She turns surreptitiously to look at Radhia, who is still engrossed in the drama playing out on the street. Like a burglar embarked on a major theft, Satwant furtively unbuttons her kameez and quickly thrusts a nipple into her child's lips.

The child, no more than a couple of months old, seems to know intuitively that it is his own mother who is nursing him. As though he has been starving for ages, he suckles ferociously, seeking perhaps to find life itself in her shrunken breast.

Satwant is in a state of bliss, savouring a range of sensations that she has never before experienced. She had given birth to the child but it is only now that she feels like a mother. Ah! The ethereal beauty of motherhood, the exhilaration, the joy, the tranquillity that accompanies it! It makes her oblivious to the fact that her sickness could perhaps make her milk harmful to the child. It also makes her forget that a sentry has been appointed to keep a watchful eye on her. Transported to this stage, she has forgotten herself and also her child.

She is focused on one and just one thing – the inexplicable sense of elation that she is experiencing for the first time in her life. She feels every pore of her body immerse itself in the delight of this moment. Her mind is bereft of all other thoughts. Even the blueness of the sky outside embodies her soaring spirits.

Lost in her own newly discovered universe, Satwant's eyes are closed. Suckling an infant for the first time can be painful for anyone, let alone for a mother who is coping with various ailments. Every time the child sucks fiercely, Satwant feels shafts of pain traverse her body. But the same shafts also carry the beauty of life itself. Can anyone other than a mother ever experience something like this?

A crackling voice emerges out of the blue and numbs her from head to toe, the shock so great that it even separates the child's lips from her breast. 'O, you accursed one! Why don't you die? You might as well have poisoned the boy. Are you a mother or the she devil herself? Even the devil does not devour the one that is born from her womb,' Gian Kaur screams as she tears the child away from Satwant's breast.

Spouting abuse, Gian Kaur takes the child and disappears from the room. Radhia, still looking distracted, tries to focus on the room. Both appear shell-shocked as they look at each other in disbelief.

Sitting by her side, Radhia whispers, 'What have you done, Bahu ji? How could you feed the baby your own milk? What on earth will happen now?'

Satwant finds herself trembling. Her body is drenched with cold sweat, not out of fear of her mother-in-law but the thought that she might have poisoned her child with milk that is perhaps contaminated by her own sickness. 'Oh god! What have I done?' she asks herself as a wave of remorse courses through her body. 'What on earth came over me? What will be the fate of this poor child now?'

Turning towards the maid, she whispers the same question, 'Radhia! What's going to happen now?'

Radhia's face is a picture of grief, her expression suggesting that she is devastated by concern for the child's well-being. The reality, however, is something else. Deep down, the child's welfare has never been her priority. Making, once again, a show of anxiety, she laments, 'Bahu ji! What a calamity! Let us pray that the child comes to no harm.'

'Radhia! For god's sake do something,' Satwant implores her with folded hands.

Smelling an opportunity, Radhia replies, 'All right, Bahu ji! I'll immediately fetch the doctor, though I have no idea what it's going to cost.'

Satwant strips the gold ring off her finger and says, 'Here! Spend whatever you have to and keep the rest. Just make sure that the child is safe. And don't you ever bring him near me again. Never! Go now, my good sister. Hurry now.'

'Yes, Bahu ji! I'll go right away,' Radhia mumbles as she leaves the room, her small eyes shining brighter than the gold she clutches in her palms.

5

It is around nine in the morning. Radhia is in the kitchen, cleaning the dishes and muttering to herself, 'God alone knows when I'll get freedom from this wretched house. You work yourself to death day in and day out, and, to top it all, you also have to listen to their abuse...'

Gian Kaur, meanwhile, sits on the doorstep nearby. Her right hand moves rapidly over the beads of her rosary but her tongue works twice as fast. 'You barren witch! You don't deserve a child! Greedy and hell-bent on looting us! Damn widow...she won't die and won't leave us alone either...'

She is still in the middle of her tirade when a ferocious Radhia approaches her from the kitchen. Hands still smeared with the ash she has been using to scrub the dishes, she glares, 'Enough of your abuses, Bibi ji. And to hell with this job! I have given birth to four children already. And god knows how many more he has in store for me. How dare you call me barren or a widow? How would you like me to use the same words on you?'

Gian Kaur had no idea that her mumbling has carried all the way to Radhia in the kitchen. She is clearly embarrassed by Radhia's outburst; but to remain quiet now would mean a further loss of face. Relying on attack as the best form of defence, she yells back, 'Why are you after my life, you miserable slut! Go and tend to your work. When have I abused you? I've only pointed out that it's time to start cooking and you've just arrived. And the child! He's cried himself hoarse. Shouldn't you at least have thought of him?'

She hasn't quite finished with her diatribe when a tall man approaches the doorway and smiles. 'What's up today, Bey ji? Why are you all worked up so early in the day?'

Waryam Singh's unexpected arrival is fortuitous for Gian Kaur. She was looking for a way to get rid of Radhia but knows that the maid was not going to give up so easily. She also realizes that in this particular instance, she may have been unduly harsh on the maid. Seeing Waryam Singh, however, makes Radhia bite her lips in seething rage and withdraw into the kitchen to resume her work. Gian Kaur immediately changes her tone. Ushering Waryam Singh into the adjoining room where Sadhu Singh is reclining on a couch, she smiles. 'I should thank the Lord that you have graced us with your presence.'

Waryam Singh leads a fairly lonely existence. There is hardly anyone around him that he can truly call his own. Yet, there are many who lay claim to his affection, call him their very own. He is a man of ordinary means, working as a pharmacist in a government hospital. He is around twenty-six or twenty-seven years old, good looking, well built and blessed with a sunny disposition. Not particularly soft spoken, his voice is known to take a gravelly edge when he is angry.

Little is known about his family, caste or home. There is speculation, though, that he is the adopted son of the late

Giani Bagh Singh who was recognized in the community as a prominent leader of the Singh Sabha. There are some who insist that the Giani, in keeping with his pre-eminent position in the community and also as head priest of the local gurudwara, had no child of his own. Others, though, discount this theory and claim that Waryam was merely the favourite disciple of the Giani. And there are those who aver that the boy had grown up in an orphanage until the Giani had taken him under his wing. But Giani Bagh Singh, till his very end, had always introduced the young man as his own son.

Giani Bagh Singh, everyone agrees, was one of those rare examples of nobility that descends in our midst once in a generation or two. Paying scant regard to his own needs and even those of his family, he had dedicated his life to serving the community around him. People say that he had come to Peshawar from some other city but nobody from the present generation can recall when. He had lived up to the ripe old age of eighty, they say. He managed to raise a fortune of almost a hundred thousand rupees to construct a beautiful gurudwara near Sadar Bazaar and spent his final years in service of the institution that he had built.

Waryam Singh, on the other hand, does not have any special claim to fame. There is one quality though that he has clearly inherited from his mentor, and he possesses it in great abundance – an abiding, untiring commitment to serve the larger community. It is this remarkable trait that distinguishes him from others, that transforms him from an ordinary mortal into an extraordinary one.

The late Giani ji was highly regarded for his disdain for the comforts of life even though he spent his life providing these to others. He endeavoured to serve everyone, without the slightest consideration of caste, creed or faith. For the destitute of the city who had no food to eat, no clothes to wear, Giani ji was nothing short of a saviour. Conversant with the traditional Ayurveda school of medicine, he went out of his way to visit anyone who was sick. He tried his best to provide medicine and healing but if he found that the ailment was beyond his own capabilities, he would arrange for the patient to see a proper doctor even if he had to pay the doctor's fee from his own pocket. It was, perhaps, for this reason that Giani ji was so keen to see Waryam Singh go to a medical school and graduate as a doctor. Waryam, however, was not inclined towards academic rigours and had to settle for joining the local government hospital as a pharmacist.

His reputation for selfless service takes Waryam into homes that would normally have remained out of bounds to someone coming from his strata of society. His work has earned him the affectionate sobriquet 'Bhapa ji' usually reserved for an older brother. It has also made him ubiquitous in this part of the town. A family could be organizing a wedding or planning a function, Waryam is the first port of call. Once he takes charge, they don't need to worry about minor details. Bhapa ji sorts out the problems, sees things through. Neither fatigue nor sleep, neither hunger nor thirst distracts him from the responsibility that he cheerfully takes upon himself.

Womenfolk tend to be particularly reliant upon him, provoking, no doubt, a fair amount of jealousy amongst a section of the male population. And in his hospital, other employees are expected to put in a full day's work but Waryam is free to come and go pretty much as he pleases. It is not unusual to see the other pharmacists and at times even a couple of doctors step in to handle his official responsibilities. As for Waryam, he can mostly be seen hurrying along the alleys and by-lanes of one neighbourhood or another, dropping off a bag of flour to one family or responding to another's plea that they had run out of firewood. No sooner has he finished one chore than he is being summoned for the next one, this time a request from the woman whose child has been coughing since daybreak. Without a murmur, Waryam lifts the toddler on to his shoulder and marches off to the hospital.

Waryam's relationship with these families goes well beyond meeting requirements like these. He is also their friend, philosopher and guide, intervening to restore peace between squabbling couples, brokering a marriage deal between two families, helping the office clerk whose wife wants to travel to her parents' place or the one whose wife is coming back after visiting her parents. Bhapa ji can always be relied upon to offer sound counsel and even volunteer where required.

Depending on their age, women in the neighbourhood relate to him as his grandmother, mother, aunt, sister or niece. He sits beside anyone and chats for hours, listening to the most personal details of the family's financial position, the relationships between the woman and her mother-in-law and much else.

The circle of Waryam's relationships also includes influential officials from various departments of the government. The main contractor at the commissariat, the head clerk at the municipality, the chief constable at the police station – all are considered his friends. Little wonder, then, that he often gets waylaid by a motley group ranging from the habitual free loaders to the genuinely needy. Like Bhanu the porter with his plea, 'Bhapa ji, I'd asked you for a pair of those thick army socks. Look at the sorry state of my feet, the way the heels have cracked.' Or Duni, the confectioner complaining, 'Must I live on your promises alone? All I asked for was a measly pair of shoes.' Or Mantua, the betel-leaf seller reminding, 'Bhai Waryam! I had requested you for a blanket.' Amidst all this, Waryam makes reassuring noises as he hurries along towards his next errand.

Waryam was heading for Sadhu Singh's house, having learnt that Kuldeep's wife had fallen ill shortly after his imprisonment. After spending a few minutes with the patient, he figured out that with the possible exception of Sadhu Singh, no one else in the household paid the slightest attention to her deteriorating health. Without hesitation, he took upon himself the duty to visit their house twice a day to enquire about Satwant's health, noting her temperature and getting her medicines from the hospital.

Immediately after ushering Waryam Singh into her husband's room, Gian Kaur starts to unburden herself about Radhia's conduct, taking care that Radhia does not once again tune into her scalding tirade. She could have gone on and on with her litany of complaints about the maid but for her husband interrupting her. Lying on his bed and wracked by a fresh bout of coughing, he calls, 'Deep's mother! Will you get me a cup of tea?'

Angered by the untimely demand, she proceeds to direct at her husband the ire that she had reserved for Radhia. 'The hell with your tea! This heat has turned the place into an inferno. Doesn't leave anyone the energy to lift a finger. And all you can think of is your tea!' Picking up her rosary, she furiously counts the beads and recites the opening sections of the Mool Mantra prayer before picking up the threads of her interrupted diatribe. 'Useless, good for nothing! Tucks in a ball of opium in the morning and snores away. Wakes up and he wants tea. Tea and opium; that's all he cares about,' she bemoans. 'Isn't he just the perfect specimen of that adage of opium lovers: *Intoxicate yourself, sleep long and deep, fret not over anything, and leave the rest to fate.*'

A few more rasping coughs, each heavily loaded with phlegm, and Sadhu Singh calls again, 'My good woman! This cough is killing me. I am sure a cup of tea will give me a few moments of relief. But if you think it is too much trouble for you, I'll try to get up and make some myself.'

'Of course! I am sure you will,' she crackles with sarcasm as she finishes the cycle of counting the 108 beads in the rosary.

'Why get angry, Bey ji. I'll go make it for him. Look how frail he's become. You should be serving your husband as you would serve god!' Waryam Singh gently chides.

Reminded of the scriptures which enjoin a woman to treat her husband like god, the religiously minded Gian Kaur mellows visibly to say, 'Veera, when have I ever said no to him? Where would I be without him? All I wanted to say was that a hot cup of tea is not the best thing for him in this blazing heat. It will only harm his innards. I will gladly make him a cup if he wants one. Whatever I said was for his own good.'

'And may I give you some good news?' Waryam Singh opens the newspaper he is carrying. 'The Guru ka Bagh prisoners are going to be released soon.'

'Really?' she exclaims, her eyes shining with excitement. 'How soon, Veera? I will shower you with sweets, bearer of good tidings. When will my son be freed?'

'Maybe another five or six days,' Waryam Singh declares after looking again at the paper.

'Rock the cradle for a while, will you. May your husband live long,' Gian Kaur calls out to Radhia as sounds of a crying child wafts across from the other room.

Radhia walks across to rock the cradle while Gian Kaur, elated by news of the release of the prisoners, speaks to her with a new-found affection. 'Look here, girl. Please don't mind anything that I may have said in anger. You know how this wretched tongue of mine goes out of control. You are like a daughter to me and daughters should never take offence at anything their mothers might say. Here! Take this money and buy something for your kids on your way back.'

Turning towards Waryam Singh, she says, 'Just think of her poor kids. Who should they look up to? Their father is drunk all day. If they are able to get two square meals a day, it is only due to the efforts of this girl. Otherwise, who knows what their fate would have been. I wouldn't even wish an enemy to be addicted to liquor the way their father is! So, Veera, is it confirmed that they will be released in five or six days?'

'Yes, Beyji. That's what it says right here, that the government will soon announce their release.'

For Radhia, the kindness in the tone of her mistress is an entirely new experience. She forgets the abuse hurled at her earlier. Beaming, she turns her attention to the cradle and starts to hum a lullaby as she rocks it.

Come hither, O sleep, come
To the eyes of my little one

Gian Kaur busies herself with tea for her husband. Waryam Singh gets up to go to the room upstairs.

6

Waryam Singh finds Satwant asleep as he enters the room. Asleep, but not quite. Her eyes, neither fully open nor properly shut, lend her face the scary countenance of a corpse. He tiptoes across the room and gingerly perches himself on the edge of the stool near her bed. Her face is pallid and the hollows beneath her eyes so pronounced that he allows himself a quiet sigh of relief when he notices her gently heaving chest.

Seeing her open her eyes, he enquires, 'So, how are you feeling, Satwant?'

'Bhapa ji?' She turns her face towards him. 'When did you come?'

'Just a few minutes back.' He picks up the thermometer from the alcove, gives it a couple of quick tugs to reset the mercury and places it between her lips.

'How's the fever today, Bhapa ji?'

'Just above a hundred.'

'No, Bhapa ji.'

'And why not?'

'Seems quite a bit higher than that to me.'

'Don't be silly.'

The worried look on Waryam Singh's face is enough to tell the patient that her fever today must be somewhere in the range of 103. It tends to be around 101 or 102 on most days, and today she feels it is perceptibly worse.

'You are going to get well soon,' he says as he reads out the story about Kuldeep's imminent release from the day's paper. Her eyes, so lifeless that they seem prepared to welcome the god of death, come alive with a new sparkle. Her lips quiver, not unlike the flame of a candle just before it dies out. She shuts her eyes.

'You are going to get well, Satwant,' Waryam Singh repeats.

She opens her eyes momentarily, before closing them again.

'Satwant!' He caresses her forehead, steels himself and says, 'If I asked you something important, will you reply?'

'Sorry. I wasn't paying attention. What did you say?' The patient turns towards him.

'What's going on in your mind these days? That's what I want to know. I've been meaning to ask you this for several days now. I get a strong feeling that you are carrying some deep secret.'

Without saying a word, the patient opens her eyes, blinks and closes them again.

'Satwant!' he says again with anguish. 'I know I'm not your real brother. But treat me like one and share your worries with me. I promise you will not regret it.'

'I have always seen you as my brother, Bhapa ji.'

'Do go ahead, then. If you don't mind—'

'That's not the point,' she interrupts. 'It's just not the kind of thing that I can share with a brother. Had you been my sister, maybe I would have...'

'In that case, please treat me like your sister. I can only assure you that various persons have confided in me with their most personal problems and none has ever had any cause to regret.'

'But, Bhapa ji...it's...it's no use speaking about this now.'

'Don't worry about that. There is no harm in letting me know.'

Satwant turns her back towards him, tired perhaps from lying too long on one side. Covering her face with her hands, she starts to sob. Waryam Singh walks around to sit next to her on her cot, trying his best to calm her down.

'Are you sure you have to know this, Bhapa ji?'

'If you have no objection...'

'He won't come home once he is released from jail.'

'What? Why do you say this?'

'Because he was unhappy with me. That's why he went away.'

'How can that be?'

'I suspected him. That's why.'

'Suspected him? Of what?'

'I failed to understand him.'

'And what did you suspect him of?'

Silence.

'Come on, Satwant. Trust me.'

Silence.

'Come, Satwant. Open up your mind, please.'

Silence.

'I can't bear this silence, Satwant.'

Silence.

'Please don't cry, my dear sister. Tell me, quick.'

'I thought he was a sinner...'

'Is that because you thought he had...he had some...with someone?'

'Yes.'

'But with whom?'

Silence.

'Please don't go silent again. With whom?'

'Saroj.'

'Which Saroj? Babu Ganga Vishan's daughter?'

Satwant nods, her eyes now swimming in a sea of tears.

'It is quite natural for you to think like that, Satwant. And you wouldn't be the only one. I know of several others who thought the same. But it's all untrue. I happen to know a fair bit about this. They grew up together, played together, studied together. They loved each other. This goes back to the days when your father-in-law lived in Babu Ganga Vishan's house, in Babu Mohalla. That was a long time ago, years before your marriage. But who told you about it?'

'No one.'

'How, then?'

'I found a letter in the trunk.'

'And what did the letter say? I still can't believe this. I know them both so well. And I can verify the facts better than most people. I know, of course, that Kuldeep can be a bit fickle. Standing firm has never been one of his distinguishing attributes. But he is not a bad fellow at heart. For all the years that I've known him, I can say quite honestly that I haven't come across any particularly negative trait in him. I've also been acquainted with Saroj for quite a while. She is so pure, that girl. You would want to recite her name along with your morning prayers. But fate has been truly cruel to her. She became a widow while she was still in her childhood. She has suffered for no fault of hers. Anyway, let's see what this letter of yours says.'

'It's there in that trunk. You can take it out and read it,' she says in a halting voice and asks for some water.

Waryam gives her a glass and walks across to the trunk to fetch the letter.

'Read it aloud, will you,' she implores, wiping with her

dupatta the drops of water trickling down the corner of her mouth.

Raising his voice to make it audible for Satwant, he starts to read.

Dear Kuldeep

I am not sure how to address you. I find myself standing at that distant summit of love where the sights and sounds of the earth below cannot reach. I only see love. Names, titles and modes of address seem meaningless here. Sometimes, even the name Kuldeep seems to float away into the distance, leaving behind just the prefix 'Dear'. But while the prefix needs to hang on to something tangible, love can stand beautifully on its own and does not depend on any props. Addressing you with a 'Dear' provokes a desire for possession. That is why I prefer to think of you only as my love.

Reading your letter that said it would be your last communication, I was neither hurt nor surprised. I am not trying to say that I have no physical or material desires. That would be untrue. But it is true that by dint of my penance, self-control and discipline, I have managed to suppress such desires if not killed them entirely. My life has not given me the opportunity to experience either material comfort or physical pleasure. Mine is a life incomplete. What would a flower know about fragrance if it has never had the chance to bloom?

Dear Kuldeep, by the time my eyes opened to be able to see and know the meaning of love, such feelings were forbidden to me. Yet, I was not unhappy. The good Lord has blessed me with an abundance of self-control and if I had one desire, it was to be able to open the locked vaults of my heart to someone who cared. But I never got that chance. There was no place for me at the home of my in-laws. And while I had my father at our home, his support was also as good as non-existent. Little wonder, then, that this responsibility has befallen upon you. When did that happen? I am not sure. You are, after all, a part of my childhood. We grew up playing together.

But our society saw our relationship through jaundiced eyes. There was all manner of comment and speculation about us which eventually contrived to wrench us away from each other.

Dear Kuldeep, let me assure you again that I have no regrets. I accept that you will soon be happily married and will have your own family. As for me, the unbreakable bond of your love is all the wealth that I need in this life. And I know that it will always stay with me. I also expect that you, with the passage of time, will begin to forget me - as indeed you should. Memories of an unfortunate soul like me can bring no cheer to a blessed one. But nothing will erode the value of the capital that I own - the precious love that you have given me.

Before I end, allow me to mention the one desire that I have nurtured for a pretty long time. I would have loved to see your bride, to embrace her as she emerges from the wedding palanquin, to dress her up and pamper her, to run a thousand little errands for her. But all of that now appears like a distant dream. As things stand, I may not even get the chance to glance towards your home.

So long, my love! May you have a happy and prosperous life. May the cool breeze bring happy tidings to your home. That is all that I can ask for.

Saroj

Keeping the letter aside, Waryam looks at Satwant. Her eyes are closed.

'Satwant,' he calls.

Slowly, she opens her eyes.

'How could this letter create any suspicion in your mind?' he reproaches.

She does not respond.

'Is there anything in it that would lead you to doubt him?'

She remains silent.

'Poor Kuldeep! This is so harsh on him.'

Tears of contrition trickle down her face.

'Do speak up, Satwant. What was there in this letter that led you to suspect him?'

Sobbing, she covers her face with both hands.

'Silly girl!' he whispers, placing his hand on her head to comfort her.

'Bhapa ji, I don't know what came over me! How could I act like that?'

Waryam Singh senses the waves of remorse coursing through Satwant. Her headstrong nature had led her to this abyss. Unable to find a way out, she had decided to sacrifice herself to the raging fires of penitence.

Gently stroking her forehead, he consoles, 'That's water under the bridge now. Kuldeep is going to be back soon and I am sure he will be delighted to know that all those doubts have been cleared.'

'But...but what if he doesn't come?' Satwant clears her throat and murmurs.

'You are such an idiot,' he remonstrates, giving her an affectionate hug. 'Why on earth wouldn't he come? Of course he will be here. And if he isn't, I'll go after him and fetch him, no matter where he is. Don't you lose heart, my dear sister.'

Her face lights up momentarily with a faint glimmer of hope and her eyes shine with the confidence of one who has unexpectedly resolved a tough dilemma. Looking at Waryam Singh, she asks, 'Will you do me a favour, Bhapa ji?'

'Of course! You only have to ask!'

'Can you ask Saroj to come over and see me just once?'

'But...well...she...I don't know.'

'Please! Do find a way. Somehow. Plead to her on my behalf if you have to. But she must come.'

'Why plead? I'll just go over to her and tell her to come with me. But you are a wise girl, Satwant. Should you really...'

Satwant remains quiet.

'Anyway, I'd better get going. It's getting late now and I still have to fetch your medicine.' Picking up the empty bottle of medicine, he makes his way down the stairs.

7

The Sadar Bazaar area has a well-known neighbourhood called Babu Mohalla, named after the large number of government employees or 'babus' that inhabit it. It is situated on the western side of the bazaar behind the old market.

There was a time when the wholesale market at Sadar Bazaar was a major trading centre for sugar and gur. Farmers from distant places like Taikal, Charkhani, Landi and Abdara would arrive with thousands of kilos of produce. But the establishment of the new market called Pipal Mandi had spelt its demise and the ancient trading post remained in name only. It is now a predominantly residential locality and most of its inhabitants are Sikhs. Its reputation as a Sikh neighbourhood is bolstered by the presence of two gurudwaras. One, known as the Mandi Gurudwara, is a fairly modest affair. The other, the Singh Sabha Gurudwara, though, is a magnificent edifice that attracts quite a few visitors. It also houses a memorial to Giani Bagh Singh.

Babu Ganga Vishan's house is located in Babu Mohalla. Aged fifty something, he is a native of Punjab but has spent much of his adult life as a government employee in the Frontier Province. Having retired about three years back, he now lives on a comfortable pension. His house and his long stint in Peshawar entitle him to see the north-western city as his new home.

His comfortable existence, his virtues and his goodwill, however, are overshadowed by one solitary blot. Babu Ganga Vishan has become dangerously addicted to hard liquor. How did a noble soul like him fall prey to this vice? Nobody knows for sure. Some speculate that he is under some severe mental stress that has driven him to drink. Others feel that his habit was under control while he was working but had grown out of hand after his retirement. His wife passed away around six years ago and the spacious home now has just two other occupants – his daughter Saroj and their domestic servant Mangtu. He has rented out the ground floor, preferring to stay on the first floor.

Saroj is twenty or twenty-one, a matriculate with a Giani degree that reflects honours in Punjabi. She has a passion for music and, apart from being blessed with a sweet voice, is adept at playing the harmonium, sitar and other instruments. She also has a strong interest in literature and is often found in the company of books.

Ganga Vishan's reading room isn't particularly large but its tasteful décor clearly reflects the owner's appreciation for the finer things of life. A wall-to-wall carpet seems an embodiment of the finest Persian craftsmanship. Its fifteen-inch border is embroidered with red and yellow flowers. Two opposing corners are shaped like a crescent and feature a comely female pouring wine from a decanter into a delicate goblet. A slender waist, long and slim neck, fair complexion and fine golden hair conspire to create an alluring picture. The central section of the carpet is a vast flowerbed ablaze with bright colours.

The walls are adorned by a variety of paintings. The fading colour of a few of them suggests that they are fairly old. But they are well looked-after, with nary a speck of dust on any of them. If anything, regular dusting had given the frames a rather attractive sort of sheen.

Although his body has become rather obese and misshapen, the gentle creases on Ganga Vishan's forehead suggest the pleasant countenance of one who has led a comfortable life. His hairstyle and precise shave suggest that advancing years and indifferent health have not made him oblivious to his appearance.

An elegant cover with floral patterns drapes over the mantelpiece, its delicate fringe fluttering with every gust of wind. A framed portrait of Guru Nanak Dev has been respectfully placed between two brass vases. Ganga Vishan's devotion to the first Sikh guru can be gauged from the fragrance of the fresh flowers resting in front of the portrait.

It's still fairly early in the morning. Rays of sunshine, streaming in through the top of the window, light up a photo frame on the opposite wall. It bears the portrait of a young maiden, her face framed by two long plaits sloping all the way down her shoulders. She is perched on a six-foot-high wall, a smile on her face and a badminton racket in her hand.

Saroj was barely twelve when she was married into a prosperous Hindu family. She was, however, not destined for happiness. Two years later, her husband died in a road accident, leaving behind a fourteen-year-old widow. Her in-laws, materialistic to the extreme, balked at the prospect of looking after a dependent daughter-in-law for years to come. Young Saroj was left with no option but to face the ignominy of returning to her parents' home and resuming her studies.

Saroj is tall and lissom, though not particularly fair skinned. Her amber-coloured eyes convey a sense of calm, quiet confidence combined with a spirit of gentleness and humility. Her smile is often accompanied by a subconscious lowering of her eyes. And when she laughs, her shoulders tend to gently pull towards her neck. Yet, it would be a mistake to consider her old-fashioned. She is open-minded and expresses herself with a confidence and clarity that enhance her attractiveness. Dimples appear in her cheeks and her eyebrows curl inwards when she is trying to emphasize on a particular point. When listening to others, she appears full of concentration, her lower lip pursed just a little bit, head tilting gently to one side. Even in disagreement, she has her own style, rocking her head ever so slightly, index finger and thumb of her right hand joined in fluid motion as she speaks. She has long, well-combed hair, supple and artistic fingers and a row of immaculate teeth that look like jasmine buds. Her attire tends to be simple but tasteful and she shuns anything that could be considered gaudy or flashy. She appears particularly partial to an aquamarine sari worn with a matching blouse and to a purplish kameez that she often sports with a white salwar.

Ganga Vishan has made every effort to protect his daughter from the burdens of widowhood so that she can try to lead a normal life. This has allowed Saroj to develop her interests in both music and literature. She has become a fairly prolific writer of poems and short stories, some of which have, of late, become something of a talking point in the Punjabi media. She is also the moving spirit behind the Ladies Satsang Association at Babu Mohalla and often takes the lead in singing hymns and even addressing the congregations at the Singh Sabha Gurudwara. Apart from this, she volunteers at the local girls' school, spending two or three hours daily to teach Punjabi.

With such a multitude of activities and interests, it is no wonder that Saroj finds herself busy doing something or the other throughout the day. The absence of any free time, she thinks, would be a sufficient protection against stray thoughts, whether old or new. She wants to make sure that the reins of a capricious and unpredictable mind remain firmly within her control. But can anyone really tame the human mind with such ease? You can put a harness on an animal to domesticate it, may be even tether or shackle it. But the human mind? Who could look at Saroj and think that she had gone through the horror of widowhood? To the stranger, she has all the attributes of an eligible young maiden.

Ganga Vishan, though, is fairly conservative in his outlook and the remarriage of a widow is something beyond the pale. It is against tradition and has never happened in their family, and he certainly wasn't going to entertain any such thoughts. He understands Saroj's plight and empathizes with her but is helpless in addressing the situation.

Sitting in his reading room, Ganga Vishan is immersed in

the current issue of a popular Punjabi monthly. He is reading a short story titled 'A Life Incomplete'. The author's name is Saroj.

Saroj comes into the room on some errand. Seeing her father read the periodical that has her most recent story, she tiptoes around the room to stand behind him. With bated breath, she waits for him to finish the story, anxiously peering at the side of his face to decipher his reaction. She thinks of the phrases that her father might use in appreciating her work after he has finished reading.

Ganga Vishan lifts his head to see the reflection of Saroj in the mirror in front of him. She is looking back at him through the mirror, the merest hint of a smile lighting up her eyes. Without speaking a word, he signals to Saroj to sit on the armrest of his chair. She obeys, still waiting anxiously to hear his comments. He remains silent, eyes closed in deep thought. When he turns to look at her, she sees two large teardrops emerge from his eyes. Are these pearls, she wonders, the reward for my story today?

Her father's appreciation is the most precious gift that Saroj could desire. Seeing that her story has moved her father to tears brings a glow to her own face. Using her dupatta to wipe the tears of his face, she starts, 'Babu ji...'

But words fail her. Perhaps she wants to ask, 'What exactly did you feel after reading the story? How did it impact you?' Maybe she still wants him to express his appreciation in words that she could cherish.

'Saroj?' he finally speaks. Casting a questioning glance at her, he continues, 'Have you truly written this story on your own?'

Saroj feels her elation crumble under the impact of that one questioning sentence. She feels like the poet who expects his monarch to shower gold coins on him, only to discover that he has received lumps of coal instead. Her pride and self-esteem have been dealt a crushing blow. Does her father really take her to be a cheat who copies the work of others to get herself published? Her left hand involuntarily starts to crumple the letter of appreciation that she had just received from the editor of the magazine. The glow of joy evaporates from her face, leaving behind a pale shadow of herself. She finds her right hand slide from her father's shoulder to rest lifelessly on her thigh.

Setting the magazine aside, Ganga Vishan looks again towards his daughter. Patting her hand, he reassures, 'Please don't misunderstand me, child. I didn't mean it that way!'

Taking a deep breath, Saroj feels her waning strength return. Her heart, still seething from the insult, starts to soften.

'How can I ever doubt the felicity of my daughter's pen?' He caresses her head as he speaks. 'I said that only because you have exceeded my wildest expectations. I want you to attain perfection in the art of writing. And I am stunned to see that despite your preoccupation with so many routine things, you have retained the passion to express yourself so freely. Such power in the words, such sophistication of thought, such depth of emotion, such noble values! Saroj, you will one day become the leading storyteller in Punjabi. That is my prediction today. I cannot shake away the vivid images of the unfortunate couple you have portrayed in your story. I wouldn't expect someone twice my age to reach such a pinnacle of narrative skills. And the title of the story is so apt: A life incomplete! But tell me, Saroj, this incomplete life...does it refer to the hero's or the heroine's? Neither seems to have had the opportunity to enjoy the fragrance of a fulfilling life. To me, both the hero and the heroine seem to be equally ill-fated.'

Her father's fulsome praise is like an elixir for Saroj. She soaks in the impact of his words, resolving to redouble her efforts to keep writing. But as he finishes speaking, his final sentence casts a strange kind of spell on her. A shadow of gloom sweeps across her face. Her eyes close and her forehead creases with the burden of some unknown hurt as she says, 'Neither the hero's nor the heroine's. It is someone else.'

Her eyes are focused on the ceiling, trying somehow to escape the probing gaze of her father. She wishes she could fly to some desolate place where she would be able to cry her heart out.

Ganga Vishan glances at his daughter and is unable to hold her gaze for more than a moment. Perhaps the prism of her eyes has suddenly given him a peek into the hidden depths of her heart. He wipes his eyes and hastily goes out of the room. Saroj nestles into the vacant chair and closes her eyes to find herself in a distant world of her dreams.

8

The seconds on a clock seem to stretch interminably as they approach a fateful moment. Will he be released today, will it be tomorrow? The seconds have dragged into minutes, hours, days and weeks. Almost a month has elapsed before the promised moment eventually arrives for Kuldeep. It is around seven in the evening when the forbidding gates of Borstal Jail slowly swing open. A lumbering queue of almost a thousand prisoners snakes out and starts to make its way in the general direction of Gurudwara Dera Sahib. Kuldeep emerges with the batch from Frontier Province but disappears soon thereafter. The batch leader is clearly annoyed that he has left without the courtesy of a goodbye. Other prisoners from the batch mumble that he must already be on his way to the station to catch the first train home. Kuldeep, however, has other plans. He has quietly stepped away from his batch to take the pathway towards the staff quarters at the jail where he has joined his friend Ahmed Khan.

Waiting outside their door to greet him, Ahmed and his wife Zubeida Bano overwhelm Kuldeep with the sheer warmth of their welcome. A Pathan woman dressed in the typical Punjabi attire of salwar-kameez, Zubeida is around twenty-five or twenty-six years of age. She has a ruddy complexion that speaks eloquently of good health and cheerful spirit. She seems to be particularly partial to silver ornaments of all sorts, which adorn her fingers, arms, ankles, ear, neck and even around her waist. Kuldeep wonders if this is her regular style or she has gone out of her way to make an impression on their guest.

Still somewhat diffident, he follows his hosts into their house. Zubeida initially appears a bit reserved and slow to engage in conversation. But in less than an hour, she is chatting with Kuldeep as though she has known him all his life. The ice-breaker, perhaps, is Kuldeep's impish comment, 'Come on, Bhabhi! Why should you veil your face before your dewar? Pathan women, in any case, are not known for this practice.'

Before she can respond, Ahmed interjects, 'She seems to have picked up this bad habit since we came to Punjab. She never bothered to cover her face until we moved here. But now that she has done so, I am afraid you will have to pay a fair price to get her to remove her veil.'

'Ah ha! That confirms my belief that you jailors will not do anything without a bribe.' Kuldeep grins.

'No doubt about that. If we didn't take bribes, how would we manage to provide for these.' Ahmed points to his wife's ornaments.

'But I have nothing to offer by way of a bribe,' Kuldeep reproaches.

'How extraordinary! If a jailor can't get a bribe from a prisoner, who else will he get it from?'

'All right, then. Let this be a loan to me. I will repay it when you come to Peshawar and Satwant will lift her veil before her jeth.'

'That's very bold of you.' Ahmed smiles. 'You are taking responsibility for her actions without knowing whether she will comply.'

'But aren't you doing pretty much the same thing? Look at bhabhi, who hasn't spoken a word. She is acting as though something precious will fall out and be lost forever if she were to open her mouth!' Kuldeep teases.

Ahmed pauses for a second, searching, perhaps, for a fitting rejoinder. Lowering her eyes towards the floor, his wife says, 'I have hardly veiled my face. I don't know what the two of you are arguing about.'

'Why then are you hiding those delicate little amulets on your forehead? Are you afraid that I am going to run away with them?' he continues in his sardonic tone.

Without saying another word, she pulls back the dupatta above her forehead and looks at her husband. He gives her a friendly glare and chides her, 'Go on, now. Get him something to drink, will you. It's so unbearably hot out there.'

'How can I serve him something? Do you think he will accept anything that I have touched? You should have ordered something from a Hindu's shop and asked their boy to bring it to him.'

'That really is the limit, Bhabhi. If we can't even share a glass of water, how are we going to develop this relationship between dewar and bhabhi?' Kuldeep smiles affectionately.

Husband and wife look at him in surprise. Seeing their expression, Kuldeep reassures them, 'If that were the case, I could have had a drink in the market itself. I didn't need to come here at all.'

Zubeida feels a new sort of affection and respect for the young Sikh. She serves him a glass of cold water, followed by a delicious meal and an animated, cheerful conversation that forges a new bond between the three of them. While turning in for the night, Kuldeep declares his intention of leaving for Peshawar the following morning. Zubeida, however, is adamant that he spend at least a couple of days with them, that he give them the chance to look after him after his long incarceration. Kuldeep is equally insistent about returning home at the earliest. His heart wants him to fly to his beloved and join her in the blink of an eye to make up for the long months of separation. Ahmed, recognizing his friend's state, interjects with Zubeida, 'Don't stop him, my dear woman. I have seen the way he has spent the last seven months, pining away for that piece of his heart. And we can only imagine the torment of the bangle-laden one as she awaits him.'

Ahmed uses the phrase 'the bangle-laden one' whenever he teases Kuldeep about Satwant. But today, that expression brings an involuntary smile to Kuldeep's countenance. He closes his eyes and sees the array of red and ivory bangles hugging the forearms of his beloved. Zubeida takes one look at his face and realizes that it is best to let him leave in the morning.

Kuldeep has found something entirely new and refreshing in the informality and friendship that has so quickly developed between him and the Pathan couple. A Sikh spending a night in the house of a Muslim, eating with them from the same plate, sharing in their joy and laughter! In his own town of Peshawar, with its polluted religious atmosphere, an experience like this would be virtually unthinkable. He marvels at the warmth and hospitality with which Zubeida has attended to him, and at Ahmed's undisguised affection. What a wonderful couple, he reflects.

Yet, there is something missing in their home. It takes him a while before he figures it out. There are no children in the Pathan home. Normally, a family like this would have had at least a couple of toddlers prattling around. Unable to hold back, he asks his friend, 'Ahmed bhai! I don't see any children in the house. Is everything all right?'

Ahmed heaves a deep sigh and replies, 'It is all in His divine will, my brother. It's close to eight years since we married and Allah has not blessed us with a child yet. I have tried my best to deal with this but I must say that I find it much harder to console your bhabhi. There are days when she feels so low that she can do nothing but cry. Maybe we are not lucky enough to have a boy. I would even be happy with a girl or two. But we have to accept our fate. We know that we are powerless before His will.'

'Do not despair, my friend,' Kuldeep comforts him. 'You are both fairly young. Have patience and trust in god. There is no dearth of anything in His house.'

They accompany him to the station the following day to see him off. As the train emits a long whistle to signal its imminent departure, Zubeida's eyes turn moist. She looks at Kuldeep and mockingly warns him, 'Don't you dare forget us after you reach your home, okay?'

Kuldeep bends down to respectfully touch her feet. 'I shall pray to the Lord that this bond remains forever. I will always remember the love showered upon me by my bhabhi.'

9

Even though the Frontier Express is steaming towards its destination it cannot keep pace with the flight of Kuldeep's imagination. The compartment was packed with passengers when he had boarded the train in the evening, denying him any opportunity to lie down or even to sit comfortably for much of the night. But several people had disembarked at intermediate stations. By daybreak, he is able to lean on the window-frame beside his seat and enjoy the luxury of stretching his feet all the way to the seat in front. Settling into a degree of comfort, he finds his eyes closing of their own volition. The train hurtles through the countryside, but for Kuldeep it isn't quick enough. He wants to close his eyes for a second, open them and find himself on the platform at Peshawar Sadar station.

To distract himself, Kuldeep picks up the newspaper left on the seat beside him by a passenger and starts to read. The effort is in vain. Each time he tries to concentrate on a word, it develops a life of its own, dancing before him, teasing as it morphs into Satwant's face. Smiling, frowning, reflecting, pensive, pouting, sleeping...each word captures a different facet of her charming countenance. The newspaper in his hands has been transformed into a cinema screen with images moving and changing in a dizzying blur. His thoughts carry him to Peshawar, alighting from a tonga at the doorstep of his home, his eyes moving towards the window on the upper floor. Gleaming bangles on a slim arm resting on the windowsill gradually come into focus. The very next second, the bangled arms are clasped around him, and Satwant is in his embrace. A steady stream of tears flows down her lovely face. Kuldeep too is in a similar state. Wordless, they hold each other, revelling in the comfort of their embrace. They feel as though they were meeting after a lifetime and who knows how long they would have stayed locked in each other's arms if it weren't for a loud rumble that shakes Kuldeep so violently that Satwant slips from his arms and falls to the floor.

Reluctantly opening his eyes, Kuldeep sees that the train had stopped at Nowshera station. 'My God!' the passenger next to him exclaims. 'What was that? I almost fell off my seat!'

Kuldeep looks around to see an elderly Pathan reclining on his side in the seat in front of him, a veiled woman next to him, dozing gently as she leans against the window. A Punjabi youth of about fifteen or sixteen sits by the window across the aisle, peering intently at the passing landscape and softly singing to himself. A Muslim family sprawls on the long seat next to him.

Kuldeep's face is buried in the newspaper but he is, in fact, neither reading the paper nor paying much attention to the passengers around him. His mind's eye has moved to a plump, three-month-old child nestling in his lap. The child's skin is like unblemished silk and soft as a ball of freshly made butter, his hair a wad of cotton wool, his large, shiny eyes transfixed on Kuldeep's own. Nuzzling the child's hair and cuddling him gently against his chest, Kuldeep feels a thrill of undiluted pleasure run down his spine. He lifts his eyes to see Satwant standing in front, her eyes sparkling with unabashed affection for father and son. Seeing his mother, the child starts to cry. She extends her arms to pick him up but Kuldeep is reluctant to let go. Instead, he holds Satwant's wrist, an array of bangles glistening under his eyes. She yells to protest against the tightness of his grip, and the child cries louder. But Kuldeep is oblivious. He can only see the bangled arms before him, the mocking words of Ahmed Khan about 'his bangled one' ringing in his ears. The train comes to a halt at the Peshawar City station and he feels both the bangled arm and the child slip from his grasp. The Punjabi boy sitting across from the old Pathan is singing:

O ye bangled one
Careful when you reach
For that stem of saffron
I beseech
O ye bangled one
I can die for thee

The Muslim family is lost in its own world. The toddler has started to cry, annoyed no doubt by the older brother who keeps tugging at his shirt. The irritated father delivers a wringing slap on the lad's face, hand making contact with cheek just as the train comes to a shuddering halt. The boy falls on the toddler and both start bawling. The mother shouts at the father for hitting the boy and cacophony rules. Kuldeep hurriedly sets aside his newspaper and leaves the train, walking straight to a public sink to splash some water on his face. Sleep refuses to leave his eyes as he returns to his seat with the knowledge that the next station is Peshawar Sadar.

10

The train finally arrives at its destination. Kuldeep hurries out of the station and hires a tonga to take him home. His mind, hitherto a captive of its own flights of fantasy, starts to come back to earth. His heart starts pounding, slow and heavy, as it captures the rhythm of the horse pulling his tonga to its destination.

The tonga comes to a halt besides his house. Before dismounting from the carriage, he glances upwards. The window is closed. He wonders why. A closed window in this heat? Could Satwant have moved downstairs to escape her loneliness? His pulse quickens and he feels his heart beat two or three times for each step he takes towards his doorstep. He wishes she would open the window to see him approaching the door. That would surely make her forget her customary reserve in the presence of her mother-in-law. She would fly down the stairs, race through the room to open the door and embrace him. He finds himself praying that Satwant would be home alone and he would be able to spend a few quiet moments with her.

He opens the door and recoils at the sight before him. His

mother sits in the middle of the room, surrounded by women dressed in white. 'Why is everyone wailing? Has anyone...?' Kuldeep mumbles as he moves forward to embrace his mother. His heart sinks as his ears absorb the sounds emanating from the mourning women and his brain begins to decipher the voices.

'O Kuldeep! She left us even as she waited for you...her eyes were transfixed on the street right until her last breath.'

'He will come soon, she kept saying even as she was dying.'

'I saw her just three days back. She was so sad. Why do you cry, Satwant? I had asked her. She said, bua ji, will I go without seeing him again, just yearning for him?'

'She could barely speak. Yet, she would keep raising her head to look out of the window. O Kuldeep! If only you had come a couple of days sooner. At least she would have seen you once before leaving.'

Kuldeep freezes. Not a tear emerges from his eyes, nor a word escapes his lips. He is like a statue chiselled out of stone. He feels himself enveloped by a fog. The women fade into the distance like shadows. He can hear the heart-rending wails of his mother but even these do not register. He is curiously disconnected from his surroundings. He doesn't remember when his father comes up to him, embraces him and leads him into the adjacent room. Nor does he recall sitting down on the bed, being offered a glass of water. He is unable to comprehend the tragedy. Again and again, he asks himself the same thing, 'Can it be true? Is Satwant truly no more?'

The sound of an infant crying in his cradle pulls him back into reality. So it's true, Kuldeep thinks. I have lost Satwant forever.

Meanwhile, word about Kuldeep's return from prison has

spread like wildfire through the neighbourhood. The gathering at their house starts to swell rapidly and soon there is no more room for anyone to go indoors. As the crowd spills into the street outside, calls for Kuldeep to emerge from his refuge begin to take a more insistent tone. He turns a deaf ear to these demands and expresses a desire to go to the room upstairs. He is told that the room has been converted into a makeshift gurudwara and the ritual recitation of prayers from the Guru Granth Sahib is in progress. It would be inappropriate for him to go there at this time.

Ignoring his mother's remonstrations, Kuldeep ascends the stairs and opens the door to enter. His head brushes against the dying stem of acacia hanging from the top of the door. It rustles for a second before falling near his feet.

The Guru Granth Sahib has been put to rest and there is silence in the room. Perhaps the priest only comes in the morning and evening hours for the recitation, he thinks. He kneels before the holy book and sits on the rug placed in front to accommodate devotees and visitors. His eyes sweep around the room. With the solitary exception of two trunks lying in one corner, nothing in the room seems familiar. Closing his eyes, he begins to see vivid images of Satwant everywhere. They had spent so much time in this room...Satwant sitting on the bed and chatting with him, sneaking up behind him and covering his eyes, humming a song in unison with him, looking ever so bashful when his mother came into the room...He thinks of all the evenings spent in small talk, in close embrace, in making love, in simply lying awake. The heat of those images penetrates deep into his heart before rising up to melt his eyes with their warmth.

He gets up and makes his way to the terrace outside the

room. The three-legged stool stands upside down near the railing. Two bottles of medicine lie on the floor next to the stool. One had cracked open while the other is still intact. Several paper wraps of medicine, covered with a layer of dust, are strewn next to the bottles. Half covered by a mat is a plastic comb that he recognizes. He had bought it for her and he notices that two of its teeth are broken. It brings images of his ailing wife to the fore. Lying week after week on her bed, her hair had become matted and her hands too infirm to comb them properly. The comb had probably got entangled in her hair, causing the teeth to break as she tugged in vain.

Distraught, Kuldeep paces up and down the terrace. He looks inquiringly at the floor, the railing, the stool, anything that might yield some clues about the last days of his beloved. In unison, every object, every particle around him appears to relay the same dying words from his wife.

He can bear it no more. The pain in his heart finds its escape through his eyes as he breaks down and starts to sob. As he comes back into the room, his cries of anguish echo around the room and make their way to the gathering downstairs. A few of them come up to comfort him and gently escort him down.

11

The human mind has an uncanny ability to adapt itself to a new reality. A mother may think that she will die if she were to lose her only child. A young bride may believe that she will not be able to last a day if she were to become a widow. And yet, there is the unstoppable cycle of life that keeps moving even after the unthinkable has happened. It keeps the body alive even when the heart is convinced that it cannot bear the grief.

Kuldeep finds himself in a similar situation. The dreams and fantasies that he had so lovingly conjured during the journey from Lahore to Peshawar, the joyful prospect of reuniting with his beloved after a long separation, the delicious reverie of being locked in embrace, the many thrills embedded in every thought – everything has been abruptly shattered by one lightning strike. Will his tender heart survive this brutal assault? But for Time, that ruthless tyrant, this is hardly something to worry about. It is like the giant bulldozer that will pursue its own path, oblivious of the fate of any stones or pebbles that may come in its way. Those that do will be crushed into powder.

Locking himself up in his room, Kuldeep often covers his face with a pillow and weeps bitterly. He goes for days without bothering to eat and spends the nights grieving over his loss. A strange fever rages in his body and he lies awake, wondering if he, too, would be consumed by the fire burning inside him. Or wondering if his penance could bring her back. Foolish thoughts, Time mocks. She hasn't gone somewhere that she can come back from.

In due course, Kuldeep manages to emerge from his solitude, only to find a lonely and empty existence staring at him. He is bereft of any desire or aspiration. The world around him increasingly looks like one of those meaningless riddles which defy any rational answer. Memories and images of Satwant lurk round the corner, springing unexpectedly to pierce his numbed senses, to remind him that he is still alive.

Family, friends and relatives are seriously concerned about his state. No one had thought that Satwant's demise would have such a profound impact on him. They do their best to comfort him, to distract him from his sorrow. Some suggest that marrying again might shake him out of his despair. A few even bring proposals for an early marriage but Kuldeep resolutely turns a blind eye to the well-intentioned shenanigans. The wounds in his heart are much too deep to be filled so easily. Looking desperately for solace, he finds himself spending hours at the cremation grounds where Satwant's body had been consigned to the flames.

It is during this period that he learns of a well-regarded saint from the Nirmala sect in Amritsar who has come to the Singh Sabha Gurudwara. The saint delivers sermons and discourses during the morning hours and recites hymns from the Guru Granth Sahib in the evenings. Kuldeep gets into the habit of attending both sessions, finding himself drawn towards the saint's message and discovering a degree of reassurance in the midst of the congregation. The sermons convey a stark and simple message: this life is a transient phenomenon, attachments and relationships are an illusion, sorrows and emotions are ephemeral. Focus on His Name. *That* is the panacea for all troubles.

While others in the congregation listen attentively to the saint's discourse, Kuldeep starts to actually experience his words. Of course, life is transient, relationships temporary and attachments a mere illusion. How could he disagree?

Tragedy has left Kuldeep's mind rather soft and impressionable. The saint's message of renunciation from the ephemeral present and his emphasis on the Eternal begin to make a deep impact on him and he spends more and more time in the presence of the saint.

Almost two months have elapsed since Satwant's death.

Thanks to the influence of the saint, Kuldeep is returning to a semblance of normalcy. He hasn't yet succeeded in erasing Satwant from his mind but he finds himself making a conscious effort in that direction. His parents, too, are relieved that he has started to emerge from his grief and is getting into a devout frame of mind. Gian Kaur, herself of a religious disposition, is particularly pleased that her son is in the company of a noble soul.

Kuldeep's son, meanwhile, is developing into an adorable child. Anyone coming home first enquires about the baby, and ladies in the neighbourhood are particularly keen to pick him up and cuddle him. Kuldeep, though, tries his best to avoid the child because he is a living and constant reminder of Satwant and a distraction from his guru's message of renunciation.

The saint is visibly pleased with the devotion of his new disciple and initiates him into the Nirmala sect by administering the guru mantra to him. Kuldeep immerses himself in the message and is often seen meditating late into the night. It is probably a bit premature to say that he has been able to push Satwant out of his thoughts. There is no doubt, though, that chanting the mantra with full concentration calms his mind and gives him solace.

There is a sprawling park behind Babu Mohalla where Kuldeep often goes in the evenings to find some peace. As darkness descends in the park and a moist September breeze blows gently, most of the habitual evening walkers return to their homes but Kuldeep lingers. He feels strangely restless. Despite trying his best to concentrate on the guru mantra, he is unable to keep thoughts of Satwant away from his mind. He sits cross-legged on the grass, trying in vain to focus his mind on the message of the One but repeatedly finds his attention drifting. He gets up a couple of times, walks a few paces to gather his thoughts before sitting down again. It is now fairly dark and he gets up one last time, wondering if he should give up for the day and go home.

He has barely walked a few paces when he hears footsteps approaching. Must be a late evening walker coming for a stroll, he thinks, moving aside to allow the stranger to pass. As the footsteps came closer, he turns around to see a female form approach him.

'Is that you, Saroj ji...?' he enquires deferentially. 'Here? At this time?' A wave of memories comes rushing into his head.

'Yes, Kuldeep, it is me.'

'But...I was under the impression that you had left for the hills.'

'I had planned to, but...'

Without a word, both sit down on the grass.

'I must apologize, Kuldeep ji,' Saroj starts. 'I know I have violated your instructions but it really was important to meet one more time.'

'My instructions?'

'You had ordered that I must never meet you again.'

'Did I?' Kuldeep queries with a hint of surprise. 'When?'

'In your last letter to me!'

At a loss for words, Kuldeep lowers his eyes for a while. But unable to avert her gaze for long, he looks up again at her. Her face is luminescent in the darkness.

'I am really sorry about Satwant,' Saroj murmurs. The heaviness in her voice suggests that her eyes are brimming with tears.

Kuldeep remains silent.

'Perhaps, to a certain extent, I too am responsible for her death,' she sighs as she speaks.

'Not you, Saroj. It's me.'

'Had I not been in your way...?'

'Oh, Saroj! Why do you bring up the past...' Kuldeep interjects, his voice cracking with emotion.

They are silent for a while, engaged in a wordless conversation.

'Here it is,' Saroj whispers, holding out a folded piece of paper to him.

'What is it?' Kuldeep rasps as he reaches out for the paper.

'It is Satwant's last...' Unable to complete the sentence, Saroj wipes her eyes with her dupatta.

'Satwant's!' Kuldeep exclaims with the voice of one who had found a treasure that he had been hunting all his life. He gets up from the grass and walks towards a lamp post nearby. Saroj follows.

Sitting down under the light, Kuldeep opens the letter and starts to read. His heartbeat quickens with elation as he reads the first few lines. Unable to proceed after the first three sentences, he hands the letter back to Saroj. Tears stream down his face, glistening as they catch the light at a peculiar angle.

'Saroj dear! You have always been so kind to me. Do me another favour and read this out to me please. I just can't...'

Saroj obliges.

'My Lord, I waited for you endlessly. You did not come and I have to depart, carrying with me my yearning to see you one last time. Try as I might, I am unable to get over that accursed moment when I dared to cast a doubt upon you. You departed, leaving me behind to repent over my folly. Even worse, I couldn't get the chance to do the one thing that I so desperately wanted: to fall at your feet and seek your forgiveness from the depths of my heart. All this time, I have waited patiently for you. Seven long months have gone by and now the Lord of Death is impatient and refuses to allow me to wait any longer. Bhapa Waryam Singh obliged me by getting Sister Saroj to come so that I could apologize to her. Will you, too, forgive me?

'My Lord, by the time you return, I will have left this world. I know the sadness you will feel over the fact that we could not meet. So many of our desires have remained unfulfilled; the marital bliss that we had hoped to enjoy for years and years will also remain beyond our reach because cruel Death now has me in its clutches...'

Saroj stops mid-sentence, unable to continue any longer. 'Here, you can read the rest,' she says, extending her arm to pass the letter to Kuldeep. But it takes no more than a glance at his ashen face to conclude that he is in no state to read anything. Pulling her hand back, she summons all her strength to continue.

'...and will tear me away from your embrace. My Lord, please don't waste yourself pining for me. I couldn't survive without you but you are stronger and I am sure that you will be able to carry on. A fish can't live without water but the water will stay even if the fish disappears. I am leaving a part of me with you. Please keep him close to your breast and take special care that this delicate flower does not wilt. It was my great misfortune that I couldn't even gaze at him to my heart's content. But you do not face any such constraint. Look at him, hold him and enjoy him to the fullest. My dearest, I am leaving my most valuable possession in your charge with the trust that you will give him the best possible care...'

The letter is fairly long and after the first few paragraphs, a change in the author's handwriting is clearly visible. Some letters are written in bold strokes, others are disjointed and quite a few are nothing more than a barely legible scrawl – an indication, perhaps, that the author was struggling to maintain a grip on her pen. With every passing line, Saroj struggles to read further. The challenge of deciphering an inconsistent scrawl was compounded by the turmoil inside her own mind. She folds the letter and lets it rest on her lap.

They sit in complete silence. Saroj's eyes are fixed on Kuldeep's face, trying to decipher his mental state. He seems to be delving into the deepest folds of his heart, searching in vain for something precious that he has lost. Saroj's concern grows as she gazes at him. How is he going to cope with this? How will he manage the rest of his life? she wonders. Who will revive his soul?

She is aware that he has already refused to entertain any suggestions of remarriage. He was also getting increasingly detached from his home and family. She worries that he might soon walk away from his home, his ageing parents and even his infant child to become a recluse. After careful reflection, Saroj seems to have arrived at some decision.

'Kuldeep ji...' She taps his shoulder to catch his attention.

'Yes?' Kuldeep emerges from his reverie at the warmth of her touch on his shoulder. But within a few seconds, he is back in his own world. He is sitting besides his dying wife, holding on to a red-bangled arm, feeling the dry bones where the flesh has all but withered away. He looks into her eyes, saddened by the burden of unattained aspirations. He hears her frail voice whisper, 'My dearest, our desires remained unfulfilled...'

He alone knows what lay hidden behind that simple sentence. Bending down to lightly kiss her icy forehead, he murmurs, 'Satwant! My life! Where have you gone, leaving me in the swirling waters of this whirlpool? I wish I could have left before you.'

'Please don't say that. I am sure you can live without me. And I am leaving behind a living part of me with you, am I not?'

He feels Satwant clasp his palm in her hands to rest it on her bosom.

Saroj is looking intently at Kuldeep's face, trying to gauge his feelings from his eyes as they dart around the distant horizon in search of his soul mate. When they blink, a flood of tears run down his face.

A surge of sympathy wells up in Saroj's breast. She feels a new sensation in her heart, a feeling that is particularly foreign for one who has borne the stamp of widowhood from the time she was a mere child. Brushing aside her hesitation, she turns towards him and asks, 'Kuldeep ji! What are you thinking about?'

'I am thinking why I have remained alive when the one who was the breath of my life has gone away. I wonder how long I will survive without Satwant.'

Her eyes shine with a new resolve as she says, 'Kuldeep ji, I shall keep you alive even if I have to give up my life. I will make sure that no harm comes to my Kuldeep.'

'Is that true, Saroj?' he responds, a look of disbelief clouding his eyes briefly before his guru's message of renunciation asserts itself again.

'Absolutely,' she affirms. 'I will make sure that you are looked after.'

'I have become disillusioned with this world, my dear Saroj. I don't want to get caught up in the web of attachments and relationships all over again.'

'I'll turn your disillusionment into love, dear Kuldeep.'

'I don't think you can fully understand the state I am in, Saroj. Satwant's demise has turned my life into a barren desert in which nothing green will ever grow again.'

'I will make the desert bloom like a garden full of flowers.'

'You are the one who first showed me the paradise that love can be. And then Satwant came into my life to reveal a world that I had never seen before and probably won't ever see again. Her demise has hit me with the force of an earthquake and devastated my mind and buried all my feelings and desires in its rubble. I can feel the sincerity and the depth of your empathy towards me, my dear Saroj. But Kuldeep has become a worthless, inanimate being. I can see the emotions, the feelings of love, the desire for a happy and fulfilling life that you nurture in your heart. But I have none of these, nothing that I can offer in return. My only possession now is the painful memory of Satwant. I hope that the strength of my meditation and penance will help me erase that too. Truly, Saroj, I am no different from the thorny shrub that stands alone in the desert. Why should a delicate vine wish to cling to it?'

Saroj's feminine heart winces under the impact of Kuldeep's words. She is tempted to walk away and leave him to himself. But she recognizes that his words are merely a reflection of his guru's influence and this makes her more determined to persist. 'I will transform this thorny shrub into the fragrant sandalwood tree. I will not shirk the responsibility entrusted to me by Satwant in her final moments. I will not allow you to renounce this world and turn into some ascetic.'

Saroj speaks with a passion that springs from the very depths of her heart. But Kuldeep appears unmoved, her words having virtually no impact on him.

'Saroj ji, I truly appreciate your infinite kindness and sympathy but I have nothing to give back. I am quite empty,' he insists.

'I will fill the void,' she responds unflinchingly.

'Alas, Saroj ji, that's a void only Satwant can fill.' Kuldeep sighs and presses his hand against his chest. He seems to be trying his best to control the fires raging inside him, to prevent the embers from escaping into the world outside.

'I will become Satwant for you,' she says with such determination that Kuldeep is momentarily jolted out of his stupor.

'But...but my wounds are still so fresh, so raw that even the touch of the softest cotton causes unbearable pain.'

'How long will it take before it can bear the touch of this soft piece of cotton?' she enquires. The compassion and anxiety in her voice are reflected in her eyes too.

'It's hard to say,' Kuldeep looks at the love in her eyes and intones. 'I get the feeling that this pain is going to be my sustenance for the rest of my life. I have begun to develop a sort of liking for it. I have no desire that my wounds should heal; in fact, I am happy to let them bleed...'

Observing the lines of disappointment on her face, he says, 'I had no idea that you have so much feeling for me. You really do seem to be turning into my Satwant for me. But...but...my salvation....?'

She brightens visibly and responds, 'Can't you nurture the hope that I can make your life blossom once again?'

There is a tremor in Kuldeep's voice as he says, 'My good Saroj! Please don't try to extract a promise from me yet. Who knows? Your love just might succeed in pulling me out of this abyss?'

'As you wish, then,' she replies, dejected. 'Just call me whenever you are ready. I will gladly dive into the abyss to pull you out.'

Kuldeep bows his head in silent gratitude. It is pitch dark as they get up from the grass and dust their clothes.

'Let me escort you back to your place,' he says as they start to walk towards Babu Mohalla.

12

After seeing off Saroj at her place, Kuldeep leaves Babu Mohalla and takes the road towards his house. It is a dark night. Saroj's comely face, her evident affection and anxiety for his well-being, and her soft voice tug at some remote corner of his heart. It is as though something new was trying to sneak into his heart without his being quite aware of it. But his defences have been fortified by the sermons of his guru and whatever it is that he is feeling fails to penetrate beyond the surface.

Barely a hundred yards after Babu Mohalla, Kuldeep leaves the main street and turns towards the market. It isn't much of a saving in terms of distance but it takes him via the Singh Sabha Gurudwara located in the market. Having made it a habit over the last few months to stop by the gurudwara whenever possible, he finds his feet subconsciously making the detour.

He has barely entered the market area when he hears the melodious notes of a hymn wafting towards him. The congregation at the gurudwara was still enjoying the evening session of devotional music, he notes. The words of the hymn start to become audible as he quickens his steps towards the gurudwara.

The fish can't survive its separation from water...

He pauses to soak in the sweetness of the melody, the pangs of separation that it invokes, the metaphor of a fish detached from water, a devotee separated from his Lord, a lover from his beloved...

By the time he reaches the gurudwara, the refrain 'the fish can't survive its separation from water', playing over and over again, is reverberating in his ears. He can hear his own beloved, trapped as she was in the jaws of Death, echoing 'Water can live without fish but a fish cannot survive without water'.

Leaning for support against the entrance of the gurudwara, he finds himself staring at Satwant, unable to remove her skeletal frame from his mind's eye. At the same time, Saroj's face also appears intermittently in his consciousness. He feels like a swimmer struggling in the currents of a river with one of its banks being decorated for a wedding even as the other plays host to a funeral pyre. Powerless against the currents, he oscillates between the two banks, drifting close to one before being pulled away towards the other.

Again, he hears the verse:

Trapped in the fisherman's net weeps
The fish, separated from its water

He sees a luminous fish trapped in the net flung carelessly on the bank by the fisherman as he leaves his boat. The fish writhes in agony but the fisherman is completely oblivious of its plight as he drags the net behind him. The fish disappears from his sight and Kuldeep is buffeted by powerful waves of anguish. Crashing against his sinking heart, they envelop him in their darkness and he finds himself struggling to stay afloat. 'Hold my hand,' he hears a voice plead. 'I will lead you out of this abyss.'

The gentle touch of a hand on his shoulder shatters his reverie. 'Why don't you come inside? You will hear guru ji properly. It is the purest nectar.'

It is Chattar Singh, the carpenter. Like Kuldeep, he is a devotee of the saint and a regular at his congregation. Eyes closed as he plays the harmonium, the saint is singing 'The fish can't survive its separation...' and explaining its meaning to a rapt audience.

The sheer beauty of the hymn, the power of the saint's oration and the devotion that he commands from his followers create a poignant atmosphere. Kuldeep is enveloped in its aura as he immerses himself in its bliss.

13

It is about 11 in the morning. The monsoon is approaching and there has been an intermittent drizzle which has brought the temperature down a couple of notches. The scalding heat of the Indian summer appears a lot less oppressive as Babu Ganga Vishan reads a novel, reclining in the comfort of an easy chair in his room. The servant has been under the weather for a couple of days and Saroj is managing the kitchen in his absence.

Sitting on her haunches in the small kitchen, Saroj arranges a handful of slim logs so that they would light up properly in the hearth. She has a matchbox in her left hand and a matchstick poised between her thumb and index finger. Her attention, though, is riveted on an unrelated activity around the high ventilator window in the kitchen. A small wasp, of a brilliant yellow hue, is buzzing in an ever louder crescendo near the glass pane of the window. It flits from one end of the kitchen to the other, always returning to the same window to probe an opening, an outlet for an escape.

Saroj is drawn towards the plight of the wasp, as she gazes at it with little heed to the growing pile of burnt-out matches near her feet, or to the rapidly emptying matchbox in her hand. Getting up, she opens the door with the wire mesh, hoping to provide a larger exit to the trapped wasp as it continues to crash against the walls and against the glass pane of the window. But her noble intent is of no avail. The wasp continues in its aimless trajectories, ignoring the open door, and buzzes in frustration against the impenetrable walls. 'What a foolish creature!' Saroj wonders. 'It can't accept the confines of this kitchen, nor does it take the obvious way out of it. What does it really want?'

To prevent flies from entering the kitchen, she closes the door and turns her attention to the hearth. Placing a pot with some vegetables on the fire, she settles down on a low stool beside the hearth and finds herself getting swept away by the tide of her own thoughts. The logs, meanwhile, have come alive with a crackling, crimson flame and the burning smell of overcooked vegetables pull her out of her thoughts. She gets up to add some more water to the pot, grumbling about a fire that is slow to start and then picks up so quickly that the vegetables are caught unawares and end up being burnt!

The meandering flow of her musings is again interrupted. This time it is a stronger smell, not of burning vegetables but of cloth. A handful of restless embers have escaped the confines of the hearth to land on a duster that is now smouldering with an acrid smell. She brushes the ember off the cloth and reflects that it is best to keep your inner flames under check. Even the smallest spark can trigger a fire and lead to all manner of damage.

The wasp has again started to dart around the kitchen, buzzing louder with every failed attempt at freedom. Saroj goes across to open the door and this time the wasp spots the opening and makes its escape. Looking at its receding form, she wonders if the time has come for her to similarly open the portals of her own heart so that the one who has been occupying every bit of its space could also exit. But who was to assure that he would leave even if the door were left ajar. She stirs the pot with a steel ladle and, after satisfying herself that the dish was ready, removes the pot from the hearth and replaces it with the griddle to make some chapattis. While the griddle heats up, she turns her attention to preparing the dough.

A determined set of footsteps approaches the kitchen. As she glances over her shoulder to check, Bhapa Waryam Singh has materialized outside the door. He enters the kitchen with his customary informality.

'Sat Sri Akal, Bhapa ji' Saroj greets and moves the low stool towards him.

Waryam Singh eases himself on the stool and comes straight to the point.

'Look here, girl. You've again started interacting with him? Haven't you already suffered enough?' he chides. 'Listen to me, Saroj. There's no point getting upset with what I am saying. I have known you since you were a child. You've grown up playing in my lap. And you have such a pure heart that anyone who points a finger at you will be accursed. But you can't afford to be so naïve. Beware, Saroj, of the terrible time through which our society is passing. It is nothing short of Kalyug, the dark age of evil. People seem to revel in the misery of others. Someone's house is on fire and what does the bystander do? It is the blessings of Basantar, the Fire God, he says! Not a word of sympathy for the owner, for the pain he suffers because his house is burning. That's how we've become. We will spit at the moon if we can, though we know that some of the spit will probably fall back on our own face. But that's not going to deter us, is it? Just think about it! You were with him till ten last night, alone and in a secluded place. What if someone had seen you? Can you imagine the salacious tales they would have spread about you?'

Waryam Singh doesn't believe in beating about the bush. If he wants to convey something, he does so directly and without holding anything back. The only thing he ever tries to conceal is his own goodness.

Within a few minutes of his entry, he has spoken his mind about the issue that has been bothering him. Saroj would have been utterly mortified if anyone else had criticized her in this manner, or had dared to speak so candidly about such a delicate matter. But Waryam Singh is different. He could be a son who acted like a daughter or a brother who was like a sister. It is easy to confide in him. Besides, he has been aware of her secret for a fairly long time and Saroj has discussed it with him on several occasions in the past. But his unexpected reproach brings a touch of crimson to her face and she lowers her eyes.

'Are you angry that I brought this up, Saroj?' Waryam Singh lifts up her chin and asks.

'Of course not,' she responds. 'How can I get angry with you, Bhapa ji? I realize that you are only concerned about my welfare, but...'

'I know what that "but" means, Saroj. I am not a child. I believe that there is nothing that anyone can do to save Kuldeep. He is determined to become a hermit. He's completely lost his mind, that fool. Blessed be the True Word of the Guru. These charlatan saints...they are the real problem...playing havoc with the lives of others and enjoying the sight of their homes burning. And Kuldeep appears to be completely brainwashed by this so-called saint. Goes around telling anybody who cares to listen that he plans to renounce his home and hearth to become an ascetic, that he will join some dera and spend the rest of his life in prayer and meditation. I told him that his aging parents need him, that caring for them at this stage of their lives is the highest form of worship. But who is going to change his mind? I made the mistake of raising the matter with him this morning and he really got after me. He had the nerve to accuse me of pretending to be a good Samaritan while...I thought for a while that I should challenge him, ask him what he meant by that. But I decided to let it be. As you sow, so shall you reap.'

Having made three or four chapattis, Saroj sets them in a plate, adds some vegetables from the pot and interjects, 'Do wait for a minute, Bhapa ji. Let me take this plate across to Bau ji so that he can finish his meal. He had mentioned that he has to go somewhere.'

'Here, give it to me,' Waryam Singh says, taking the plate from her hand and going over to Ganga Vishan.

'Why don't you have some too,' Saroj offers when he returns. 'After that, we can relax and chat to our hearts' content.'

'No thanks. I don't feel hungry right now. I'm also in a bit of a rush today. Do carry on with your work and we can keep chatting,' he responds, picking up the threads of the conversation again. 'Saroj, I understand the state of your mind. But you must recognize that the path that you are pursuing is utterly futile and it will be best to abandon it. I believe you and Kuldeep must have discussed this matter when you were with him last night. I happened to see you together when I passed that way.'

'Bhapa ji, Satwant assigned an important responsibility to me,' she murmurs, her voice trailing off.

'I am aware of that, Saroj. Satwant also said a lot of things to me. She even asked me to prevail upon you and ensure that their home remains alive and inhabited.' Waryam sighs. 'But Saroj, I know Kuldeep better than you. You have only seen one aspect of his heart, while I have observed him from every different angle.'

Saroj listens silently, trying to gauge the unusually solemn look in his eyes.

'Kuldeep has one major failing in his character that hasn't yet come to your attention,' he continues. 'I have known him for many years now. There was a time when we may even have become close friends. But this flaw of his persuaded me to step back.'

'What flaw, Bhapa ji?' she enquires anxiously.

'He has no control over himself. He has no clarity of

purpose, no firmness of mind. When he desires something, he must have it at any cost. But it doesn't take long for him to get bored with it and act as though he has never been interested in it. I've seen this trait in him since he was a child. Have you ever been to his old room on the ground floor of their house? It is nothing less than a pawnbroker's shop. He'd buy a piece of furniture or some other item for the house, use it for a while before losing interest in it. A month later, he'd be off to the market to buy something else. Anything that catches his fancy, he has to acquire. Whether he needs it or not is secondary to him. He's had this obsessive trait in him for many years. After buying all manner of objects, he was suddenly bitten by a new bug of simplicity and reserve. So off went all the furniture and other stuff to the auction house to be put on sale. This also applies to his dress. He caught the English fad and started to dress in fancy jackets and trousers. This lasted for a while before he announced that wearing those clothes was nothing more than aping the British. I've seen these fads of his so many times now!' Waryam recalls wearily.

Saroj feels a rising sense of irritation and distaste over his description but makes no attempt to check him. He continues, 'He's been like this since he was a kid. It is his impetuousness that has prevented him from settling into any profession. He thought he wanted to be in the textiles business, so he started a clothing merchant's establishment but gave it up within months. Next, he set up a general merchandise store but that too didn't last and he moved on to open a grocery store. He's tried so many different things but never sticks with anything long enough to make it work. This volatile and restless nature of his is also reflected in his human relationships – in friendships and even in love. You may see him today, ready to sacrifice his own life for the sake of a friend. And ten days later, he can behave as though he has never seen that very person. Over the years, he has made many friends, and lost many too. And the same applies to his behaviour towards you. After all, he was in love with you, wasn't he? So how could he fall so easily for someone else?'

Saroj finds this unpalatable and objects, 'But Bhapa ji, under the circumstances what else could he have done?'

'That's just nonsense and excuses,' Waryam Singh replies tersely. 'Had he been disinclined to marry Satwant, he could have objected and his father could have done precious little about it. Look at the present situation and tell me if he is paying any heed to the wishes of his parents! They've been trying to persuade him for months now that he ought to get married again. But what does he do? Says he wants to go off and become a hermit!'

'But Bhapa ji...towards Satwant he was genuinely...'

'The brilliance of the full moon lasts four days. And then...? Darkness!' Waryam Singh retorts. 'Wait for a while and you'll see that Satwant doesn't even figure in his dreams. Please don't take me amiss, Saroj. I don't mean to sound overly critical about him. Poor fellow can't help it. That's how he is!'

Saroj finds it difficult to digest such censure about Kuldeep. Such unfair criticism of one who permeates every pore of her body! She is hurt and wants Waryam Singh to stop. But unable to muster the courage, she tries to suppress her own feelings. Her mind, though, has started to wander into unknown areas, wondering if there was a trace of jealousy underlying Waryam Singh's harshness.

Oblivious to such concerns, Waryam Singh continues, 'You

can expect a person like him to shower love and affection upon you in the short term. Just don't expect that he will remain faithful to you for any length of time. Would he have left Saroj for another person if he possessed an iota of faithfulness in his fibre? Does he see the beauty of the mind? Or is it just the beauty of the skin that attracts him?'

Scenes from the previous night start to crowd into her mind. 'My dear Saroj! Please don't try to extract a promise from me just yet...' She discerns a glimmer of truth in Waryam Singh's words, but not enough for her to believe everything he has said. She wants to say something to counter his thesis but restrains herself.

They are silent for a while, before Waryam speaks again. 'Listen, Saroj. You don't really have a whole lot of experience with the vicissitudes of life. You can find plenty of companions who will profess their love for you. The challenge is to find one who will remain faithful through thick and thin. Infatuation that is based on external beauty is like a shimmering pool, while true love has the purity of the natural spring. The pool looks pretty but it can dry up and it can also become dirty. But the spring...it may lack the lustre of the pool but it will keep flowing and it will remain clean.'

Saroj listens quietly, her head lowered. Waryam Singh pauses, trying to read her mind.

'Saroj!' he says with renewed determination.

She lifts her head. The glow of a mature wisdom appears to have replaced the shining innocence in her eyes.

Still trying to probe her gentle emotions, he persists, 'What is the point of subjecting yourself to pain when you know that nothing positive will come out of it?'

Saroj remains silent.

Waryam Singh's probing questions are beginning to look like a tough exam.

'Do you need a companion?'

Silence.

'You know that you can be completely candid with me. You do know that I only wish you well.'

'No, Bhapa ji, I am quite satisfied without a companion too...but...'

'But aren't you troubled by your lonesome life, by the emptiness in your heart, by your comatose soul?'

Saroj recoils, assailed by a familiar horror. As she turns an inquisitive glance towards Waryam Singh, her heart cries, 'Is this man sitting before me truly a noble spirit, or...?'

Looking deep into his eyes and at his face, her heart answers its own doubts. 'Of course. He is truly a noble soul.'

Undeterred, Waryam Singh continues, 'You are a widow. And as far as our society is concerned, you are barred from enjoying the beauty of love, from fulfilling your desires. Do you understand this?'

She lowers her eyes, unable to conjure a response.

'But if you are determined,' Waryam Singh asserts, 'you can break the shackles of society. You are no longer a minor. There is nothing that society or indeed even the law can do to stop you. That leaves your respected father. I don't see him coming in your way either. He cares too much for you and will be content in whatever brings happiness to you. My own view is that you must take a decisive position. You will gain absolutely nothing by trying to straddle two boats.'

Saroj lifts her head to look at his face, her eyes narrowing as they focus on the lips uttering such harsh words. She moves her gaze towards his eyes, noting that they are firmly fixed on her own, waiting for a decisive response from her. His look is direct, honest and guileless, infused with the nobility of his soul. It erases any residual apprehensions that she might have harboured about sharing her innermost feelings with an outsider.

'Bhapa ji', she pauses, searching perhaps for words that would best express her feelings. 'I have no physical desire. Indeed, I find myself quite free from it. But still...'

'Go on! Do say whatever you have in mind without any hesitation.' He pats her on the back in encouragement.

'But my heart...' She pauses in mid-sentence, reflecting once more on what she wants to say.

'Why have you gone silent again? Don't you trust me fully?'

'No, Bhapa ji, it's not that.'

'So what is it? Anyway, I can't really compel you if you don't want to share this with me. Let it be.'

'But I do think that I must discuss it with you. There is no one else that I can share it with.'

'Go ahead then. Open your heart!'

'A woman's heart beats in my breast, Bhapa ji. Maybe I can explain myself better if I write to you about it. I may not be able to speak about it.'

'All right then. As you please,' Waryam Singh says, rising from the stool. 'Perhaps I have already discerned whatever you wanted to convey to me. Your heart yearns for true love but you haven't been able to find it. You are troubled by the loneliness that occupies your heart. But you can't speak openly about it; there is nobody that you can share it with. Without the warm touch of a loved one, your heart appears to float around in a state of despair. And you are attracted by memories of Kuldeep that belong to the distant past. Who knows? Kuldeep might even agree to marry you but that thought is not what excites you. What you desire is a share of his heart. Silly girl! You know that's not going to happen. Your infatuation with this idea has already led to the needless loss of one innocent life. You just don't understand how our society works. They won't even hold back from pointing their ugly fingers at an angel like you. Can't you appreciate this reality? Do you really want to go through that?'

Tears stream down Saroj's face.

'Do you agree with what I say?' Waryam Singh asks.

Saroj closes her eyes. 'Of course you are right, Bhapa ji. It appears that you can read my mind.'

'In that case, you must take a clear decision on the path that you wish to pursue – of detachment or of domesticity?'

She is silent.

'There is no guarantee, Saroj, that a life of detachment will be bland or tasteless, nor that a family life will open the gateways to heaven. You discover the reality only after you have started your journey on the path that you have chosen. Either possibility can become a reality, and maybe neither.'

'In that case, Bhapa ji, I am happy to follow your advice. You can tell me what my path should be and I will follow it. I don't think I am able to take this decision on my own.'

'Don't be silly.' Waryam Singh smiles. 'How can you ask someone else to choose your path for you? And you want to take the counsel of one who has never chosen his own course? I am afraid you will have to map your own destiny.'

'I think I'll need to reflect on this a little bit longer before I can decide,' Saroj responds after a brief pause.

'Yes please. Do think it through carefully,' he cautions, stepping out of the door.

'And I have to ask you a small favour, Saroj. I hope it won't be too much of an imposition.'

'Do tell me, Bhapa ji.' Her eyes light up with enthusiasm.

'Will you be able to come to my place tonight?'

Stunned, she looks at him quizzically. His countenance radiates the same sense of serenity and assurance. She knows that he has posed a tough question. To visit the home of a single man, and that too at night! Why? Her mind lurches around, confused, as she mumbles, 'I'll come, Bhapa ji.'

Saroj sits down on the low stool in the kitchen, looking after him long after he had left. What have I done now? she wonders. Why did I promise that I will come?

14

It has been raining since mid-day and dusk is descending. Saroj is restless, her mind in turmoil. Several issues conspire to keep her in this state. First, the state of affairs with Kuldeep. Second, the thought of having to go to Waryam Singh's house that night continues to nag her. And third, she is increasingly concerned that Babu Ganga Vishan had been gone since breakfast and there is no sign of him. With the rain still continuing, there is little chance that he would come home dry. The rumble of clouds seems to drive an alcoholic towards his bottle much the same way that the sound of ducks takes a hunter towards his gun.

She has already sent the servant to the liquor store twice to inquire about her father's whereabouts. He has also gone to some of his other favourite haunts but has drawn a blank. She knows that her father tended to avoid coming home when he was drunk because he didn't want to face her. This wasn't out of fear that the daughter would get angry with her father. Anger and rudeness simply aren't part of Saroj's nature. But she does have one very formidable weapon before which Babu Ganga Vishan finds himself defenceless. He simply cannot bring himself to see tears in her eyes.

But could her tears keep him away from liquor? No, sir. If her tears alone could have performed this miracle, Saroj would have gladly shed every teardrop that she could muster and make him drink a glassful of them. Alas! That her tears alone could provide him the intoxication that he craved!

Her mind turns towards Kuldeep. Waryam Singh had brought forth a number of startling elements. Had these affected her feelings towards Kuldeep? Not really. Kuldeep has left a very deep imprint on her and it cannot be erased so easily. But she is willing to concede that his picture may have become a little bit hazy since the morning's conversation. Maybe, also, that some of its sheen has worn off, its glow dimmed somewhat. But he has occupied such a prominent place in her heart for so long that removing him from there so abruptly is simply out of the question. Besides, how can she disregard the responsibility that Satwant, in her dying moments, had assigned to her with the words, 'Saroj! You are the only one who can look after Kuldeep.'

She is still trying her best to erase the effects of the previous night but her efforts so far have been in vain. Her love for Kuldeep and her sense of duty towards Satwant exert a strong influence. But after seeing his attitude, she despairs that she will neither get love nor manage to discharge her obligation. Waryam Singh had further complicated matters by showing her the other, previously unknown dimension of Kuldeep's personality. And by asking her to come to his home that night.

She grapples with this entirely new situation. Why has he called her and what is she expected to do there? Besides, there is no sign of her father. If he didn't show up soon, how could she just leave the house and go? And if he did turn up, what would his condition be? Would it be right for her to leave him alone if he were in no state to look after himself?

Like the coiled paths on a hillside, her thoughts meander along indistinct tracks that often intersect in ways that make the traveller lose his bearings. Agitated and unsure, she gropes for a way through the tangle.

It is beginning to get dark and it is pouring. She goes to her room and picks up a book to read. A moist breeze takes advantage of the open window to enter the room, gently blowing her dupatta over her shoulder. She is unable to fix her eyes on the pages of her book. Images of Kuldeep float up to her eyes, his words from the previous night echoing in her ears, 'Dear Saroj! I have lost all interest in this world. I don't want to get caught up in the web of relationships and attachments.'

Has he really lost all interest, she wonders. Has Satwant's demise really left such a large void that no one can fill it? But why am I so worried about it? What is he to me? Nothing, really. There is no dearth of men in this world, and he is just one of them. If it is his misery that binds me to him, I am sure I can find other men who are even forlorn. Why am I so obsessed about helping him out of his misery? Is there a hidden motive of my own that lies tucked away in some mysterious fold of this story? If so, what could it be? And if not, why do I find myself frequently swept away in this flood of thoughts about him? Then, there are those revelations that Bhapa Waryam Singh made about him this morning. How do I know if all of that is true?

Night has fallen and it is still pouring. The streets in the neighbourhood have started to get flooded and the drains are beginning to overflow. Her thoughts dart from Kuldeep to her father's continued absence before settling on Waryam Singh. Maybe this heavy rain is a good thing. It gives me an excuse to avoid going to his house. But why should I have to offer any excuse at all. I am not beholden to him or to anyone else. All I need to say is that I wasn't able to come!

Getting up from the chair, she peers through the open window to see if she might catch a glimpse of her father coming down the street. There is still no sign of him. Where could he be in this weather? she frets.

She has barely settled back into her chair than she hears a clumsy knock on the door. It hadn't been bolted and she sees her father push it open and stumble into the room. Looking at his wretched condition, she steps back and takes a deep breath. He is drenched from head to toe and his clothes are covered with mud at several places. He is barely in control of himself. An unfinished half-litre bottle of liquor sticks out of his pocket.

There is no point in saying anything to him at this time. She calls the servant and together, they help Ganga Vishan change into his night clothes and settle him into his bed. Saroj goes to her own room to lie down but there is too much going on in her mind to allow any hint of sleep. Nor does she have any appetite for dinner. A strong current of thoughts carries her in its flow. Should she go to Waryam Singh's house or should she stay back? Maybe if the rain eases up, I'll go, she reasons with herself. But the rain tonight is in no mood to cooperate. It continues to pour, maybe even harder than before.

The clock strikes ten and she gets up with a start. Looking through her window, she sees that the downpour appears even more menacing thanks to the strong gusts of wind. It is pitch dark and the solitary street light is a feeble glimmer that only serves to light up the inky black water all around it. The noise of the rain batters at her eardrums.

Moved by some inner force, she gets up and reaches for an umbrella. The servant is washing dishes in the kitchen. She goes across to him and instructs, 'Mangtu, I have to go out to see a patient. You can bring your cot downstairs and bolt the door from inside. But stay awake till I get back, will you. I don't want to be standing outside and knocking the door down with you fast asleep. Understand?'

'Okay, Bibi ji,' the boy mumbles and continues with his chores.

Saroj braces herself against a looming fear as she steps out of her house. It is dark and there isn't a soul in sight. The wind howls around the street, making it a challenge to open the umbrella and to hang on to it. Not that it offers much protection against the swirling rain which seems to come at her from every direction. She pauses for a minute, contemplating the possibility of retreating back to the comfort of her home before gritting her teeth and setting down the street. She has barely walked about fifty paces or so when a strong gust almost snatches the umbrella out of her grasp. Clinging on to it, she sees that it has been wrenched inside out and rendered virtually useless against the rain. Her clothes are completely drenched and her sari billows in the wind. She flings the upturned umbrella in the general direction of her house and makes a determined bid to tie the errant fringes of the sari in a tight little knot around her waist.

She is now striding directly into the wind. The showers come straight into her face, blinding her with their fury, making every step an uphill task. The temptation to turn back towards her home again presents itself. Besides, what would people say if anyone sees her out on her own at this time of the night and under such conditions? But a strange kind of power has taken hold of her as she brushes aside her fears and continues on a path fraught with risks.

She is shivering with cold by the time she reaches the gate of Babu Mohalla. Her teeth chatter but there is a firmness in her steps as she leaves her neighbourhood behind and moves towards her destination.

She is now on the main road and the wind is behind her, pushing her forward with a force that makes it difficult to maintain her balance. The wet sari, clinging around her legs, also does not help matters as she tries to sidestep one puddle after another. Twice, she stumbles and almost falls but somehow manages to regain her balance in the nick of time.

Babu Mohalla has been left far behind and she is now going past Kunj Lal Street before approaching Maakhnia's Centre where Waryam Singh lives. She can see a light coming from his house, indicating that the front door is open.

She is going to turn towards his house when she sees a man cross the street a few yards away. She has traversed the entire journey from Babu Mohalla without running into anyone and thinks that she has safely managed to overcome an important hurdle. But her heart skips a beat as she sees the silhouette of the stranger. Is it someone who might know me? she wonders. Peering into the darkness, she realizes to her horror that it isn't just anybody. It is Kuldeep. Wearing a raincoat, a kerosene lamp in hand, he seems to be hurrying somewhere. Their eyes meet for a brief second as they cross each other before they avert their glances, pretending that they have seen nothing. Kuldeep's footsteps slow momentarily before regaining speed as he goes past her. Struggling to get a grip on herself, Saroj approaches Waryam Singh's house.

Heart still pounding, she enters his room. This is the first time that she has actually stepped inside his place. It is a fairly small room, with a door at the back that seems to lead into an even smaller chamber. A cursory glance reveals a minimalist set-up that certainly appears inadequate for the needs of any individual. One corner is occupied by a cheap sort of bed, covered by a rough-looking sheet. An alcove in the wall next to the bed provides a base for a small lamp. Some well-worn clothes and two pairs of old shoes are strewn in another corner. The untidy appearance of the room suggests that it has been quite a while since anyone has bothered to clean it and put things in an orderly fashion.

A doorless cupboard with three wooden shelves nestles against the wall opposite the bed. An assortment of medical supplies – bandages, cartons with medicines, some cotton, a few bottles with tincture, lotion and such like – occupies most of the space on the shelves. The room has no windows, a small ventilator shaft near the ceiling providing the only possible access to some fresh air. With the bed occupying much of the room, it is clearly a place that the inhabitant uses for sleeping only.

As she takes in her surroundings, Saroj recoils with a sense of disgust. I had no idea that Waryam Singh was so careless, that he maintained such a shabby lifestyle, she thinks. The sounds of a painful groan emanating from the little chamber at the back of his room interrupt her thoughts.

Waryam Singh is standing near the bed in drenched clothes. Seeing her enter, he gives her a rolled-up newspaper and gestures towards the chamber. 'Take this lamp with you and change your clothes first,' he instructs.

Without saying a word, Saroj takes the roll, picks up the lamp and goes into the chamber. She is taken aback by the sight that greets her. A young woman, apparently on the verge of death, lies on a cot, groaning. Her emaciated body is little more than a skeleton. It is tough to tell how old she is but Saroj surmises that she must be at least twenty. A stench similar to that of rotting flesh comes from the dirty rags in which she is clothed. Saroj shrinks in her corner, assailed by a wave of nausea. She wants to immediately flee from this hellhole. Holding her breath, she unwraps the newspaper to discover a plain cotton sari and vest. Clearly, Waryam Singh had no doubt that she would brave the rain to come to his place and had gone to the market in anticipation to buy these articles. But how could he be so confident that I would come, she muses.

She changes into the dry clothes as quickly as she can before returning to his room. Shuddering at the thought of the putrid stench in the chamber she takes a deep breath. Waryam Singh has collected a selection of medical items from the shelves of the doorless cupboard and appears to be waiting for her.

'Please come inside, Saroj,' he bolts the front door shut and asks her to follow him into the chamber. Disregarding her own revulsion, she quietly obeys and follows him.

'Who is she, Bhapa ji?' she asks.

He sets the medical supplies on a newspaper and settles down besides the head of the patient. 'We'll come to that later.

Let's first attend to the task for which I have called you here,' he says. 'Pull up her shirt along the back and all the way up to her shoulders.'

Looking at the girl's back as she lifts up her shirt, a shiver goes down Saroj's spine and she feels dizzy. A wound as large as her hand and as deep as her fingernail is spread across the middle of the girl's back. Neglect over an extended period of time has caused an infection so acute that even specialized surgeons would have hesitated to tend to her.

With a determined look in his eyes, Waryam Singh ignores the wails of pain and spends the next half hour trying to clean the wound and putting a bandage around it with Saroj's help. He helps her sit up for a minute to give her some milk before allowing her to lie down in a slightly more comfortable posture.

Saroj is beginning to feel extremely uneasy about her prolonged absence from home. Turning towards Waryam Singh, she implores, 'It is getting really late. Do help me get home, Bhapa ji.'

He can see the worry, nay fear, writ large on her face but replies firmly, 'I'm sorry, Saroj. You can't go home tonight and leave me alone with an unknown young woman in my house.'

'I understand that, but I really can't stay here any longer,' she protests.

'In that case, please take her home with you. For tonight only. I'll make sure that she gets admitted to hospital first thing tomorrow,' he pleads with a hint of desperation.

What does he mean? That I should become the custodian of her corpse for the night, Saroj wonders. 'I'm sorry, Bhapa ji. I can't do this,' she replies firmly.

'All right, then. Let's go.' Waryam Singh bends down to put on his shoes. He opens the door to get a sense of the weather. The rain has eased a bit, though the wind is still pretty strong. Saroj can see the disappointment in his eyes as he steps out of the house. She feels ashamed that she is letting him down. But she knows she simply doesn't have the stomach for the groans of pain and the combined stink of rotting flesh and formaldehyde permeating the room.

Without further comment, she follows him as he escorts her home, before trudging back to the patient.

15

Kuldeep hasn't experienced a moment of happiness since his return home from prison. Satwant's demise has destroyed his aspirations much like an unseasonal hailstorm devastates a ripe spring crop. His life is like a boat caught in the turbulent midstream of a river in flood. Neither bank of the river is in sight to offer some sense of hope.

Barely a few days back, he had been like a bird on song, winging its way towards its beloved. But his entire little universe had been shattered by the shocking news of her death. Now, thanks to the guidance of his spiritual guru, his boat is acquiring new purpose and direction, and moving towards salvation. The pain is still there, though its intensity seems to be diminishing with each passing day. The colour of his attachment to the world around him has also started to fade under the soothing balm of salvation that his guru is administering to him. The unexpected encounter with Saroj that night, however, appears to have applied a fresh coat of paint to it. He feels himself like the wretched soul who is forced to remain astride not one, not two, but three boats.

The sight of Saroj has created such turmoil in him that he thinks he is losing his mind. Helpless, he falls at the feet of his guru and seeks his protection. After about two and a half hours of discourse, he feels his sinking spirits propped up by a new force. Under the power of the guru's sermon, his misgivings start to subside and he is imbued with a fresh energy. He is impatient to get away from the familiarity of his home, his surroundings and to make a fresh start in his life.

So when did he fall in love with Saroj? He isn't quite sure. But he does remember the time when they were deeply involved with each other, a time when they had exchanged vows of everlasting love, when they had even glimpsed a part of heaven somewhere in their distant future. It was, however, nothing but a mirage – one that not only disappeared in an instant but also changed everything around them.

Saroj wasn't particularly wise or mature at the time. Her early experience with widowhood had left her with the firm belief that marriage wasn't meant for her. Even when her innocent mind fell for Kuldeep, she was looking for little more than the fulfilment of love. Kuldeep, on the other hand, was at a stage of life where he was expected to acquire a life companion and settle into married life.

Saroj had surrendered her heart and soul to Kuldeep. And maybe Kuldeep had also done the same. But there was a big difference in their minds and in their perceptions about self-interest. Kuldeep was keen on marriage and even though the idea ran contrary to Saroj's belief, she found it hard to turn him down. She promised that if she could obtain the consent of her father and of society, she would gladly be his wife. That stage, however, was never reached.

Kuldeep's parents were the first to get upset when they learned of his intention. His proximity to Saroj was already becoming the talk of a neighbourhood where the very mention of a widow's name was considered a bad omen. They swung into action and started pursuing every possible option to find a suitable match. For a while, Kuldeep resisted and turned down several proposals. But that lasted only until he was shown Satwant's photograph and he agreed to marry her. Saroj learnt of this unexpected development only after he was formally betrothed to Satwant. Was it because she was fair-skinned, while Saroj had a darker complexion? one wondered.

The news came as a shock to Saroj. Yet, she was not overly distraught because she felt that she could still retain her association with him. She was being naïve, the foolish girl, not realizing that her place in Kuldeep's heart would quickly be supplanted by another one. Her hopes that she would continue to stay in contact with Kuldeep also did not materialize. There could be two reasons for this. First, Kuldeep was completely captivated by the beauty of his bride and Saroj didn't quite measure up on that particular yardstick. Second, the neighbourhood had been rife with gossip about his relationship with Saroj and he found this completely intolerable. To bring matters to a close, he wrote a stern letter to Saroj advising that she should neither try to meet him, nor correspond with him. Saroj replied with her own final letter to him, and we know that as a consequence, Kuldeep stormed out of his house and Satwant left this world forever.

For Kuldeep, this was the first time after Satwant's death that he had once again felt some stirrings towards Saroj. The Saroj that he had met the other night was so different from the exuberant young maiden that he had known. She had spoken with such maturity, almost like the ideal woman of his imagination. The Saroj of yore was only the girl next door that he loved. This one was so much more – an epitome of self-sacrifice, a guide and a reformer too.

The evening after he met her, Kuldeep is sitting in his first-floor room for his usual meditation and recitation of verses from the holy book. His concentration is broken by a sharp spray of rain that splashes over the back of his head and trickles down his neck. Irritated, he looks back to see that rain is coming in through the open ventilator shaft. He gets up to close the ventilator before settling down once again into the cross-legged posture that he employs for prayer and meditation. It is about nine and he can hear the rain pelting down. Getting up once again, he starts to pace up and down. Everything in the small room appears scattered and out of place. He thinks of Satwant and the way she'd make sure that everything was kept in an orderly fashion, when the room was dusted not just once but several times in the day. Images of Satwant fussing around the room are so real that he wonders if she really had left this world for ever, that she wouldn't come back soon to set the room in order again. Out of the blue, he hears a voice very close to him, 'For your sake, dear Kuldeep, I shall become your Satwant.'

His pace quickens as he peers closely at every object in the room with a new-found interest. A pile of books are stacked haphazardly in the cupboard. He picks up one and finds several more tumbling down to the floor. The way the books had been arranged defied any method or classification. The hardbound little gutkas with verses from the holy Guru Granth Sahib are at the bottom of the pile. A few religious tracts are placed on top of the gutkas, followed by commentaries and explanations of a few other scriptures, a substantial sort of book on the life of Guru Nanak and a few assorted publications. The table near the cupboard is as chaotic. A few old newspapers and magazines, along with a couple of gutkas and a few books – all scattered in a manner that getting to any particular object would have been a real chore. The cot and its bedspread, clothes, shoes and pretty much everything else appear similarly out of place. There are pegs to hang the clothes properly, yet the jacket is struggling to cling on to the leg of the cot and the trousers dangle from the top of the door. His turban and one of his shirts compete for space with the books and magazines. The shoe rack with three shelves seems to belong to everything other than shoes. The top shelf has a small clock that waits for someone to wind it so that it can resume its habitual ticking. The middle shelf is home to an ink pot, a tube of toothpaste, a writing pad and various other odds and ends. A bottle of aspirin and a tin of Ovaltine occupy the bottom shelf. One pair of shoes gathers dust near the foot of the bed while another has settled down next to the steel trunk. One of his slippers sits absurdly on the chair, apparently abandoned by its companion that is nowhere to be seen. A small tin of shoe polish and a brush sit disconsolately next to a duster. Everything is as Kuldeep had discovered it that fateful day and he has not allowed a soul to enter his room and set it right.

'Kuldeep! Please come down for a moment!' his mother calls out from below. Overcoming his reluctance, he makes his way down the stairs.

Entering the room downstairs, his eyes first fall on his ailing father. They move to his child, sleeping peacefully in the cradle. And they settle on his mother's crestfallen countenance. Their eyes meet briefly and he knows in an instant that all his efforts to cultivate a sense of tranquillity has come to naught. The familiar noose of family ties and attachments stares him in the face.

'Looks like nothing bothers you, my son,' his mother begins her harangue. 'Are you concerned about your father's failing health? Sure, you should continue with your prayers and your meditation. No one is going to obstruct you from following that path. But you must also think of your home and of your own health. Just look at the way this sickly pallor has spread over your face. You haven't eaten a morsel in five days. How long can anyone survive in this state? Maybe we should get someone to counsel you. After all, who else do we have but you to look after us at this age? Ever since that witch Radhia left, this child of yours doesn't let me do anything in the house. Waryam Singh, at least, used to drop in once in a while to check if we needed something. He too hasn't showed up for days now and I wonder if he has gone off on leave or something.'

Kuldeep is barely taking note of his mother's outpourings. His mind has already moved on to his guru and he can see himself sitting at his feet, listening intently to his sermon. His body, meanwhile, ambles across to his father and sits by his bed. 'How are you feeling today, Bapu ji?' he hears his voice say.

'Deep,' Sadhu Singh sighs deeply as he speaks. His eyes are moist with tears. 'What am I seeing, Deep?'

'What is it, Bapu ji?' Kuldeep's foot taps the floor idly. Sadhu Singh is silent, tears streaming down his face as he gazes at his son. Kuldeep knows what his father will say.

Sadhu Singh clears his throat before speaking. 'I had such

high hopes of you, Deep. I had these dreams that my son would grow up and be the support that I need in my old age so that I can spend my final years in comfort. We saw you grow up, one day at a time, and we cherished these hopes. But...' His voice cracks and he is unable to continue.

The tears in Sadhu Singh's eyes, the pain so evident in his voice would have been enough to melt any son's heart. But Kuldeep is unmoved. There is no visible effect on his face or, indeed, in his demeanour. Nor does he utter a word in response. Instead, it is his guru's words that echo in his ears:

It is mine, it is mine, they always say
So attached they are to this way!

'Why don't you speak up, son? I am your father, after all. I do have some claim on you. Say something, please. Talk candidly with me and maybe I can...'

Kuldeep's mind is still focused on his guru's sermon.

Mother or father, son or brother
Relatives near or far, even your wife
None will matter once you are gone
And you will be no more than a ghost

Tears course down the old man's cheeks as his trembling hand tries to caress his son's back. 'Speak up, my precious. Do talk to me. Let me know what's going on in your mind.'

'Talking much only produces evil,' Kuldeep hears the words in his head.

Once more, Sadhu Singh sighs deeply and puts his arms around his son. 'Look at me, my dear. Don't you have any idea about my condition? If you insist on remaining mum like this, I swear I will bang my head against this wall and breathe my last right before your eyes.'

His father's voice carries a strange kind of resolve that Kuldeep can no longer ignore. Looking up, he asks softly, 'What do you want me to do, Bapu ji?'

'I want to see my son flourish and be happy.'

'In other words, you want me to get married, right?'

His father nods in agreement.

'But I have already fulfilled this desire of yours once, haven't I?'

'It wasn't fulfilled. It was terminated halfway.'

'And who can guarantee that it will fructify this time?'

'There is never a complete guarantee for anything. But it is hope that sustains this life of ours.'

'Bapu ji, don't our scriptures say that every breath we take is precious and that we are the most fortunate of all creatures because we were born as human beings? Why not use every breath of ours to remember His Name and make our life a true success?'

Sadhu Singh is at a loss for words. A part of him tells him that he has no reason to be unhappy. Under similar circumstances, young men of Kuldeep's age have been known to go completely astray and even destroy their lives prematurely. His son, at least, seems to be following a noble and righteous path. But the other part reminds him that what he needs most at this time is to have his son by his side. Instead, he can see the writing on the wall. Kuldeep is rapidly slipping out of his grasp.

Father and son chat for about an hour, until their conversation is abruptly interrupted when Sadhu Singh breaks into a violent bout of coughing. It turns out to be much worse than his usual attack of asthma, and they can see his condition deteriorate sharply. He needs an injection, which means getting hold of the doctor.

Kuldeep grabs his raincoat and sets off in the direction of the doctor's house without giving a second thought to the raging storm. As he approaches Maakhnia's Centre, he sees someone on the other side of the road, braving the rain with small, unsteady steps. As they get closer, he sees that it is Saroj and his heart lets out an involuntary cry. 'Where is she going at this time of the night?' he asks himself in a trembling voice. His steps falter for a second before gathering pace once again as he crosses her. He takes another ten or fifteen steps before pausing momentarily to look over his shoulder. Saroj is nowhere to be seen and it takes him a split second to figure out that she could only have gone inside Waryam Singh's place. He winces in pain, as though a dagger had been driven through his heart. 'Going into the house of Waryam Singh? A man who is single and unattached? At this hour?'

He had been nursing some doubts about Waryam Singh's character. He considers him a self-serving, good-for-nothing busybody who is constantly trying to be the centre of attention. He is of a lowly status, excessively chatty and a person girls from decent families should avoid for the sake of their own reputations. Kuldeep is aware, of course, that Waryam Singh had been quite helpful during Satwant's illness. But who could be sure that he wasn't pursuing some ulterior agenda of his own. It is suspicions like these that had led him to do some plain speaking with Waryam Singh the previous night.

Thoughts about Saroj have temporarily displaced concern about his ailing father from Kuldeep's mind. He is assailed with unexpected misgivings about her, driving him crazy.

Accompanied by the doctor, he takes the same road on his way back, slowing down as he approaches Waryam Singh's house to gently nudge the door. It is shut and he thinks he can hear the cries of a female voice, struggling perhaps to escape from a stronger person's clasp. The clattering sound of the rain and the noise of the howling wind, however, make it impossible to know for sure if it is Saroj's voice.

He is in a daze and would probably have stopped right there if it hadn't been for the doctor by his side. Weighed down by disappointment with Saroj and contempt for Waryam Singh, he reluctantly wills himself to keep moving.

The doctor administers the injection to Sadhu Singh, collects his fees and leaves. Under the effect of the medicine, Sadhu Singh drifts into a fitful sleep, allowing Kuldeep to go up to his own room. He tries to sleep but in vain – the entire evening has been hell and it plays on his mind which is spinning out of control. Sleep appears a distant and unrealistic possibility.

16

There are times when embers from the fires of suspicion can turn an entire edifice of hope into ashes. Kuldeep is in such a situation. The sight of Saroj that evening has destroyed his peace of mind. Doubts about her motives and her true character would have continued to gnaw at him if it hadn't been for another misfortune – the demise of his father within a few days of that asthmatic attack.

During the couple of months that have elapsed since the death of Sadhu Singh, Waryam Singh has visited their house on several occasions, to offer his condolences or just because he happened to be passing by. The rage in Kuldeep's eyes whenever he comes face to face with Waryam Singh is unmistakable. His words of sympathy to Gian Kaur over the demise of her husband are like spears hurled at Kuldeep's heart.

'Why am I so bothered about this?' Kuldeep would often ask himself. 'Why should I allow this fire to consume me from within? It's their life. If Saroj has an unholy relationship with this man, if he is acting in a manner that will destroy her life, so be it! This world is full of sinners and immoral characters. It isn't for me to decide upon their punishment. As you sow, so shall you reap. And what kind of a relationship do I have with Saroj that I should get so worked up about her affairs? I am the one who decided that I would break off with her. And yet, I find myself unable to concentrate on my prayer and meditation. What kind of a fool am I?'

It is difficult and perhaps impossible to fully comprehend one's own mind. If one could, the world would have been a different place. In reality, though, there are situations where you cannot do what you really want, and end up doing things that run contrary to the very core of your being. Kuldeep wants to wipe the crisscrossing thoughts from his mind's slate so that he can sit in seclusion and enjoy the bliss of meditation. But no matter how hard he tries, they refuse to dim and some become even sharper than before. His mind seems constantly preoccupied with one issue or another – pining at the loss of Satwant, struggling to escape the web that Saroj has cast around him, fretting about his little child or worrying about his mother. To make matters worse, there is no one around to help him steer his boat to safety. He has become accustomed to falling back on the support of his guru whenever accosted by doubts and dilemmas. But Sant Prem

Singh has gone off to Amritsar and Kuldeep finds himself more alone than ever.

It is around ten in the morning. The cool October breeze carries a hint of the approaching winter. Kuldeep appears in a better mood as he lies on his bed to savour once again a letter that he had already read several times.

> *My dear disciple Kuldeep Singh*
>
> *My blessings to you. I received your letter and was worried about the turbulent state of your mind. You have mentioned that you are unable to focus on meditation and that your mind tends to drift towards the woman, towards your son, towards other mortal beings. The only way to cleanse your mind is to immerse it in hymns and in meditation and to surrender yourself at His feet. And beware of the company of women. Always remember that the woman is the source of all troubles. The meditation spells of some of our greatest sages were destroyed by women. If you seek the path of righteousness, you should study books like the Vairag Shatak which explores the joys of renunciation through one hundred verses. Stay away from the company of the sinful and learn to recite His Name with every breath you take.*
>
> *Your guide*
> *Sant Prem Singh*

Still in a reverie, he hears Waryam Singh's voice echoing in the room downstairs. It pricks the bubble of tranquillity in which he had surrounded himself, bringing a surge of anger in its wake. For a moment, he thinks of marching down to deliver the ultimatum that Waryam Singh should stop coming to their home and start minding his own business.

He is restrained by the fact that his mother is clearly fond of Waryam Singh and even draws solace from him.

Against his will, Kuldeep rises from the bed and quietly makes his way down the stairs. Waryam Singh is sitting on a low stool before Gian Kaur and explaining, 'What can I say, Bey ji? It's just one thing or another that keeps me preoccupied. Otherwise, I'd love to come over a lot more often. Please don't think that Waryam Singh has forgotten you. You may only need water but I won't hesitate for a moment to shed blood for you. Bau ji has left us and it isn't in my power to bring him back. But I will make sure that all your requirements are met. Call me in the middle of the night if you need me and I'll be there.'

Kuldeep finds it painful to digest Waryam Singh's words. To him, they reek of flattery, duplicity and craftiness. He hears his mother respond, 'My son, I only have you and my guru for support now. Your father may have been bedridden since quite a while but there was a comfort in his presence, like a strong umbrella over your head to protect you. Whatever he earned, he handed it over to me with never a question about where I spent the money.'

Glancing towards Kuldeep, she pleads, 'The only thing I can ask now is that this son of mine should become sensible, that the doors of this house should again be open and welcoming. He's hardly had the chance to enjoy a happily married life. Look at our own desires and aspirations, the cruel way in which they have been crushed. And look at this poor child. Deprived of the love and nourishment that he would have received from his own mother. He is now the only joy of my life. I wish I could get up and play with him but my wretched arthritis doesn't let me. At least while Radhia was here, the child was getting some care and attention. But look at him now. He's reduced to half his earlier size and has to depend on milk from outside to survive.'

'Why did Radhia leave, Bey ji?' Waryam Singh looks kindly at the child as he enquires.

'What can I say, my son?' Gian Kaur sighs. 'It is like a snake that has a lizard trapped in its mouth. If he eats it, he becomes a leper and if he lets it go, it will blind him. Radhia was like that. It was like being caught between the devil and the deep sea. She had to steal anything on which she could lay her hands. I let it pass once, twice, thrice...But how long can you afford to keep ignoring such thievery? To top it all, she had also started to act pricey. She didn't appreciate that she was getting fistfuls of cash for doing next to nothing. These people! I tell you they just can't climb out of their little minds. Give them an inch and they want the whole yard. I know them well! Just watch for a few days and see what happens. She'll become straight like an arrow once that brood of hers has to go hungry for a couple of days. Pilfering stuff from the kitchen had become a habit for her. You see a pot one day and the next day it's gone. You leave some cash around and it's disappeared. Can't you find someone else, god bless you?' Suddenly remembering her rosary, she picks it up and starts counting the beads furiously, trying perhaps to make up for lost time.

'I'm sure I can find someone who can look after the child. In fact, I do have a woman in mind for this. But she won't be able to nurse him like Radhia could,' Waryam Singh observes.

The hand counting the beads of the rosary slows down for a while as Gian Kaur counters, 'The child now gets his milk from a bottle so breast-feeding is no longer needed. What I really need is someone who can attend to him. Even an elderly woman would work just fine, god bless you.'

'The woman that I have in mind is not an elderly one. She is quite young, in fact, and what she needs from you is some love and tenderness. I am not sure if she can take your scolding the way Radhia could. But if it works out, she may be able to handle your household chores in addition to minding the child. I think you'll find her a willing and competent worker. She is a bit frail right now because she is recovering from an illness but she's no slacker when it comes to work.'

'Why would I scold her?' Gian Kaur responds. 'You've brought up Radhia but that witch was a troublemaker right from the beginning. She would always be complaining, about one thing or another, and had the most vile temperament. She would eat like a pig all day and still have the nerve to glare at me. But I never spoke a harsh word to her. Never!'

'All right, Bey ji. What will you pay her?'

'I am happy to pay whatever you say. If she is good, we'll go the extra mile to look after her. There is no dearth of anything, by the grace of god. And if she turns out to be a cheat like Radhia, I'll have to deal with her.'

'She's no cheat, Bey ji. You'll know this for yourself when you see her. She is a sight for sore eyes. Comes from a decent family but has fallen upon bad times. Anyway, tell me what you want to pay her so that I can try to settle this.'

'Whatever you say, I told you.'

'How much were you paying Radhia?'

'Ten rupees a month plus food and clothes.'

'That should be fine, to start with. If she performs to your satisfaction, you could give her a raise.'

'Certainly. It is her work that matters to me, not her looks.'

'Fine, then. I'll bring her over tomorrow.'

'Perfect. Make sure you don't forget.'

'I'll make sure,' Waryam Singh promises as he gets up to leave. 'Do let me know if there is anything else that I can do, Bey ji. I am like your own son.'

Overwhelmed, Gian Kaur raises her hand to bless him. 'May you live long, my son. May you remain the true epitome of righteousness. May others look up to you and emulate you. You are the one that people should remember first thing in the morning. May my son Kuldeep also live long, and his son too. Who else does this old woman have to support her?'

Waryam Singh turns back to glance at Kuldeep. 'Bey ji, I suggest that you shouldn't bother Kuldeep too much.' He smiles. 'Why should you interfere with his meditation when you have me around to tend to these mundane worldly chores?'

Waryam Singh is about to step out of the house when a sharp retort from Kuldeep stops him in his tracks. Kuldeep's reservoir of patience has finally overflowed its banks.

'For someone who is always so tied up with so many sincere and honest tasks, where is the time for mundane chores?' Kuldeep taunts.

'Honest tasks? What honest tasks are you talking about?' Waryam asks, looking closely at Kuldeep.

'The ones that are the talk of every street and neighbourhood and which...' Not wanting to vent all his pent-up anger at one go, Kuldeep checks himself in mid-sentence.

'And the talk is about me or about you, Kuldeep?' Waryam Singh asks, seething with anger. 'Shravan Kumar earned fame for his sense of duty by carrying his disabled parents to places of pilgrimage around the country. You, Kuldeep, will go beyond even Shravan Kumar. You will wait till you have nothing but the ashes of your parents to carry on a pilgrimage.' But he starts to repent the moment he finishes speaking. In his anger, he has made the mistake of humiliating Kuldeep before his own mother and that is not the right thing to do.

But his words provide Kuldeep with another opening. 'Nobody has the right to interfere in the affairs of our house. And anyone who wants to show to a mother that he is more true to her than her real son is nothing more than a pretender,' he thunders.

Matters seem to be getting out of hand, and realizing this, both decide to remain silent after this outburst. Kuldeep withdraws to his room upstairs and Waryam Singh departs without saying another word.

Distraught, Gian Kaur calls helplessly after Kuldeep, 'No, Deep. Waryam is like your elder brother. You shouldn't mind what he said. He was talking sense.'

Kuldeep wants to quell the fire of anger still raging in him. He is distressed that he has unnecessarily opened his mouth to say things that have only upset his own peace of mind. Trying to regain his composure, he reaches out for the first available book and starts to read it. It turns out to be a translation of the one hundred verses of *Vairag Shatak.*

Those that loom in my mind all the time
They don't belong there at all
They consort with others, like prostitutes
And to me, shouldn't matter a dime.

Images of Queen Pingla and King Bharathari from the book appear before his eyes.

17

The maid appears the following day. Kuldeep feels that she deserves even more appreciation than Waryam Singh had implied in his introduction. She introduces herself as Prakashwati and is around twenty years old. She has a fair complexion and attractive features. Although her face still shows signs of her illness, it is difficult to keep one's eyes off her. Every limb of hers moves in a way that seems intent on provoking desire. And there is something about her eyes that can inflame the passion of a young man the way the sharp rays of the sun can a patch of parched grass – they cause a strange kind of stirring in Kuldeep's heart. During the early stages, her presence isn't much more than a gentle tickle on the surface, but before he knows it, she is imperceptibly penetrating the deepest recesses of his soul.

He thinks of Prakashwati and wonders, 'What kind of a magic wand does Waryam Singh have that enables him to ensnare beautiful birds like these?' His musings are tinged with more than a hint of jealousy as he reflects on his adversary's visit to his home the previous week. 'Will her presence give him the excuse to frequent our place whenever he likes?' he worries. 'Is there anything I can do to save the lass from the clutches of this devil?'

Kuldeep had observed from his vantage point upstairs that Prakash had followed Waryam to the front door after he had formally handed her over to Gian Kaur. She had edged close to him and the two were engaged in a seemingly intimate conversation. What were they talking about, he frets. He is strangely bothered by the fact that they were talking so privately to each other.

'Why should I be concerned? What is she to me? She's only been hired to tend to my child. I should only be interested in ensuring that she does her work properly. What she does in her personal life should be of no import to me. And besides, what business do I have with Waryam Singh?' he reasons.

Prakash takes charge of her work and wastes little time in getting a grip on her responsibilities. She handles the baby and when he is asleep, she tends to the other household chores. Her performance brings an unusual cheer to Gian Kaur's countenance.

Kuldeep now has a fresh preoccupation as he tries to figure out the new maid. 'Who is she? Where has she come from? Is she married or is she still single?' His apprehensions about Waryam Singh, meanwhile, are also coming true. He has become a regular visitor to their home and Kuldeep finds his intrusions a real nuisance. As long as Waryam Singh is in their home, Kuldeep's eyes follow him everywhere, not missing anything that might transpire between him and Prakash. He also steps up his own efforts to get closer to her so that he can unravel her mystery. He often steps forth and asks her to pass the child to him, or goes across to the cradle to pick up the child before handing him over to her. Or just calls her to inquire if the child has been properly fed, and so on. His conjecture that a young woman like her would be extremely shy and reserved in the presence of a male in the house proves incorrect. With each passing day, he discerns an element of warmth in her response to his overtures.

A month goes by. It is late November and the chill of winter is starting to make its appearance. Sitting in his room on the upper floor, Kuldeep is lost in a flood of thoughts. Why hadn't his guru replied to his last letter? he wonders. But then, his mind moves to Prakash and his face brightens up. Of late, she has started to converse quite freely with him. Yet, he cannot bring himself to ask the kind of direct questions that might shed some light on her. Is his curiosity limited to her relationship with Waryam Singh? he wonders. Or does he secretly hope that her response to his question will open the door for their relationship to move to another level? Why is he allowing her to enter his thoughts in this manner? Shaking his head, he points an accusing finger at his own mind, charging it with fickleness and lack of resolve.

There are times when a relatively minor incident can have a major impact. It is fairly early in the morning. Sitting cross-legged in his room, Kuldeep is trying to concentrate on his prayers when he hears her footsteps come up the stairs. Entering his room, she hands the child to him and says, 'Can you please look after him for a while? Bey ji is feeling unwell and I need to attend to her. But this fellow doesn't want to lie on his own in the cradle.'

Getting up to accept the child, he extends his arms and his fingers brush against hers. The fleeting touch sends an electric sensation through his body. Undoing his fervent effort at restraint, he hears the words escape his lips: 'Truly, Prakash! You are fast becoming like a mother to him.'

She lowers her head in silence before looking up at him with radiant eyes and the slightest hint of a smile. Turning around with a shrug of her shoulder, she makes her way down the stairs without uttering a word, stealing Kuldeep's peace of mind.

It is around 8 in the evening the same day and he is trying, once again, to concentrate on his meditation when he is distracted by Prakash's voice wafting up to his room through the open window. He gets up to switch off his light so that he can stand in complete darkness and observe her without fear of getting noticed. Standing next to the railing, he sees her in the corner of the courtyard below as she squats on the floor to clean the dishes. A faint light from the kitchen lights up a side of her face, highlighting the beauty of her silhouette.

He gazes at her for a while before dragging himself back to his bed where he sits cross-legged and tries to focus on his prayers. He wants to calm himself but feels pulled away from his moorings by the turbulent currents raging inside him. Unwilling to give up, he forces himself to sit there for about an hour or so and may have continued longer if someone hadn't come up to turn on the light.

He finds himself looking straight into her eyes. In barely a month, she has lost all trace of her illness. He notes that her attractive face is now complemented by a buxom and healthy body. Today is the day, he decides. This is the time to have my long-desired conversation with her.

'Prakash!' he calls with a new firmness in his voice.

'Yes,' she answers with a touch of reticence.

'Please take this milk back,' he says by way of his opening gambit.

'Why?'

'I don't feel like having it today.'

'Please drink it. You haven't eaten properly either,' she says as she starts to leave the room.

'Wait!' he says. A host of new thoughts enter into his mind. How does she know that I haven't eaten well? Does she care that much for me?

'How do you know that, Prakash?'

Halting near the door, she turns towards him. 'You used to

have four chapattis. Then, it came down to three. And today, you've had just two.'

'You've been counting my chapattis?' Kuldeep asks incredulously.

'A maid who does not care about her master's meals can never be truly loyal to him.'

'But...but...' Kuldeep finds it strangely difficult to translate his thoughts into words. After a brief interval, he makes another attempt. 'But perhaps you don't know why my appetite has been diminishing over this period.'

'I have tried to find out but...' she says with a look that goes straight into the deepest corner of his heart – the corner where so many other memories are already piled up in an unseemly heap. Disturbed by the commotion caused by this newest entrant, they leap up towards his throat. He chokes. But then, like the waves that build up in their race towards the seashore, they crash against the land and quietly dissipate.

A tremor of remorse goes through Kuldeep's body, calmed only by the soothing query from Prakash, 'So why do you remain so gloomy?'

'What makes you say that I am gloomy?' He looks closely at her, trying perhaps to read some meaning into the indecipherable text etched on her face.

She does not reply, and both stand silent for a while. Kuldeep opens his mouth to say something when Gian Kaur's voice crackles, 'Prakash! Bring the child down, will you!'

'Take the glass will you,' he calls out as she steps out of the door.

'Finish the milk first. I'll fetch it after that!' she replies.

The sound of her feet prancing down the steps is like music to Kuldeep's ears. Her voice continues to echo in his ears long after she has left the room. He looks at the glass of milk and smiles. His refusal to drink it was only a ploy to start a conversation.

The glow of her presence has kindled a new light in him. In its gentle radiance, he realizes that he has forgotten to ask her any of his principle questions. 'What is your relationship with Waryam Singh? Where are you from? Why did you accept the lowly job of a domestic and where did you learn such graces?'

Lying down on the bed, his head is abuzz. 'First it was Satwant, then Saroj and now this one. Am I falling for her in the same way? Shame on me! Think of the noble path where Guruji was trying to lead me and where I am headed! I turned down Saroj because I wanted to avoid getting caught up in the web of attachments. And today? Today my mind is inundated with thoughts about this maid...What a devil's mind I possess...So lowly...So set in its own ways!'

I need to resume my meditation, he decides. Getting up, he spreads a sheet on the floor and is about to sit cross-legged when his eyes fall on the glass. He is about to pick it up when he pauses. 'Hadn't she said that I should finish the milk and that she would come later to fetch it? If she comes and sees that the milk is still in the glass, she will ask me the reason and I will again be able to start a conversation! No! I don't care if she comes or not. I shall not talk to her. I shall not even look at her.'

Armed with a new resolve, he sits down and starts to chant the verses he has learnt from the guru. He isn't sure how long he has been meditating before his attention is distracted and his eyes again fall on the glass. Prakash is standing before him, asking, 'How come you still haven't finished your milk?'

'I didn't want to,' he replies.

'Why not?'

'Didn't feel like.'

'Why?'

'Just like that.'

'And what does that mean?'

'Nothing.'

'What do you mean by "nothing"?'

He opens his eyes to discover that there is nobody in his room. The glass is still perched on the stool. 'I was meditating. Where have I drifted?' he curses himself. He closes his eyes again, only to hear the plaintive wail of a beggar, 'Give something to this beggar, O Mother of children! May your coffers expand when you give to a beggar!' Kuldeep grits his teeth in anger. 'These beggars are so insensitive. Don't they have any idea about the disturbance they cause with their shrieking? Even if they have to beg, why can't they lower their voices?'

He gets up to shut the window and sits down for one more attempt to resume his prayers. He concentrates hard and for a while the breathing and chanting move in unison to produce their unique harmony. But the sheer joy of meditation that he used to experience earlier is missing. Is it the light? Is the room too bright? He gets up again to turn it off.

No sooner does he sit down in the pitch-dark room than the relentless chatter of a cricket distracts him. Upset, he turns on the light and scans the walls. The sound seems to come from the wall in the front, and then from the right. Unable to locate the elusive creature, he frets in helpless rage. I've never heard this fellow before. From where did he decide to make his appearance today? He picks at a little hole in his mattress and pulls out enough cotton wool to plug both his ears. Instead of shutting out the sound of the solitary cricket, he feels as if he is surrounded by hundreds of them. The sharp chatter of one has been replaced by the relentless drone of many. Restless, he takes out the earplugs and reasons that someone might come up to call him. He doesn't want to be deaf to such a call.

He drifts into a fitful sleep before being awakened by the steady ticking of the clock. It must be 3 a.m., he thinks, time for his habitual early-morning meditation. Peering closely at it, he sees that the two hands had merged into one. Just 12, he wonders. Is something wrong with this clock or has this night decided to extend itself into eternity?

Lying down again, he tosses around for a while before finally surrendering himself to sleep.

18

Life has a strange tendency of getting affected by developments in a manner that is completely beyond the comprehension of the human mind. The gut-wrenching scene Saroj witnessed in Waryam Singh's house three months back has had a similar sort of impact on her life. She has developed a profound respect for the man and for the selfless nature of his principles. Would any man, any human being have attempted what Waryam Singh was trying to accomplish that night? A curious mix of repentance, yearning and intent grow within her heart. The repentance is provoked by a feeling that she had let him down that night and also missed an opportunity to help a stranger in distress. The yearning comes from the recognition that had she been a man, she would have been in a much better position to accompany him on his mission without attracting adverse comment from society. And she intends to meet him and mend fences at the earliest.

She has not seen him since that fateful night three months ago. 'Could he save that poor woman's life?' she wonders. 'Such a deep and putrid wound! Could anyone have survived it? Could I have helped? He had asked for my assistance with so much hope and confidence. Could I have spent that night at his place? Only if I am prepared to be his companion for the rest of my life, which is impossible. So what is the purpose of my life? If I can't be of use to myself or to anyone else, I must be quite worthless. What, exactly, am I? Who am I, and for what purpose?'

Early next morning, she asks her servant to carry a message for Waryam Singh. She requests that he visit her home that evening, and the boy comes back with an affirmative response.

She spends the day waiting for him. Ganga Vishan returns from the club around 5 p.m., a deep frown creasing his forehead. 'You look worried, Bau ji. Is everything all right?' she asks.

'Nothing, really,' he replies and goes towards his room to remove his trousers and jacket and get into a comfortable dhoti. He settles into his favourite chair and fixes his eyes at the ceiling. Saroj stands behind his chair, rests her hand on his shoulder and probes, 'What's the matter, Bauji?'

He heaves a deep sigh but refrains from speaking. She pauses, knowing that pestering him would be fruitless. An uncomfortable silence pervades the room.

Ganga Vishan finally looks at his daughter and begins, 'Saroj, my child...'

'Go on, Bau ji. Why have you stopped?'

'I was thinking...' His voice trails off in a haze of uncertainty. 'I hope you won't get offended by what I am going to say.'

'Don't worry, Bau ji. I won't.'

'And you won't be afraid either?'

'Of course I won't,' she says even though she realizes that her heart is beating faster.

'Did you go to Waryam Singh's house that night?' His voice is grim as he reflects on the loss of face that he would suffer in the community.

'I did.' Saroj overcomes her anxiety to speak with a courage that is sometimes bred by faith in your own innocence.

'But you didn't tell me.'

'It was ten at night and you were in no condition to understand.'

'And what was the emergency?'

'Bhapa ji had sent for me.'

'Bhapa ji calling for you was an emergency? I don't understand.'

'He needed my help to look after a patient.' Saroj ignores the darkening clouds of anger on his face and replies boldly.

'Do you think you have acquired a medical diploma or something?' There is an unmistakeable edge in his voice.

Much as she wants to, Saroj finds it difficult to disregard his sarcasm, laced as it is with a distinct undertone of suspicion. Trying to check her own rising anger, she demurs, 'It isn't a question of medical knowledge. The patient was a young woman and Bhapa ji thought it important that I should be there.'

'Do you have any idea what people are whispering?' he asks in anguish.

'What are they whispering about, Bau ji?'

'They are saying that Waryam Singh is not a good person,' he says with barely concealed anger. Before she can respond, he continues, 'Do you know who that patient was? Did you know her?'

'No.' She is dismayed. Could it be that my own father is suspecting me? she wonders.

'Did anyone see you that night while you were going or on your way back?'

'Only Kuldeep.'

'And I considered Kuldeep a decent person. Who would have imagined that he would go all over town to slander us in this fashion!'

'Let's leave Kuldeep out of it, Bau ji. But tell me what is *your* view about Bhapa Waryam Singh?' She looks quizzically at her father.

'Waryam Singh?' He lowers his head and goes into deep thought. She asks him again and he looks up with a deeply worried face.

'Waryam Singh...he is not a bad man...but...but...perhaps he is not quite respectable.'

'Bau ji!' Saroj asks philosophically, 'would you say that all respectable people are good? That they don't have any flaws? And can you be considered good only if you come from the higher strata of society?'

Saroj's questions make Ganga Vishan reflect on his own character. He, too, is considered respectable. But is he good? Isn't he a drunkard of the first order? Pondering these issues, he remains silent.

Emboldened, Saroj continues. 'Let's set aside what people say, Bau ji. If you think that Bhapa Waryam Singh is not a good person, please say so and I will have nothing more to do with him. But I do know your views. You do not consider him a bad person and that is what matters.'

Her transparent honesty shines on her face and Ganga Vishan finds it difficult to look into her eyes. 'No...that's not what I meant...I would never have any questions about Waryam Singh's goodness,' he ventures sheepishly.

'And can you doubt my goodness, Bau ji?'

There is a hypnotic glow in Saroj's eyes that forces Ganga Vishan to lower his own. He realizes that he has wronged his daughter and has to find a way out of this predicament. 'I need to go for a walk,' he mutters, picking up his walking stick.

Waryam Singh walks in about half an hour after Ganga Vishan's departure. Saroj is sitting in a corner, tears streaming down her cheeks. She raises her face to look at him as he hurries towards her. 'What's wrong, Saroj? What happened?'

Saroj clenches her teeth and remains silent. It takes a fair bit of persuasion by Waryam Singh before she agrees to speak.

'Bhapa ji, I would have found myself in a really difficult spot if you had arrived half an hour back. I wouldn't have been able to bear anyone insulting you in my presence.' Her recounting of the conversation with her father a short while back has little effect on Waryam Singh. He was, in any case, wearing a rather stern expression when he arrived at her house and Saroj's words don't seem to make it any worse.

'When the whole world is talking about it, what difference does it make if your father also feels the same way,' he remarks dourly.

'What are people saying?' There is a note of concern in Saroj's voice.

'The same...whatever your father said...' Waryam Singh murmurs. 'I have never done any harm to Kuldeep. Why does he...? Anyway, let him do as he wills...' His voice trails off in obvious dismay and when he gets up, Saroj can see tears glistening in his eyes.

Unable to bear his pain, Saroj says, 'Why do you take such troubles on yourself, Bhapa ji?'

Misunderstanding her concern, Waryam Singh retorts, 'I don't particularly care about what the world says against me. But I didn't expect this of you. I know I am strong enough to deal with the lies that society might hurl at me. I am afraid, though, that I'll lose my will to persevere in my tasks if I get the feeling that you, too, have started to view me with suspicion.'

'Bhapa ji, how could I ever stoop so low? I would rather die than face such an allegation. As it is, I am being consumed by the fires of repentance for having let you down that night. I am willing to face the torment of a burning cauldron, or be hung upside down in a well. But believe me, nothing can make me fail you again. Ever. As for my actions that evening, I stand ready before you to face any punishment.'

Waryam Singh's serious countenance breaks into a smile. 'Such hyperbole! What kind of a martyr do you take yourself to be, silly girl? And what kind of a butcher would I be to put you in a cauldron or in a well?'

'So you think I am being melodramatic?'

Waryam Singh nods in gentle affirmation. Infuriated, she protests, 'In that case, you are the one who is being unfair to me. You don't think I can sacrifice something for you?'

'I am sure you can, but...'

'What do you mean by but...?

'But...to sacrifice your love is harder than you think. Ask your own heart, and you might even find yourself in agreement with me.'

'I am afraid I don't quite understand, Bhapa ji.'

'Not everything can be explained by mere words. There are a lot of things whose meaning is revealed by time and not by words.' He pauses for a while before changing the subject. 'Anyway, let these matters be. Hadn't you sent for me?'

'I did.'

'Is there anything that I can do?'

'Can't I send for a dear one without having a specific errand?'

'You can send for a dear one, but not an outsider.'

'Why sprinkle salt on my wounds, Bhapa ji?'

'Would you have been in such a hurry to return home that night if you hadn't considered me an outsider?'

Once again, Saroj feels the hungry flames of repentance leap at her.

'Anyhow, do tell me why you had to send for me,' he asks.

'I wanted to see you so that I could apologize for my folly that evening.'

'If you want to apologize to someone, Saroj, you go to his house. You don't send for him.' Waryam Singh smiles.

'In that case, I am ready to come wherever you ask me to,' she replies even as her mind hovers over the unwarranted harshness of her father's comments a little while back.

Reading her mind, Waryam Singh interjects, 'Truth shall prevail, Saroj. One must side with the truth even if the whole world were to turn against it.'

'Certainly, Bhapa ji. Truth will always prevail. And even if the whole world turns against it, I will stay on the side of truth.'

'There is one other matter that I have just remembered. I need you to help that Radhia, the one who looked after Kuldeep's child. She has really fallen on hard times. Her husband picked a fight with someone after getting drunk and injured him. He's been arrested and I have deliberately not made any effort to get him released. A few days in prison might just do him some good. I hope he gets some sense and leaves his drinking habit. But meanwhile, Radhia's little one is starving.'

'And why was she sacked from Kuldeep's place?'

'She had got into the habit of stealing stuff, Bey ji felt.'

'So you want me to help a thief?'

'Yes! Because if she gets a square meal and her troubles are heard with a sympathetic ear, she may give up stealing.'

'And how much help does she need?'

'Not a whole lot. Just a kilo or so of wheat.'

'But that's hardly enough to feed her family.'

'That's not what I meant. I want her to be helped in a way that she can earn for herself, that she should get a job. Maybe you can keep her with you until she finds regular work.'

'Instead, why don't I simply send her a bag of flour and some other necessities?'

'Because that would only make her lazy and dependent. I understand your reluctance to bring her into your home. You fear that she may end up pilfering at your place too. But I think that if you were to give her some proper attention, you will not only cure her habit of stealing stuff but you may actually make her a better person.'

'All right. I'll either keep her myself or will make sure that she gets a job with someone else. It might have been better, though, if you had counselled Kuldeep's mother to retain her for the sake of his child.'

'I've arranged for someone else to stay with them.'

'Who?'

'That girl...the one whose condition terrified you that night.'

'She survived, Bhapa ji?' Saroj looks at him in disbelief.

'Not just survived but recovered sufficiently to take up a job. Though I do see a danger lurking there as well.'

'What?'

'Kuldeep seems to be eying her in a funny sort of way.'

'Kuldeep? How can you say that, Bhapa ji? I am sure you have misunderstood,' Saroj cries out. It is as if a dagger has pierced her heart.

'No. I haven't misunderstood anything. But I do worry. Anyhow, we will cross that bridge when we come to it. So, shall I send Radhia across to you?'

'Sure. Please do,' she replied. Her mind is already flying in another direction. Kuldeep? Could he really be falling for a maid? Who is she? How does she look? I didn't even get a chance to see her properly that night. Not that there was much to see in that corpse!

'Bhapa ji! What makes you think that Kuldeep might be....'

Aware of her feelings, Waryam Singh explains, 'I might have made a blunder. I wanted to make sure that the poor girl gets a regular job so that she does not slide back into a life of sin. But I am beginning to realize that you can't wash away the sinful deeds of your past unless you undergo a rigorous penance.'

'Who is she, Bhapa ji? Where did you find her?' Saroj asks in consternation.

'It happened one evening. I was returning from the city when I saw her under a tree by the side of the road. She was writhing in pain and her cries of agony were absolutely heart-rending. I must confess that I was lost in my own thoughts and when I first heard her screams, my instinct was to keep walking. I couldn't see her clearly in the darkness and I thought that this is just one of those clever beggars who pretend to be in severe distress so as to fleece a bit of money from an unsuspecting traveller. Yet, something persuaded me to retrace my steps. I had a flashlight with me and I have to say that a shiver went down my spine when she came into my view. Her clothes were in tatters and seemed to be soaked with blood and pus. The condition of her back was beyond description, her face was ashen, her cheeks hollow and it was quite clear that she was struggling for her life. She was conscious but her eyes were closed and she had no energy to utter a word. I tried to talk to her but her eyes remained shut. She heard my voice, though, and somehow moved her hand to her lips to indicate that she needed water. A tin mug and a small bundle of soiled clothes lay next to her. I picked up the mug and walked to a tap some distance away to fetch water. She took a couple of sips as I set the mug against her lips and seemed to draw some energy from the water. I asked her to let me know what ailed her so that I could try to help her if possible. She opened her eyes to look at me and mumbled something but I failed to decipher her words.'

Saroj heard him with rapt attention, her eyes wide open as though she was trying to visualize every scene of the unfolding drama. Waryam Singh paused for a while before resuming. 'She reached behind her back to gradually pull up her shirt. It was horrible. I honestly felt my heart in my mouth when I saw that wound, so deep and rotting. It was so badly infected that I could actually see worms crawling around in that cesspool of blood and pus in the glow of my flashlight. Surely, that wound was too far gone to be cured and she wouldn't last more than a few days, I thought. To spend time and effort on someone in that condition might end up being a total waste. Yet, I couldn't leave her to die in that state. I carried her to a nearby house and propped her up against the verandah before going to fetch some milk for her. She felt a bit better after drinking it and I left her there to return home. It was only after I got your promise to help that I went back to the spot with a tonga and brought her home. That's when you saw her. And next morning, I took her over to the hospital where she was able to get proper medical care.'

Saroj is overwhelmed by Waryam Singh's narrative of that traumatic night. He is no ordinary human, she thinks. He is an angel who has descended from the heavens. In reverence, she bends down to touch his feet before raising her hands to her own forehead. 'Bhapa ji, this world is not meant for beings like you. Your abode should be up in the heavens, along with the angels and the gods. I regret that until that evening, I had only met your physical form, not your soul. Perhaps that is the reason I held back and proved to be of no use to you.'

'Saroj, why do you give so much importance to a small person like me? If I have done something good, the credit must go to my guru, my mentor who was also like a father to me. It was Giani Bagh Singh who made me realize the value of community service, of putting others before self. And I've been both unfortunate and ungrateful that I could not appreciate the importance of his words while he was still around. I would have spared no effort to serve him. Alas, it's too late now.'

Saroj bowed her head in memory of the departed guru before continuing, 'Bhapa ji, she must be so grateful to you. You've virtually given her a second life. I wish I had also used the opportunity to be of some service.'

Touched by her words, Waryam Singh smiles. 'Saroj, I can assure you that there is no dearth of opportunities to serve. There are so many of god's creatures who die an unjust death without even feeling the warm touch of a helping hand. You could dedicate your entire life to the cause and they still wouldn't get a minute each.'

Saroj feels a ray of light descending to illuminate her soul and purge her mind of all her fears, her worries and her sorrows. Her eyes shine as if they have had a glimpse of heaven itself.

'But how did the poor woman come to such grief? She must have told you something about herself,' Saroj enquires.

'Yes, she did,' he replies. 'She's narrated her entire tale of woes. She comes from the hills, from a fairly well-to-do Hindu family. But she was barely five when she was lured away by some pimps.'

'What do these pimps do, Bhapa ji?'

'They are elderly women who used to be prostitutes and who have spent their lives carrying the burden of their sins. Once they are past their youth and their earnings dry up, they start working as agents for prostitution rings. They frequent poor villages in the hills or other areas affected by hunger or famine. Or they show up at big country fairs where they abduct young girls or buy them from desperate parents. Thereafter, they often sell them to other touts who will take them away to big cities and introduce them into the flesh trade. At times, they will also keep the girls until they mature so that they can be put to work as prostitutes and these pimps can live off their earnings. And it's not limited to women alone. I've also known of men who are engaged in this business. Prakash is one of those unfortunate girls who ended up wasting precious years of her life in this wretched profession. She fell ill and got a nasty boil on her back that kept getting worse until she ended up in that miserable state.'

'But Bhapa ji,' she asks with a tremor in her voice, 'didn't anyone bother to get her treated?'

'Who would have bothered to do that? The people she lived with were only interested in her earnings. They made some half-hearted sort of attempt in the beginning but when they saw the ailment linger, they threw her out like a fly out of milk. Who cares for anyone else these days? She spent some time in a charity hospital but even they had a mercenary attitude. If you can't pay, you don't get treated. She suffered for over a month before being labelled a hopeless case and getting shunted out. Soon, she was back on the streets, her condition deteriorating by the day. After I found her, I was able to get her admitted into a hospital and use some of my connections and also some money to get her treated.

'Mercifully, she survived. I wanted to make sure that she didn't sink again into the same morass. She, too, was desperate that she should stay out of the clutches of those greedy wolves who had kept her in a life of sin. She promised me that if I could find her some kind of employment, she would use the opportunity to change her life for good. So when Kuldeep's mother asked me to find someone who could work at her home, I thought this would be the perfect chance for Prakash. I advised her that she should never reveal her real name or her past to anyone and, if necessary, she should describe herself as a widow. In the bazaar, she was called Putlibai but I suggested that Prakashwati would sound more respectable. But I am worried now that her flirtatious nature is again emerging from the shadows. My advice to her was like water off a duck's back. To make matters worse, Kuldeep seems to be playing his own games with her. The whole business has got me regretting my decision to have her employed there. I just hope that Kuldeep doesn't fall for her. I know that boy's nature well. It's like water lying in a flat plate; you never know which way it will drift.'

'This is a real cause for worry, Bhapa ji,' Saroj agrees.

'Anyway, let me see what I can do.' Waryam Singh gets up to leave but Saroj asks him to wait.

'The other day, you had wanted me to make a vow to you and I had said that I needed some more time to think about it.'

'Well! Think a little more about it, Saroj,' he cautions. 'To live your life within the confines of a vow is a lot harder than merely taking a vow.'

'The confines of a vow?' she calls after him as he leaves. 'What is that, Bhapa ji?'

'Time will tell you!' he replies.

19

If an animal goes out of control, you can use ropes and sticks to rein it in, but once the human mind has gone berserk, there is no rope that can shackle it. Once it leaves its moorings, it's gone for good.

Several days have gone by without yielding any opportunity for Kuldeep to probe Prakash about her antecedents. Nor has she given him a chance to progress in that direction. The hunter, after casting the net for its prey, had quietly stepped aside to observe the prey move steadily in the direction of the bait. Prakash is skilled in the art of enticing men. Having lured Kuldeep, she has retreated a few steps so that she can observe him move towards her.

Kuldeep is confused and restless. Having toyed with him over the glass of milk, she has neither raised her eyes to look at him nor provided an opportunity when he could have a quiet word with her. Even when he calls for his customary glass of milk in the evening, she feigns some other preoccupation and requests Gian Kaur to take it up to him. The change in her attitude perplexes Kuldeep and intensifies his desire for her. He is assaulted by an entirely new set of doubts. 'Why is she avoiding me like this? Was I too forward and is she afraid of me? Did she take offence at something I said? Maybe she was right to take offence. Is it right that I should have taken such liberties with another woman? Should I apologize to her? But I need an opportunity for that too.'

He is on the lookout for a suitable opportunity which eludes him for several days. And then fate provides him the opportunity quite unexpectedly. A rash has broken out on the child's back. Conventional treatment has failed and despite various medicines and ointments, it shows little sign of abating. The child is in pain and Gian Kaur suggests that he be taken for a bath at Bhai Joga Singh's gurudwara. The gurudwara has a formidable reputation for the healing properties of its large, open well. Its water, viscous and milky white with a strong smell of sulphur, is believed to be particularly effective in curing skin ailments.

It is a Sunday morning when his mother comes up to his room. 'Son, the gurudwara is going to be pretty crowded today. I'd love to take the boy myself but I'm afraid my arthritis will make it really tough for me to carry him all the way. Why don't you take him and give him a quick bath. The child is suffering.'

'I have no problem with that but what do I do if he starts to cry. I don't think I'll be able to handle him,' Kuldeep pleads.

'Take Prakash along.'

Her words send a current through Kuldeep's body but feigning disinterest, he mutters, 'Oh, all right.'

Gian Kaur goes down to ask Prakash to change into something decent and accompany Kuldeep to the gurudwara. Kuldeep sees her as he descends the stairs from his room. He cannot believe his eyes. Dressed in a deep turquoise salwar and a canary-yellow kameez with a matching dupatta with elaborate chikan embroidery, she looks like a nymph that would fly away at any moment. She seems to have paid special attention to her hair which cascade down her shoulders and back. He pauses in shock. The clothes look familiar. Of course, they belonged to Satwant and have been happily given over to Prakash by his mother.

A few minutes later, they are on their way to the gurudwara, sitting on the ample rear seat of the tonga. Prakash's dupatta is draped over her face, veiling it but not completely. Each time the tonga hits a little bump, he gets tantalizing glimpses of her cheeks, the sight plunging a fresh arrow of desire into his heart. The closed gate at a railway crossing brings the journey to a temporary halt. They are surrounded by a couple of lorries and a few other tongas. The tongawallah dismounts to tighten the harness, giving Kuldeep an opportunity to start a conversation. They haven't exchanged a word so far. Kuldeep turns around to face her, his eyes burning with desire.

The child is asleep, his head resting comfortably against Prakash's shoulder. She catches Kuldeep's glance and lowers her eyes. He loses his nerve and looks away.

He turns his face to the other side, suggesting that he was trying to see if the gate was about to open. His mind is humming with a jumble of thoughts. What did I read in that split second when our eyes met? he wonders. Anger...? No, it wasn't that. Love, then...? No. Not that either. There was no real trace of that. Hatred, perhaps...? No, it couldn't be that. She would have turned her face away instead of gently lowering her eyes if she felt that way.

The gate creaks open with a shudder and the tonga resumes its journey. Kuldeep feels his heartbeat pick up in unison with the hooves of the horse.

The tonga comes to a halt near the Dabgari Gate and they alight. They walk through the gate, Prakash following a few steps behind Kuldeep. She has pulled the dupatta further down her face to veil it properly. Every now and then, Kuldeep catches a glimpse of her dress through the corner of his eye. He has a surreal feeling that it is Satwant, not Prakash, who is behind him.

As they approach a fork in the street, Kuldeep takes the lane on the right, while Prakash keeps going straight. 'It's this way, Prakash,' he calls out. 'Looks like you've never been to Bhai Joga Singh's gurudwara.' In response, she tilts her head towards him and raises her veil. Their eyes lock and Kuldeep feels his pulse racing. She looks at him in a way that leaves him breathless and weak in the knees. Anything could have happened but a horde of Sunday visitors heading for the gurudwara envelops them from all sides, carrying them in its flow. The magical moment comes to an abrupt end.

Passing though several by-lanes and alleyways, they reach the street that leads into Bhai Joga Singh's gurudwara. The crowd here is so thick that it is difficult to move. Managing the child in the midst of the swarm of devotees is a challenge and Prakash tries to carry him on her shoulder so that he does not get pushed around. It works for a while, until a surge in the crowd causes her to stumble and the child almost falls to the ground. Kuldeep reacts quickly to grab him and positions himself next to Prakash to protect her. Progress is difficult, the limited space in the lane squeezed further by vendors trying to hawk a variety of street foods and bric-a-brac to the visitors, and by beggars trying to extract some alms out of them. The multitudes coming to the gurudwara each Sunday are a real bonanza for them.

For the women of Peshawar, the assortment of samosas, spiced gram and other mouth-watering savouries that accost them on their weekly visit to the gurudwara pose a real challenge. Each vendor has his own portable stall that comprises of a rickety bamboo tripod standing about chest-high. A large, shallow basket is perched on the tripod, displaying the chutneys, spices and other ingredients that accompany the savoury. The scrawny fellow making the gol gappas seems to be one of the more popular ones. Next to his basket, on a smaller tripod, is a small earthen pot containing spicy kanji. He is surrounded by about a dozen women arranged in a tight little circle around his twin tripods. His hands move at lightning speed, stuffing small bits of potato into the round gol gappas before scooping a dollop of kanji into them and placing them on a palm leaf that serves as the plate for the customer. The ladies focus on the tricky business of popping the whole gol gappa into their mouths without spilling any of the kanji on their Sunday-wear. But the crowds bearing down on them are unforgiving. An elbow knocks the gol gappa out of a woman's hand inches before it reaches its destination, leaving her mouth open in unfulfilled anticipation. Another has her plate crushed against her neighbour's stomach, unleashing angry accusations of carelessness and worse. A third, unbalanced by a push from a burly passer-by, almost falls on the vendor's basket. Lightning reflexes, honed by years of practice in working in similar environments, has the wiry fellow dive in time to save his wares. 'Watch out, Bibi!' he yells as the matron, mouth filled with a gol gappa, mumbles an incoherent response. The situation is no different for the vendors selling an assortment of cosmetics, buttons, threads and other similar stuff, though this pales in comparison to the scenes outside the shoe-keeper's stall. There is a melee in the narrow space where visitors struggle to balance on one leg to remove their shoes and hand them over to the volunteers manning the stall so that they can wash their feet before entering the gurudwara premises.

Pushing and jostling through the crowd, the trio eventually reach the sacred well. Kuldeep holds the child in his left hand, while clasping Prakash's hand in his right. Prakash is in a real state. Her dupatta has slid off her head and her hair, the recipient of so much attention a while back, is dishevelled.

She is clearly uncomfortable with the sheer mass of people surrounding her and annoyance is writ large on her face. Taking a deep breath as they reach the clearing near the well, she adjusts her clothes, pats her hair and takes the child from Kuldeep to head towards the well.

The child is given a quick dip in the waters of the well, after which they proceed to the sanctum sanctorum inside the gurudwara. They prostrate before the Guru Granth Sahib to pay their obeisance, make the token offerings recommended by Gian Kaur and quickly withdraw, wrestling once again with the multitudes to make their exit.

Kuldeep is desperate to share his feelings with Prakash. He needs a quiet spot and a few minutes alone with her to express himself. As they approach Dabgari Gate, Kuldeep enquires hesitantly, 'If you agree, Prakash, we could make a brief visit to Panj Teerath before we return. It's been a long while since I went that way.'

'Ok, let's go,' she replies without looking at him.

Relieved, Kuldeep summons a tonga and tells the driver to take them towards Panj Teerath.

20

As you emerge from the Courts Gate and cross the main road, you enter an ancient garden that is popularly known as Panj Teerath. Locals believe that it has been around since time immemorial. Fables about the garden are steeped in antiquity but there is no agreement about its precise place in history. It does not find mention as a major site of pilgrimage in any of the ancient Hindu texts. Yet, oral tradition is resolute in its belief about the antiquity of the place. Some say that the Pandavas, the five legendary heroes of the Mahabharata, spent some of their years in exile at this precise location. Others believe that an ancient sage known as Pancham, a derivative of the Sanskrit word for 'five', performed his penance at this location.

The historicity of the place may be in doubt but there is complete agreement about its popularity amongst visitors. Spanning over half a mile in its circumference, it is characterized by mature, shady trees and springs and wells that provide an endless supply of cool, clear water to little streams crisscrossing the park. The wide open meadows are dotted with small temples, platforms and traditional twelve-door structures that stand testimony to the antiquity of the place.

Panj Teerath is a particular favourite with the locals during summer, attracting hundreds of residents seeking refuge from the enervating heat in its cool environs. Peshawaris have developed this habit of going for a picnic in the summer months. Whenever the heat becomes unbearable, a couple of friends get together with their families and plan a picnic in the park. A typical weekend would see small groups sprawling about in the lawns or congregating under the magnificent old trees. It is not uncommon to see a family or two walking in with their groceries and other provisions to make a small fire and cook their food right there. True, they have a good time. But, over a period of time, this has also sullied the environs and polluted the garden. Some groups come solely for the purpose of merry-making, while in others liquor flows faster than the waters of the streams. But for such anomalies, the place could have truly lived up to its noble nomenclature.

The onset of winter, though, brings a kind of solitude to the atmosphere in the park. The number of visitors comes down significantly, and the ones who do come want solace or a quiet spot for meditation. A contrast, indeed, from the noisy groups in summer whose sole purpose is to entertain themselves!

Katori Khuhi, a well lying within a bowl-shaped structure, nestles in one corner of the park. The water in this well always comes up to the brim of the bowl and often overflows it. A small twelve-door building stands near it.

Kuldeep and Prakash stroll in the park for a while before ending up near the Khuhi. There is hardly a soul around and it offers Kuldeep a perfect opportunity to open up his mind to her. Turning around to look at her, he pauses.

'Prakash!' He finally summons his courage.

'Yes please!' she replies with a gesture that is pregnant with meaning.

'Are you angry with me?'

'Me? Of course not.' She turns her face away from him.

'I hope you aren't lying, Prakash.'

'I can never lie to you,' she turns back towards him and responds. This time around, she looks directly at him in a way that sweeps away any remaining bits of hesitation that he might have harboured.

'Why have you been hiding from me? Ever since that day?'

'Which day?'

'That day, when you returned after giving me the glass of milk.'

She stays silent.

'I worry that I may have exceeded my limits that evening,' he says, his forehead shining with a layer of nervous perspiration.

'No,' she replies simply.

'There is so much that I wanted to ask you but...' he continues. 'Will you answer my questions, Prakash?'

'Go ahead,' Prakash responds with the same inscrutable look.

Kuldeep's curiosity is getting the better of him. 'Why did a girl like you, from a decent family, accept such a lowly job?'

Instead of 'from a decent family' Kuldeep probably wanted to use a word like 'beautiful' or 'attractive' but better sense prevailed and he held his tongue. He doesn't want to say anything that might be taken amiss. But there is no reason to be concerned. Prakash shows no sign of anger or reserve. Instead, she sighs and says, 'It is nothing but fate that makes us do what we do.'

'If you don't mind, I really want to know more about you,' he asks with the trepidation of a subject facing his master. Why am I so diffident before her? he agonizes. She is merely a maid.

The child is sleeping peacefully in her lap. When she looks at Kuldeep again, it feels different. He senses an element of familiarity, even a feeling of companionship in her eyes. With an effort that is no less than climbing an insurmountable mountain, he attempts to move closer to her. The palpitation in his heart rises to a crescendo as he gently holds her hand.

'Prakash, if you can open your heart to me, maybe I too...'

Prakash makes no effort to withdraw her hand. He sees this as the first sign of victory in his quest for her affection. But looking into her eyes, he also discerns a sense of helplessness.

'What will you gain by asking me?' she says, her eyes indicating her reluctance to reveal her benighted past. 'My parents passed away while I was still a child. I came of age in an orphanage and was fifteen when the managers at the orphanage entrusted me to a sickly old man...'

'Entrusted...?' Kuldeep empathizes. 'Or married off to him...?'

'You can interpret it as you like. Entrusted...! Sold...! Anyway, he didn't last for more than four or five years.'

'Oh I see!' Kuldeep murmurs in sympathy. 'So you were left a widow after that?'

'And it became difficult to protect myself from evil eyes. Several hoodlums were intent on getting hold of me. But I was determined to avoid falling into another trap that would destroy me. I eluded them by secretly leaving the town. I succeeded in escaping from them but fell grievously ill.'

'Where do you come from?'

'I am from the Multan region. My parents were moneylenders.'

'So you landed up here. And how did you meet Waryam Singh?'

'I can never repay him for the kindness that he showered on me. I don't think even my blood relations would have done more for me, the way Bhapa ji came forth to help me. If I am still alive today, all credit must go to him.'

Kuldeep notices that her eyes had lowered with the burden of her gratitude to Waryam Singh.

'Did he just get you the job with us or was there something more as well?' he asks in a tone laced with the rising flames of jealousy.

'Getting me a job in your house was in itself no small matter. Who would care to help a stranger in a new city in this manner? And that too when it comes to a single woman. You can imagine her plight. Spending a single day on your own in an alien city can be a challenge.'

Both remain silent for a while. Kuldeep has the look of a man steeling himself for an important new step.

'But Prakash,' he wills himself to put his thoughts into words. 'You are still so young, so beautiful. How will you spend your life? I often worry about you.'

'It will pass,' she sighs deeply. 'So many years have passed, and the remainder will also pass the same way.'

He pauses to muster his courage. 'And what if I said that I need your companionship? You know, Prakash, the child really can't stay without you. He's become so attached to you that I wanted to ask if you can become his mother.'

Kuldeep waits for her response with bated breath, like a prisoner before the judge pronounces his sentence. She is silent for a while, before replying, 'If I knew for sure that you will not abandon me midstream, what could be better for me...but I don't think your mother will agree to this.'

'Oh don't be silly.' His voice is unable to conceal his elation. 'How can my mother disagree on a matter like this? She will be delighted when she learns. Ever since Satwant passed away, she has been pestering me to get married and I am the one who has been resisting and saying that I am not interested. But you, Prakash, are an enchantress who has cast a spell on me. Promise me, before this lovely spring that your love for me will be perennial like its waters.'

A parakeet perched on a tree near Katori Khuhi is busily pecking away at a large green berry. Clearly enjoying its meal, it glances at the couple and, with a satisfied look, drops the remaining part of the berry into the bottomless depths of the well.

Prakash leans her head against his shoulder, sending fresh currents through his body. A thought crosses her mind and she sits upright. 'Wait! I have to first consult Bhapa ji on this matter. I can't take such a big step without his consent.'

The child turns in her lap and looks like he is going to cry. She turns her attention to him and gently pats his head. Kuldeep seethes with rage. His hatred towards Waryam Singh, temporarily submerged by the giddy feelings of love towards Prakash, again leaps to the surface. This could be a real problem, he thinks. How can she feel that way towards my sworn enemy?

Waryam Singh is a devious fellow who cannot be trusted. Kuldeep is convinced. No matter what kind of respect or affection Prakash holds towards that man, it is likely that Waryam Singh befriended Prakash only because of her beauty and to satisfy his own desires.

'Consent from whom? From Waryam Singh?' he turns towards Prakash and enquires. 'There is no need to speak with him about this, Prakash. He is hardly the noble soul that people make him out to be. He might have provided you some assistance when you needed it and that, perhaps, makes you think that he is a good man. But I will sit with you one of these days and tell you stories about him that will make your hair stand on end. I also feel, Prakash, that when two souls are uniting in love, there is no room for any third person. I want your agreement that from this day, you are mine. I can already visualize the joy on my mother's face when I break this news to her. There is no reason to delay matters and I feel that we should prepare for a simple wedding ceremony this Sunday itself.'

Prakash is uncomfortable with the vehemence with which he speaks against Waryam Singh. She also doesn't see any cause for the undue haste with which he is moving. But these thoughts remain in her mind and she doesn't say a word. Vows are made and tied into a knot without any certainty about their strength or endurance. The depth of feelings in their hearts may not have been clear but the glow in their faces is eloquent testimony to the way in which they have so quickly immersed themselves in the dangerous rapids of passion.

By the time they reach home, it is 11.30 and they are soaked with the desire created by their new proximity. It would be no exaggeration to say that the air around them is suffused with craving for each other.

21

'What's the matter, Bey ji? The house seems to have a lonely look about it today?' Waryam Singh asks, stepping inside to greet Gian Kaur.

Looking up from her rosary, Gian Kaur replies, 'The child has developed a nasty rash all over his body. I thought it would be good to give him a bath at Bhai Joga Singh's gurudwara. Kuldeep and Prakash took him there and have been gone since morning.'

Waryam Singh is engrossed in deep thought. Seeing the signs of worry writ all over his face, Gian Kaur asks, 'And what's wrong with you today? You are not the kind who can stay quiet for such a long time.'

'Nothing, Bey ji. I've had a bit of a headache since morning. Anyway, tell me how is Prakash doing? Has she picked up a bit of the work that you expect her to do?'

'Oh! She is an angel, a real angel!' Gian Kaur beams. 'May the Lord shower His blessings on you, in this world and in the next! She has brought us so much comfort from the day she arrived. She is like a lucky charm who has relieved me of much of my burden. I don't have to worry about anything now. She runs this house like it is her own. And I love the way she fusses over me all day. It seems that she hails from quite a decent family.'

Her breathless description of Prakash's virtues only aggravates Waryam Singh's dilemmas. He is happy that she has settled well into her work, but knowing what he does about her and Kuldeep only adds to his worry.

'You had suggested a pay rise for her,' she continues. 'That is no longer an issue. I have entrusted the entire house to her. I am happy to pay her whatever you say. The amount is immaterial when someone gives you so much comfort and happiness.'

'I think, Bey ji...' Waryam Singh pauses to measure his words carefully. 'I also think there is no harm if you would consider re-employing Radhia. She is facing a really tough time. Her children are on the verge of starvation. It would be an act of nobility on your part to take her back.'

Gian Kaur shudders. To her, Waryam Singh's request is like asking a traveller in the peak of winter to remove his warm woollen coat and replace it with a wet blanket.

'You want me to take back that trouble-maker after I managed to get her off my back with such difficulty? And for her, I should sack this angel? Oh my god!' she whispers fearfully.

'But Bey ji, employing Prakash in this house could lead to further complications.'

'Why?'

'I have a feeling that Kuldeep has developed...that he may be inclined towards...'

'How can you say that about Kuldeep? My Kuldeep has the virtues of seven daughters. He is so pure of heart that he hardly raises his eyes towards her. He is always so engrossed in his own meditation that he barely has time for anything else. What makes you say something like this, my son?'

'All mothers think that their sons possess the virtues of their daughters but...'

His words are like poison to Gian Kaur. 'But you know Kuldeep so well,' she protests.

'I do know him well. But I also know Prakash...'

'Why? Are you implying that something is wrong with her?'

'I suggest,' Waryam Singh ponders for a bit before speaking, 'that you should try and arrange a suitable marriage for Kuldeep.'

'And you think I haven't tried? We've had offers from some of the most respectable families but he refuses to entertain the thought. Let him give one indication of his willingness and we'll arrange everything. But I don't know what's got into him, whose spell he has come under. He has become so stubborn that trying to change his mind is like banging your head against a brick wall. Anything that I say on the subject seems to bounce off his ears.'

'Bey ji,' Waryam Singh speaks softly. 'If he refuses to get married, I will not allow Prakash to stay in this house. I will do whatever I can to prevent Kuldeep from burning himself in this fire. I know that he will treat me as his enemy. But I will not let him besmirch his reputation in this affair.'

Gian Kaur listens to him carefully. Her mind is also sifting through a number of other episodes in Kuldeep's life and she recognizes that there is a kernel of truth in what Waryam Singh says. It would be wrong to dismiss his concerns out of hand.

'If you are intent on keeping Prakash in the house, you will have to keep a close eye on both of them. Had Prakash been a reliable person, I might even have suggested that you let the two of them marry but...'

'Heavens forbid! Hai Ram!' she cries as though she has been struck by someone. 'Imagine! We refuse noble families who would be happy to provide heaps of gold and dowry and let our only son marry a maid?'

'That is precisely why I suggested you should think of getting Radhia back. And if you don't like her, I can try to find you someone else.'

Seeing Gian Kaur reflect on the matter, Waryam Singh continues, 'So how long have they gone to Joga Singh's gurudwara?'

'About three hours now,' she replies with a touch of anxiety.

'And how long do you think it takes if you hired a tonga?'

'Maybe an hour, or an hour and a half.'

'Do you think they are sitting at the gurudwara all this time?'

'And where else?' Gian Kaur looks at him with growing apprehension.

'They are enjoying themselves at Panj Teerath.'

'Really?' she cries in anguish. 'At Panj Teerath!'

'Absolutely. I decided to come straight to you after seeing them there with my own eyes.'

Gian Kaur feels that she has been buried alive under a mountain of shame. 'If you knew that she was this kind of woman, why did you bring her to our place?'

'It was my mistake, Bey ji. I blame myself more than I blame her for this turn of events.'

'Your mistake?'

'Yes. I don't want to blame her because she has been in bad company since her childhood. You can't expect more from someone who has grown up in a certain kind of environment. If I had higher expectations from her, I am the one who has erred in judgement. Without having any experience in this field, I thought that a month or two of counselling could correct traits that have been acquired over ten or fifteen years. And even if I had succeeded in addressing some of the problems, who can be sure that they won't crop up again? How can anyone guarantee this? I had honestly thought that I had been able to bring about a considerable change in her character over the last month but I can see now that the change was merely superficial. So I am the one who made the mistake.'

Gian Kaur could read between the lines and understand clearly what he wanted to convey about the girl's character. It was hard for her to disagree with Waryam Singh's assessment.

She sighs. 'So what can we do now?'

'Let me think a little more about it,' Waryam Singh replies uncertainly. 'It would also be wrong to discard this unfortunate woman unless I can find some other place for her. I will let you know when I have something in hand for her. But be prepared to wait because it might take a couple of days. I will also try to find a dependable maid for you, but if none is available immediately, you could call Radhia back. For now, I have fixed her up in Babu Ganga Vishan's house. She was in a bad state, the poor woman.'

22

Gian Kaur slumps into her chair, head buried in her hands for a long while after Waryam Singh had left. She is beside herself with worry. How does one get a wayward son to mend his ways? she broods. He's no teenager who can be rebuked by his mother. He is an adult, and one who has already showed an inclination to renounce his home and family. How does one know that he won't react in some unforeseen manner to his mother's advice? He may end up doing something even worse.

Kuldeep and Prakash return a good hour or so after Waryam Singh's departure. They had left before 8 in the morning and it is now past 12. Gian Kaur's suspicions turn into firm conviction the moment they enter the house. Kuldeep's face radiates with a light she hasn't seen for months. Prakash, too, seems unusually cheerful and even a trifle bold in her demeanour. Gian Kaur is on the verge of saying something but for once, she decides to hold her tongue. 'It's taken you a long time, son,' is all she says as she looks closely at him.

'There was a very well-known group of devotional singers from Punjab at the gurudwara today. The hymns they sang were divine and we decided to sit there for a while and listen to them,' Kuldeep answers.

The lie is apparent to Gian Kaur. The morning session of hymns and devotional music at the gurudwara never lasted till mid-day. But she holds her counsel and asks them to have their lunch, her eyes following them wherever they moved.

It is around 8 in the evening. The child has gone to sleep,

Gian Kaur is busy making dinner while Prakash cleans the dishes that have piled up since morning.

'Kuldeep! Come down and have your dinner,' Gian Kaur calls out to her son.

'Send it upstairs,' he replies. 'I am reading.'

Hmm... Gian Kaur thinks. He usually says 'bring it upstairs' but today it is 'send it upstairs'. The difference is not lost on her.

She places his food on a tray and is going to carry it when Prakash quickly washes her hands, takes the tray from her hands and runs upstairs with it. Each new act strengthens her suspicion but she wants to be completely sure.

When several minutes pass and Prakash is still not back with the tray, Gian Kaur takes a hot chapatti in a plate and starts to ascend the stairs quietly. When she reaches the landing, she finds the door shut. The sound of hushed voices fuels her curiosity. Setting her ear against the door, she hears Kuldeep urge, 'Come now! Shed this unnecessary shyness and restraint, darling.' Prakash responds, 'Let go of my arm, please. Bey ji will think something is amiss.'

Gian Kaur has heard enough. She tiptoes down the stairs to the kitchen and sits on the low stool. A few minutes later, Prakash also returns and tries to busy herself in the kitchen. Gian Kaur lowers her head, unable to summon the courage to look directly at her. 'Why don't you go up and offer him another chapatti?' she suggests.

'No need, Bey ji. He says he's not hungry today,' she chirps. Gian Kaur closes her eyes. She has this horrible vision of her son sliding inexorably towards a dangerous abyss. She knows that she has to make an earnest effort to save him, recognizing too that there is no assurance she will succeed.

She drags herself through the motions of winding up her work in the kitchen before sitting down to have her own dinner. But it is only to put up an appearance. She finds it impossible to swallow a single morsel.

Setting the plate aside, she gets up with a new resolve and makes her way up the stairs. Kuldeep is neither sitting cross-legged in meditation nor reading. He is lying on his bed, gazing straight at the ceiling as though it is his gateway into some distant universe. Startled to see his mother walk in, he sits up and asks, 'Come, come, Bey ji. Is everything all right? You seem a bit disturbed today.'

She is quiet. Does she suspect something, Kuldeep wonders. 'Is something wrong? Why don't you saying something?'

Fighting to keep her emotions in check, she says gently, 'What should I say, son? You no longer listen to me and I am so restless. I can't eat, can't sleep. Besides, how long can you trust this body to go on? It seems to be deteriorating with each passing day. If the Lord decides to take me away tomorrow, who is going to look after baby Baljit? Your father left this world pleading with you but even his last words fell on deaf ears. Thanks to his stature, you can still get proposals from respectable families. But don't count on them to wait forever. Who knows what we'll get after they turn away. My son, you are no longer a child. Listen to me.'

Kuldeep smiles silently. Fate is indeed being kind. His mother had broached a subject that has been occupying his own mind. She had given him precisely the opening that he had been searching since his return from the gurudwara.

'Fate has its own ways, Bey ji. Otherwise, why would Satwant have died?'

'Life and death are in His hands, son. But it is hope that sustains life. You see a leaf dry up on a tree and no sooner has it fallen to the ground than two fresh ones have sprouted in its place. That's life. How would this world go on if everyone started to speak like you?'

'Bey ji, I am fairly comfortable the way I am. But if you still want me to be tied down, I will insist on choosing the shackles that are going to bind me. I hope you can accept this condition.'

She recoils, afraid that the words he would utter would cling to her like a poisonous serpent. 'You can make your choice,' she says. 'But there is no harm if you also take my counsel...'

'Fine,' he interjects. 'I am happy to take your counsel right now.'

'It's okay,' she sighs. 'Tell me what you have in mind.'

'I want to marry Prakash...'

'What?' she shrieks in utter disbelief, unwilling to comprehend that her own son could be saying this.

'Why, Bey ji?' He smiles.

'Prakash! Instead of bringing shame on me like this, why don't you just plunge a dagger into my heart? Do whatever you like,' she simpers. 'Oh! What a curse upon us! That we have to face such shame.'

Kuldeep was prepared for a certain amount of opposition from his mother but the sheer vehemence of her reaction takes him by surprise. She has always been appreciative of Prakash for her diligence and sincerity towards her work. How could she speak so hatefully about her now?

'Why did you hire her if you dislike her so much?'

'I didn't know about her past misdeeds when I agreed to take her.'

'And how have you learned about her past now?'

'From the one who brought her here.'

'Waryam Singh? What did he have to say?'

'Oh! How can I tell you what he said about her character and her misdeeds?'

'Wrongdoings?'

'Yes.'

'What wrongdoings? When did he come here?' Kuldeep asks, his voice rising with anger.

'This morning, around the time the two of you were walking hand in hand at Panj Teerath.'

'Really?' Kuldeep feels sweat breaking over his brow. 'That liar...that scoundrel...that troublemaker who is an incarnation of Narad Muni himself...he lights one fire, extinguishes another...that's his hobby. I've had enough of that rascal, Bey ji. I can't understand why he is after my life, why he accuses an innocent girl in this manner. I'm going to teach this devil the lesson of his life...'

He gets up from his bed and begins to pace up and down the room, his heart thumping with rage. Gian Kaur makes a quiet exit from his room, terrified that yet another calamity is lurking round the corner.

23

As usual, Prakash is up before Gian Kaur to attend to her chores. Picking up the broom, she goes upstairs to clean Kuldeep's room and is surprised to see him walking about slowly. His face bears a look of great anxiety.

Hearing Prakash's footsteps, Kuldeep looks up at her and

signals that she should come near him. 'Let's sit down, Prakash. We need to talk about something important.'

'Come closer to me,' he murmurs as she sits next to him on the bed. He puts his arm around her shoulder. 'Prakash, I see a major obstacle looming in the path of the promises we—'

'I know. I heard everything,' she interjects.

'You did?' He is astounded. 'How?'

'I stood in the stairs to listen, when you and your mother were speaking so loudly about it last night.'

'And so...?'

'So I'll leave this house today...so that...you...'

Kuldeep feels as if his flesh is being wrenched off his body. Clasping her in his arms, he implores, 'If you really want to go, it's up to you. I can't really stop you. But please put an end to my life before you leave this place.'

'May you have a long life! But for a bad character like me, why would you...?'

'But you are not to be blamed, Prakash. Nor is my mother at fault. This havoc is the handiwork of that scoundrel Waryam Singh. Yes, the same Waryam Singh that you never tire of praising. At least you now recognize the true colours of that devil.'

'I had no idea that he could be so treacherous, that he could act like a friend but still stab you in the back.'

'You said you are going to leave this house, Prakash! I won't let you do that so long as I am alive.'

'And I won't let myself become the reason for discord in your house. You don't have to worry about me. I've already faced plenty of misfortune. After finding shelter in your house, I did think for a while that my life might take a turn for the better. But who knows what else fate has in store for me?'

Her voice breaks and she wipes a tear from the corner of her eye with her dupatta.

Kuldeep's world seems to be slipping away from him. Impatient to regain control, he urges, 'Prakash! I know I won't be able to live without you. If you attach any value to my life, you should banish the thought of leaving this house. And as far as the issue of discord is concerned, please leave it to me. I am sure I will be able to resolve it.'

Prakash leans her head against Kuldeep's shoulder and keeps sobbing even as he caresses her face and tries to comfort her. He continues to simmer about Waryam Singh though he relishes the thought that his adversary has been roundly exposed in the eyes of his beloved.

'After everything that Bey ji has said about me, how do you think she will agree to my presence in this house?' Prakash whispers.

'You don't have to worry about that,' he asserts. 'I intend to sort out this matter today itself. Just be patient for a while. I need to go downstairs and have a chat with Bey ji.'

Gian Kaur isn't awake yet. Or maybe she had just gone to sleep, having stayed up much of the night. Kuldeep sits next to her and nudges her shoulder. She gets up with a start, eyes widening with surprise as her son comes into focus. Having worried about him all night, she isn't sure if she is merely imagining him there.

While she is still rubbing her eyes, Kuldeep starts boldly, 'Bey ji! I want to tell you something important.'

'What would that be?' she asks, fighting back her fears.

'I have decided that I am going to marry Prakash. And I am ready to give up my life if anyone tries to stop me from doing so.'

Gian Kaur recoils under the impact of the blow. Gasping for breath, she struggles to regain her composure and absorb the meaning of his words.

'I am ready to give up my life.' With that one phrase, Kuldeep has turned the tables on her. Arguments about family, honour, dignity and dowry are swept aside by the rising tide of maternal love.

Throwing herself against Kuldeep's chest, she cries, 'Your Bey ji is a poor widow. Don't leave her alone, son. You can do as you like. I will not say a word against it. All I want is that you should have a long and healthy life. I want to see you before my eyes as long as I live.'

Kuldeep is delighted with the ease with which he has changed his mother's mind. The anxiety and restlessness of the previous night vanish in a trice. He leaves the house with a new spring in his step.

24

It is about four in the afternoon and despite the bright sunshine, there is a nip in the air. Ganga Vishan reclines in his favourite chair, lost in his own world, savouring the company of his favourite companion – his bottle.

In the room next door, Saroj is in an entirely different world as she lies on the bed and ponders her future. She hasn't eaten anything since morning. The servant's entreaties have fallen on deaf ears. 'What kind of fate awaits us?' she contemplates. 'Bau ji's condition seems to be deteriorating by the day. The alcohol is destroying him. His liver is a mess, his eyes have turned pale and he is losing his appetite too. He is all I have and who knows when I am going to lose him too. It's no use trying to force him to quit drinking. He just can't, and I am not sure he will survive long even if he does stop now. Who can I depend upon once he's gone? What will my fate be?'

She goes into her father's room and sees him pouring the last couple of tots of liquor into his glass. His eyes are fixed on his glass and he is singing in a low, uneven voice:

You know for sure, I'll leave nothing of you
And so should you, leave nothing of me
For sure, I will end your existence
And urge you too, leave no trace of me

'Bau ji!' she cries and falls on his chair. Head on his chest, she sobs inconsolably. His inebriated mind takes a while to register her grief but when it does, his song trails off into the nothingness that it spoke of and he too starts crying.

Arms wrapped around her, Ganga Vishan weeps as he hasn't for a long time. 'Saroj...don't cry, my child...you know I can't see you cry...I promise not to touch liquor again...I will die but I won't drink...you are all I have since your mother died...Don't...I won't drink again...'

He continues to mumble incoherently for a long time, and Saroj keeps crying until her tears have drenched his shirt and she can cry no more. She helps her father get to his bed, covers him with a sheet and splashes her eyes with some cold water.

She has heard his assurances so many times that she has stopped taking them seriously. Each time he drinks himself into a stupor, she vents her anger through tears and he responds with similar promises. Only to be forgotten within a few days.

She hears a knock on the door. It is the messenger from the Singh Sabha Gurudwara bearing a note for her. It reads:

> *Respected Saroj ji*
> *A young couple is getting married at the gurudwara tomorrow morning. We hope you can come early and join the group of devotional singers who will perform the kirtan before the marriage ceremony. We would also be grateful if you can conduct the Aasa di Waar kirtan and the prayers during the ceremony.*
>
> *Your servant*
> *Secretary, Singh Sabha*

Saroj is feeling so low that her first instinct is to scribble on the back of the note that she is indisposed and won't be able to come. But she reasons that she is in desperate need for a change of setting and maybe the pious ambience of the gurudwara is just what she needs to lift her sagging spirits. She acknowledges the message and goes inside to resume her lonely vigil in her room.

25

Saroj reaches the gurudwara around five that morning. Settling down with the other girls in her group, she sits facing the Guru Granth Sahib and begins the kirtan. She and another girl play the harmonium, with Saroj also providing the lead voice while the rest of the group backs her up.

Saroj is well known in the neighbourhood for her melodious voice and for the devotion with which she sings the hymns. Regulars at the gurudwara, aware that she would be singing that morning, have turned up early to soak in the experience. They know that by the end of the morning service, their minds would be calm and their soul transported to a state that could only be called divine. By the time Saroj has completed the first two hymns, the hall is bursting at the seams but the usual commotion is missing. A cursory glance at the audience reveals that many of them have closed their eyes as they sit cross-legged on the floor, swaying gently with the celestial power of the kirtan.

The morning service is drawing to a close and Saroj is on the concluding verse of the hymn when her attention is distracted by the entry of the bride, resplendent in wedding finery and ornaments that tinkle with each step as she advances into the hall. She kneels in obeisance before the Guru Granth Sahib and sits down a short distance away from Saroj and her group.

Saroj has completed the final verse and is playing the concluding notes of the hymn when the girl accompanying her on the harmonium leans over and whispers in her ear, 'Saroj, do you know who is getting married this morning?'

'No.'

'It's Kuldeep.'

'Really?'

'Yes. With his maid.'

'His maid?'

'Indeed.'

Saroj goes numb all over. The left hand freezes on the fan of the harmonium, while the right struggles to find the appropriate keys. She goes off-key and misses the rhythm that she had captured so effortlessly earlier in the morning.

A few minutes later, the bridegroom walks in to pay the

customary obeisance before sitting down beside the bride. A clutch of marigold garlands covers his chest, having left telltale signs of saffron on his virile pink turban as they made their way towards his neck. A ceremonial plume adorns the pointed tip of the turban. A fringe of golden strands streams down from the turban to cover his face but Saroj can catch a fleeting glimpse each time he moves his head. It is enough to send shockwaves through her body.

The couple rise to begin the ritual perambulations of the Guru Granth Sahib. The group resumes the kirtan with a fresh set of verses. But Saroj is in a trance, barely aware of her surroundings and unsure if she is singing at all. The fingers of her right hand continue to behave erratically on the keys and it is left to her companion to raise her voice and make sure that her harmonium provides the music to accompany the verses.

The couple complete their first round and sit down to receive blessings. Kuldeep turns his head and his eyes meet Saroj's for the briefest second before he looks away. He appears calm, curiously unaffected by the encounter. Saroj feels the blood drain from her body. Her face is pale, her eyes refuse to open and her fingers tremble uncontrollably on the harmonium. Her companion gives her a worried look and asks, 'Are you feeling okay, sister?'

'Yes...No...felt dizzy for a moment...' she mutters, trying to control herself. Realizing that she has no choice but to fill in for Saroj, the girl goes back to the kirtan.

The second and third rounds of the holy book are completed without much contribution from Saroj as far as the kirtan is concerned. She is still in a daze when the final round starts, accompanied by the verse 'I am now tied to you forever...' She reels under the impact of the words and faints. Her head slumps on the harmonium, creating a stir among the other girls. A couple of them step up to carry her out of the hall into a small room at the back of the gurudwara. She lies on the cot for a while, recovers a little and returns to the hall to resume her seat. The marriage ceremony has ended and the prayers are concluding. Still weak and unsure of herself, she feels she is at the mercy of dark and ominous waves.

26

Sunday may be a day of rest for government employees but it is the busiest day of the week for Waryam Singh. This is the day the government hospital receives its supplies of medicines. Waryam Singh is the first to be there so that he can obtain whatever his wards need. He can ask for the most expensive of medicines or the most basic ones; no doctor or pharmacist in the hospital turns down his requests. Quinine along with a medicine for fever; eucalyptus oil in case of a bad cold; a pneumonia mixture and white oil to tackle pneumonia; zinc lotion for the eyes; borax, cotton wool and bandages for the injured...he draws his requirement as he wants. He takes these home, wraps them into small rolls of paper and dispenses them to the needy.

The hospital staff are willing accomplices in this arrangement. They acknowledge that Waryam Singh does more for the poorest folk in the town than their own hospital. Besides, the hospital has no real empathy for the unfortunate. From the doctor to the pharmacist, from the nurse to the sweeper, all seem to be intent on fleecing the destitute. You don't grease their palms, you don't get treated. That is the norm at the hospital. But when you don't have enough to manage two square meals a day, how do you satisfy the greed of these vultures?

Under normal circumstances, taking even the smallest of supplies out of the hospital without proper authorization would be considered a crime, attracting stiff punishment. Waryam Singh, though, has been helping himself to an assortment of medicines for years and nobody at the hospital seems to mind. They know that much of his meagre monthly salary of thirty rupees is spent on the impoverished and the needy. He does the same with the gifts that he receives from patients who have benefited from his medicines. Relatively affluent families have given him ten or even twenty rupees as a mark of their gratitude. Without the slightest thought, Waryam Singh has used the extra cash to help someone in distress.

His personal life is austere to the extreme. He usually eats at a small dhaba near his home. A couple of chapattis from the tandoor and a bowl of lentils or some vegetables don't cost him more than ten rupees a month. He washes his own clothes if he finds the time. And he has no other expenses worth mentioning. Yet, he is always in debt, borrowing five rupees from one, ten from another to tide over some pressing problem that someone is facing.

This particular Sunday morning too is going to be a busy one for him. He has spent the morning preparing small rolls and pouches of medicines which are then carefully placed into a larger bag. He is on the verge of leaving for his chores when he realizes that his clothes are all rather dirty. He goes out to fetch a bucket of water and is about to sit down to wash a few of them but changes his mind.

Getting up, he puts on his clothes and picks up his shoes and socks.

With the retreat of the monsoon, the months of September and October see a steady fall in the incidence of malaria. But this is cold comfort for those who have been exposed to the debilitating impact of the malarial parasite for a prolonged period. Their resistance diminished, they find themselves susceptible to a host of other ailments including typhoid and influenza, or even asthma and tuberculosis. The approaching winter is a particularly serious threat to such patients. If they can't be cured in October and are still on the sickbed in November, there is every chance that it will become their deathbed.

The dirty, narrow by-lanes of the town are populated with dozens of such cases, groaning away in their sickbeds without anyone to care for them. And the rare patient who isn't on his own typically has someone who is indifferent to his fate or unable to provide any real help or, worse, convinced that nothing can be done to save him.

Waryam Singh takes it upon himself to tend to such unfortunate souls. His problem, though, is that the patients are scattered all over the place and he has to shuttle from one end of the town to the other. He wants to visit each one of them but how? There are only twenty-four hours in the day and there is only one of him. Alas, if only he can clone himself into four so that everyone can be given the attention they deserve. But that isn't possible and so he simply neglects his own person and his appearance. He does have one clean pair of clothes that is mandatory for a hospital staffer, though there are times when even this modest requirement falls by the wayside.

Noticing a gaping hole in his socks, he picks up a needle and hurriedly starts to darn it with long, untidy stitches. The door opens a couple of inches and through the gap he sees an eye peering at him. Awkwardly holding the sock in one hand and the needle and thread in the other, he rises to open the door.

Saroj stands before him, still as a statue. He is startled by her unexpected appearance. Her face is ashen and bears an indescribable sadness about it. Her eyes still carry traces of the tears she has shed, with telltale streaks visible around the corners. Even the lips, usually blessed with a pinkish hue, look dark as the monsoon clouds.

'Saroj!' The sock falls from his hand. 'What's wrong?'

'Haven't you heard, Bhapa ji?' she whimpers, perching herself on the edge of his bed.

'Heard what?'

'Kuldeep has married.'

'What?'

'He has.'

'Whom?'

'The same one.'

'Prakash?'

'Yes.' She turns her face way, afraid that Waryam Singh will read the torment in her heart.

'Damn!' he cries in anguish. 'Just what I feared!'

Seeing the state Saroj is in, he sets aside his thoughts about Kuldeep and turns to console her. 'When did this happen?' he asks softly.

'This morning,' she says and again turns her face away from him.

Standing beside her, he gently pats her head. 'There...there... maybe this was inevitable.'

She is lost in her own thoughts. While she has given up on her own aspirations towards Kuldeep, how can she remain unaffected by the events of the morning? She feels like the bankrupt businessman who has not only faced the tragedy of having his home auctioned in public but also the humiliation of seeing a new owner move in before his eyes.

'Why are you so upset, Saroj?' Waryam says, his hand on her shoulder to calm her down. 'You'd lost him long ago.'

Still silent, Saroj can feel her overwrought emotions unravel. Waryam Singh knows that there is nothing that he can offer by way of advice or arguments that could assuage her hurt. It is difficult to see her grapple with pain of this magnitude.

'Where are you coming from?' he asks.

'From the gurudwara.' Saroj looks into his eyes.

'From the gurudwara? At this time?'

'Yes. I went there early with my group of devotional singers.'

'I thought your group goes there in the evening.'

'The secretary of the Singh Sabha had asked us to come this morning, for the kirtan during the Anand Karaj ceremonies.'

'Anand Karaj? Don't tell me it was your group that provided the kirtan at the wedding!'

Waryam Singh's heart, seasoned as it is by many an ordeal, struggles against its moorings. Gazing straight into Saroj's eyes, he probes, 'So you actually participated in their wedding ceremonies?'

'I did,' she whispers and raises her hands to cover her eyes. It does little to shield her emotions from him. The dam of her resolve gives way and she starts to sob helplessly. Looking at her, Waryam Singh's eyes also become moist.

'Forget about this, Saroj. Tell yourself that it hasn't happened,' he counsels, gently caressing her shoulder.

Worried that she is still sobbing and his words are having no visible effect, he lapses into thought for a while. 'I hope you aren't in a tearing rush to go home?'

'Why?'

'Just asking...'

'Well...there is nothing particularly urgent. But I am worried about Bau ji. He's been busy drinking for almost two days now.'

'Is your servant at home?'

'He is.'

'And Radhia is there too?'

'Yes.'

'In that case, come with me for a couple of hours. What I have to do might give you a different perspective.'

Saroj remembers that she had turned down a similar request earlier. How often has she repented that? Saying no a second time will only add to her guilt. She really is in no mood to go anywhere, and her concern over her father's condition looms large. Yet, she finds herself unable to decline his suggestion.

'I'll come,' she consents.

Without saying another word, Waryam Singh puts on his shoes, picks up the medicine bag and closes the door behind him as they leave the house.

27

The Kali Bari Bazaar lies a short distance from Sadar Bazaar as you head towards the railway station. It derives its name from an ancient temple dedicated to Ma Kali and is much revered by the small Bengali community. The street itself is narrow and straight as an arrow. About halfway down the street, an alley to the right takes you into an opening called the Gallu Mal Square, a small locality of about fifty houses. 'House' is actually a misnomer for the humble dwellings in the locality since many of them are thatched huts and a few are shacks with mud walls and a sheet of tin that passes off as a roof. Virtually all of them are occupied by cobblers, sweepers, grass-cutters, daily wage labourers, horse-keepers and others who make up the lowest strata of society.

Walking briskly through the bazaar, Waryam Singh – with Saroj following a couple of paces behind – turns into the alley and reaches the dilapidated neighbourhood. A few minutes later, they arrive at a ramshackle little hut that has nothing more than a loosely hung gunny sack posing as a door.

Saroj is hit by waves of nausea. During the short walk from the bazaar, they have seen heaps of decomposing garbage on either side of the alley. The stench rising from them is almost palpable. The low-lying area has no visible outlet for water. The drain on the side of the alley has overflowed and the fetid water has occupied every pothole to create cesspools that have to be negotiated with extreme care. The monsoons have taken their toll on the mud-plastered walls, lacerating them with gashes that only add to the misery of the occupants.

Already finding it difficult to breathe, Saroj struggles to retain control as she follows Waryam into the hut and takes stock of her surroundings. The place is little more than a tiny cell with neither a window nor a ventilator shaft. The absence of light gives it a strange, smoke-filled aura. Groaning in obvious agony, a man of about thirty-five is lying on a rickety cot. An assortment of rags is tied to the wooden frame at various angles to keep the cot in a horizontal posture and prevent it from collapsing. Half-a-dozen round cakes of cow dung, some crumbling but a few still fairly intact, are strewn under the cot. Undeterred by the arrival of the intruders, three or four largish rats scurry around the floor as though they own the place.

The cot occupies most of the hut, barely leaving enough space for a bench or an even smaller cot. One corner is occupied by a small hearth, a couple of earthen cooking pots, a wooden ladle and a mud pitcher. A hookah with a somewhat crooked pipe hangs from a small hook on the wall. Two brooms, a basket unravelling from one side, some animal bones and a few rags occupy the rest of the floor. The wall next to the cot is splattered with the spit and phlegm from the patient's relentless coughing. A few score flies hum busily around the wall. An army of large black ants swarms all over the floor, leaving little space to move without stepping on them.

Seeing the visitors, the patient folds his hands in respect and tries in vain to get up but is stopped by Waryam Singh. His chest rattles with phlegm when he coughs. His muffled voice forms some words but neither of them can decipher anything. Contorted by weeks of pain and coughing, his face causes Saroj to step back in fear even as Waryam Singh moves up to him to enquire, 'So how's it going, Jawanda?'

His words are still not intelligible but the shake of his head leaves them in little doubt. His condition has not shown any improvement.

A young woman of about twenty-five walks in, carrying a cake of dung strangely adorned by a burning coal that sits in the middle. She places it in the hearth and bows before Waryam Singh with folded hands to welcome him. Her eyes dart around the room, looking for something on which they could sit. A person as important as Waryam Singh has come to her dwelling and she has to keep him standing! She shrinks in his presence. Rushing outside, she returns a few moments later carrying a small bench.

'Please sit down here,' she offers. 'That's all we poor folks...'

'But how is he feeling, Attiya? Has the medicine I brought the other day provided any relief?'

'Not really,' she replies despondently. 'May the Guru preserve your glory! But there is no perceptible improvement yet. He coughs constantly and his health seems to be failing by the day. He used to eat at least half a chapatti till a couple of days back but now, even that...'

'Come on, Attiya. You can be such a fool at times,' he rebukes. 'What made you think that he is any condition to digest a chapatti? A bit of milk is all that he can take at this time.'

Attiya stares blankly at him, her silence providing an eloquent riposte to his reprimand. 'And pray, where do I get the money to buy the milk?' her eyes seem to ask.

Saroj feels her heart sink in despair as she takes in the woman's appearance. Is this how helpless, how hopeless things can become when one is mired in abject poverty? She looks at the woman's clothes and then, out of sheer embarrassment, eyes her own. Her kameez has lost its buttons and barely covers her bosom. Her salwar, too, has given way around the knees and is completely frayed near the ankles. The dupatta is tattered and falling apart.

Waryam Singh gives the man the thermometer and takes

the reading. Opening his bag, he fishes out two little rolls of paper. 'Here! Give him this one right away with hot milk and the other one at night before he sleeps. It should give you some relief from the cough and also ease up the phlegm a bit. Give this for four days and I hope he'll get better.'

'Thank you and may the gurus bless you, Sardar ji. But do take a look because his eyes seem a bit strange to me today.'

'Don't you worry. He is going to be fine. Just make sure that he takes the medicine regularly.' He takes out a one-rupee coin and hands it to her.

Attiya lowers her eyes in gratitude, unable to say anything that can remotely express her sentiments.

Waryam Singh caresses the patient's head and smiles. 'Get well soon, Jawanda! And don't lose heart. You have to give strength to your wife too. May the Lord bring you relief soon.'

Jawanda's lips move as he folds his hands and tries to say something.

Waryam Singh collects his bag and leaves the hut, followed closely by Saroj. Once they have left its vicinity, Saroj observes, 'He seems to be in a pretty bad condition, Bhapa ji.'

'I doubt if he will survive this night, Saroj,' he says softly.

She looks back at the forlorn hut and asks, 'What will she do if he dies in the middle of the night? That poor, poor woman!'

Waryam Singh sighs and slowly trudges down another alley.

Saroj stops in her tracks. 'Bhapa ji, I think I ought to stay with her tonight.'

Waryam Singh looks at her in wonder. She appears transformed by her visit to the hut. 'Really? Are you sure you'll be able to spend an entire night in that hovel? You won't pass out?' he mocks gently.

Reminded of the earlier night at his place, Saroj lowers her head, embarrassed.

'That Saroj is gone for good, Bhapa ji. I'll spend the night here.'

'But don't you have to inform your home about your absence?'

'That's not a problem,' she replies determinedly.

'And how many houses will you stay in, Saroj? As Sheikh Farid said, *there's a fire in every house, that I can see from my vantage point*. There are many persons in this locality itself who have death hovering over their heads. And think of the number of other similarly godforsaken localities in this town. How many souls will you be able to assist? You can fulfil your desire another day. We have so many other houses to visit today. Let's go!'

As they plunge deeper into the neighbourhood, word about their arrival spreads like wildfire. Men, women and children, a small crowd is soon following them as they make their way through a narrow alley that leads into a clearing. An old pipal tree stands in the middle of the clearing. No sooner have they stopped under the tree than someone produces a cot on which Saroj and Waryam Singh are asked to sit. The residents assemble in a tight circle around them, their eyes filled with a kind of reverence. The two of them are twin angels who have descended from the sky and landed in their midst.

Opening his bag, Waryam Singh starts to dispense his wares. If it is eardrops for one, it is eyedrops for another and an anti-pyretic for a third. He moves from taking the pulse of one patient to peering into the eyes of a second and examining the festering wound of another. The crowd around him continues to swell.

It takes him about two hours to attend to the needs of the crowd before they visit the homes of those who are critically ill, who have no one to look after them and who crave for nothing more than the healing touch of a warm-hearted soul.

By the time they finish their house calls and make their way back to the bazaar, it is close to six in the evening. In the midst of the bustling bazaar, Saroj senses a strange kind of calm envelop her. The visit has opened a new window into her innermost self, giving her a glimpse into hitherto unknown parts of her soul. She has actually seen and experienced the 'hell' that people only speak about. And she has also experienced heaven, not somewhere distant in the skies but right here on earth, in her own town. She has discovered that the road to heaven passes through the hell that she has just visited. This hell, she concludes, is the real doorway to heaven and the attainment of heaven is possible only by serving these wretched souls, giving them love and receiving their blessings and good wishes.

A few months back, she had witnessed a small miracle at Waryam Singh's house. It had given her an insight into the greatness of this unassuming man. But today, she has seen the full spectrum of his nobility, and seen too that his soul is riddled with the pain of those around him. She marvels at the influence this has on her. Earlier in the morning, she had felt rejected, worthless. And yet, all of that seems so distant and trivial. She feels a deep sense of contentment that stays with her even after she returns to her own home.

28

Kuldeep is discovering a whole new bed of flowers in his garden of paradise as his mind returns to earth after a long and exhausting flight in the land of renunciation. In the lush green branches of a tree in his garden, he spots a chirping nightingale. Upon catching his eye, the bird flutters its wings and settles down next to him, preoccupying itself with building a new nest.

Gian Kaur, meanwhile, is desperately trying to come to terms with the transformation of Prakash from a maidservant to a daughter-in-law who is rapidly assuming total control of the household.

Kuldeep is completely smitten by her good looks and by the ever-flirtatious sparkle in her eyes. His months of penance and meditation, his desire for renunciation of the material world have all evaporated into thin air. And what about Satwant, who had spent two years with him, whose simplicity and devotion had given him so much joy? Are mere simplicity and devotion enough to make a woman an exceptional wife, he reflects. Or does she have to intoxicate her husband with every action, with every gesture, with every move that she makes? Does she have to be a woman whose eyelashes can create a flutter in the man's heart, whose words are like the lyrics of a song, whose charm unsettles a man from head to toe, whose smile makes him heady, whose passionate embrace can make him lose his self-control and even his senses. Satwant, Kuldeep reflects, had none of these attributes. She was a simple, honest, devoted and even a beautiful woman. But that was it, no more and no less.

And what does the world think of his marriage to Prakash? Kuldeep has no time for such matters. The comments are unsparing. Hasn't he displayed undue haste? How could he think of a wedding while the embers of his father's funeral pyre are still warm? Kuldeep, though, is in his own world. To his friends, he sells the yarn that he married Prakash because of his own idealism and his desire to bring about social reform. As for his mother's unhappiness, he reasons that this is entirely Waryam Singh's fault. That man, indeed, is his worst enemy in the world. So evil that even Prakash has developed a dislike for him and tends to avoid him wherever possible. Kuldeep's mind occasionally flirts with the idea of revenge, relishing the thought for a while before setting it aside.

Their room, meanwhile, has got a fresh coat of paint and Kuldeep's old habit of buying new things and throwing away old ones resurfaces. A new sofa has been ordered, along with a revolving chair, a dressing table and beds with the new-fangled spring mattresses. He has left the selection of these items to Prakash.

They have been married for little over a month. It is January and winter is at its peak. It is about nine in the evening and the newly weds are chatting away in their room upstairs. Much of the conversation is about themselves – about their love for each other, their hope that it would endure forever, their admiration for each other's virtues and about their own beauty. Silently, though, another issue is brewing in Kuldeep's mind. His curiosity about the relationship between Prakash and Waryam Singh remains undimmed. He had wanted to ask her about the matter on the very day she had arrived, and with each passing day, the desire to get an answer becomes more intense. If he has held back until now, it is only out of fear that it might unduly provoke her, make her angry.

Tonight, though, he finds it impossible to restrain himself. Bringing up an oblique reference to the object of his ire, he asks, 'So how long have you known Waryam Singh, Prakash?'

'Not for very long,' she replies, looking closely at him as if to read his mind.

'But how did it come about?'

'He saved my life,' she says. Her thoughts go back to those horrible days. She hasn't allowed recent developments to obliterate those memories.

'And how did he do that'? There is an urgency in Kuldeep's voice.

'I had this really terrible boil on my back. I was lying by the roadside, fighting for my life. He carried me to his home.'

'So how long did he treat you at his home?' Kuldeep's voice betrays a hint of nervousness.

'Just for a night. He had me admitted to the hospital the following day.'

'And did he apply medicine to you and bandage you all by himself?'

'No. He had sent for another girl to assist him. But she didn't stay very long. I think she couldn't bear to see the ghastly state I was in at that time. In fact, he had to go out again to escort her to her place.'

'Who was that girl?'

'I didn't know her but I think Bhapa ji called her Saroj a couple of times.'

Kuldeep's mind goes back to that eventful night. 'And when did this happen?' he asked.

'About five months back, I think.'

It all falls into place as Prakash explains how the poor girl was completely drenched when she arrived after braving torrential rain. But she had barely stayed for an hour. Bhapa ji had pleaded with her to stay the night because he had a single woman at his home. But she didn't agree. She was feeling sick and wanted to get back to her house.

Kuldeep remembers the downpour that night and Prakash's narrative leaves no room for any further doubt. A wave of repentance flows through his body, numbing every nerve as it travels from head to toe. He had suspected Waryam Singh and Saroj without knowing the entire story. And worse, he had then taken it upon himself to slander them in every street and locality of their neighbourhood.

Keen to hide his feelings from Prakash, Kuldeep goes downstairs and sits in the kitchen for a while, pondering over his own actions. When he returns to his room, his face is pale and suffused with an air of gloom. 'Nothing to worry,' he responds to Prakash's solicitous inquiries. 'I seem to have an upset stomach. It has been hurting for a while but seems to be better now.'

He remains depressed and guilt-ridden for several days. He wants to go across to Waryam Singh, place his head on the man's feet and beg his forgiveness. But an act like that needs courage, which he is unable to muster.

Kuldeep had taken little interest in business during his father's lifetime. On more than one occasion, he had attempted to start a small retail establishment for general merchandise or other products but the enthusiasm had only lasted for a short while. Most ventures would survive for a month or two before being closed down with some accompanying losses to the family. Only because Sadhu

Singh had prospered from his bulk trading in sugar and gur could Kuldeep indulge in his half-hearted ventures. As of now there is no dearth of money in the house and the gold and other ornaments owned by Satwant and by his mother alone would be worth ten or fifteen thousand rupees. Yet, fired by the new zeal in his life, Kuldeep now wants to do something productive. Textiles, he thinks, is the answer. He wants to set up a shop to retail textiles and fabrics. Spurred by the idea, he decides to make an early trip to Amritsar to acquire stocks from the wholesale market there.

Gian Kaur's life, meanwhile, has taken an unexpected turn for the worse. Long used to supervising the running of the household through her maidservant and daughter-in-law, she is trying to cope with all the responsibilities that have suddenly been thrust upon her. Prakash, who had earlier taken it upon herself to look after every little thing in the house, refuses to touch anything at all. She has even abandoned the care of the child, leaving it to a young boy who has been hired for this purpose. One by one, Kuldeep has handed over to her all of Satwant's belongings, including her valuable clothes and ornaments. Some items of gold jewellery that Prakash regarded as old-fashioned have been taken to the town's main jeweller to be melted down and shaped into fancier designs. New clothes are also purchased on a regular basis so that her besotted husband would see her decked up in the most alluring colours and fashions. Seeing her like this drives Kuldeep giddy with desire. She resembles a fairy straight out of paradise, enchanting him with her airs and graces.

The couple spend much of their time in their room on the upper floor. Prakash has made it a habit to have their meals brought up to the room by the boy. He also brings up her tea whenever she needs it. Gian Kaur longs to spend time with her son but such moments are few and far between. It isn't long before she starts making the inevitable comparisons between Satwant and Prakash. She remembers the way she would chide, rebuke and even abuse Satwant but she would take it all with dignity and without ever reacting in anger. If she wanted to buy anything, even if she wanted to spend just a rupee, she would first consult her mother-in-law. With the benefit of hindsight, Gian Kaur starts to regard Satwant as an angel when compared with Prakash, who considers it below her dignity to talk properly to her mother-in-law. Expensive garments and jewellery are being bought without so much as a by-your-leave. Taking an elder's permission has become an extinct ritual; even consulting the elder is deemed unnecessary. Having run the house with an iron fist for much of her adult life, Gian Kaur can see the steady erosion in her authority. She cannot help feeling suffocated and uncomfortable in her own home.

She recognizes that her predicament is the result of her own desire for the health, happiness and longevity of her son. That desire had clouded her judgment and caused her to turn a blind eye to the dangers that she could see so clearly. She had allowed Kuldeep to go ahead with his plans even though she could perceive the havoc they might wreak on their household. Waryam Singh's common sense and wisdom could have provided some succour at this critical juncture but he has steadfastly avoided coming to their house since the day of the marriage.

Kuldeep has rented a shop but his plans to visit Amritsar to purchase stocks are yet to fructify. Each time he plans the journey, Prakash says something that causes him to defer the visit. How can he go when she speaks so lovingly, 'Oh, Kuldeep! I can't live a day without you' or 'Please don't go yet. Or take me with you if you have to go.'

Several days pass in this indecision. Meanwhile, things at home have deteriorated rapidly. Obsessed with his wife, Kuldeep neglects his mother. Clashes between mother and son on relatively minor issues are a daily occurrence and Gian Kaur is seldom shy of deploying her famous temper and colourful vocabulary. The troubles escalate sharply when Prakash begins to jump into the fray. Her willingness to match her mother-in-law's decibel level and trade insult for insult sees everyday conflicts spiral into full-fledged battles of attrition. The mother is abused in the presence of her son, but Kuldeep couldn't care less about her plight. Instead of restraining Prakash, he often ends up upbraiding his mother.

Gian Kaur could have probably acted with greater wisdom. Instead of wading straight into danger, she could have taken a detour and tried to avoid strife. But she is one of those cantankerous old women who derive pleasure from splitting hairs, from pursuing the 'why' and 'why not' of every issue until it has been exposed threadbare. There are times when she rants or weeps right through the day, and then some more at night. And at other times, when a spell of peace appears round the corner, Prakash seems quite willing to pour oil on troubled waters and even light a match to it to keep the fires burning.

The incessant strife is taking its toll on Kuldeep. He knows that his mother is incorrigible and any attempt to reason with her runs the risk of aggravating matters. Thinking that he may stand a better chance of success with Prakash, he tries his hand at gentle persuasion. 'You are so kind, Prakash. Be a little patient with Bey ji. She is already in her seventies, you know...'

The tactic fails and, on occasion, even backfires. Prakash, he discovers, could be every bit as loud, as voluble, as tempestuous and as unreasonable as his mother. The discovery comes as something of a shock. He has regarded her as the epitome of love, even of perfection. Her harshness and her unwillingness to listen to reason are annoying. Repeated complaints and arguments introduce a new dimension into the relationship – periods of sullen silence when they avoid talking to each other.

That's the strange thing about love. When it blossoms, lovers look at each other through spectacles specially made to block out anything that appears dark or unpleasant. The view they get is of a beautiful, unblemished world that is bright and sparkling. Wouldn't it be wonderful if things remain that way, that the spectacles become a permanent part of their lives? But that's not how the real world works. With time, the specs start to lose their power and reveal things that were inconceivable earlier. The sparkle begins to dull and dark spots appear on the surface of objects that used to be perfect. How long do the glasses retain their power? Funny that nobody has the answer. It can vanish in a matter of days, or endure for years.

Or you could say that when lovers start their journey, it is like a walk in an enchanted garden. But as the journey continues, the terrain becomes uneven and after a while, the gentle walk turns into an arduous uphill ascent. The clearest sign comes when lovers start blaming one another, erecting barriers in communication that impede the flow of love and start polluting it with elements like suspicion, jealousy and anger.

Are they spending too much time too close to one another, Kuldeep ponders. Maybe he needs to go away for a few days so that they can re-ignite their passion. It is time to go to Amritsar, he decides. Prakash protests, as she had done in the past. But this time Kuldeep is more determined. Her pleading still affects him but fails to dissuade him from his objective. With bedding, a small bag and about two thousand rupees in his pocket, he boards the night train to Amritsar.

The line between agreement and disagreement can be so fine that it can only be measured through the eye of a needle. Take a step forward and the disagreement turns into an agreement. Move a step back and the reverse happens.

29

Alighting from the train in Amritsar the next evening, Kuldeep finds himself in two minds. His spiritual guru, Sant Prem Singh, lives in Amritsar and shouldn't he first go to pay his obeisance and seek guru's blessings? Or should he just go about his business? A porter picks up the holdall and leads him to the exit. A tongawallah calls, 'Anyone for the Golden Temple, for Baba Sahib Chowk? I have place for one passenger!'

The guru lives adjacent to the chowk, in the vicinity of the Golden Temple. Kuldeep takes a few steps towards the tonga and pauses, assaulted by a new set of thoughts. How can I show my face to him? He had such expectations from me! And look what I have done! Alas! Those days when my mind was immersed in the nectar of his blessings! Thanks to his sermons, every waking moment was bliss, my thoughts directed only towards Him. This material world was no more than an illusion. I had found the real meaning of life in His Name. Nothing else mattered. I turned down numerous proposals for marriage. I even declined Saroj's love. And now? How do I carry this accursed face of mine before him?

And yet, the pull to pay his respects to his guru is irresistible. The guru is blessed with infinite kindness, he reasons. He has thousands of devotees and surely there will be some who are still tied to the material world, who have sinned and still receive his blessings. I will lie at his feet and ask for his forgiveness, acknowledge that I have failed to live up to his expectations, allowing myself to get trapped in the web of family life. I will ask the guru to show me the way...show me how I can remain committed to my family and yet follow the path of righteousness. I am sure he has the key to this problem.

He climbs on to the back seat of the tonga, his mind still preoccupied with his thoughts.

The journey to Baba Sahib Chowk takes about half an hour. Dismounting from the tonga, his attention is drawn towards the Golden Temple, its dome glistening in an ethereal glow as it captures the crimson rays of the setting sun. Tearing his eyes away, he finds a porter to carry his holdall and starts towards Shaheed Bunga lane. It is getting dark and he has to ask a couple of people for directions. Followed by the porter deftly balancing his holdall on his head, Kuldeep walks for about a hundred yards in the narrow, unlit lane before coming to a halt. With his guru's dera nowhere in sight, he asks the porter to set the baggage on a ledge outside a small house and wait. Alone, he goes past a few more houses before stopping outside one that has a strong light shining in its first floor. Standing in the lane below, he hears the muffled sounds of an argument taking place in the upper floor. One of the voices has a familiar ring to it but he isn't sure.

Undecided, he pauses. He sees an approaching figure in the shadows some distance down the lane. The man is carrying a small steel bucket and sports the small turban, flowing beard, long tunic and shorts typical of staff working at the various deras and other religious establishments in the neighbourhood of the Golden Temple.

'Sat Sri Akal, Sardarji,' Kuldeep steps up to greet the stranger. 'Could you guide me towards the Dera of Sant Prem Singh?'

'You are standing at his doorstep,' the man replies gruffly, looking at Kuldeep from head to toe. 'Where are you from?'

'From Peshawar.'

'And what business do you have with Sant Prem Singh?'

'He is my guru.'

'Really?' the man says with barely concealed sarcasm. 'How did a fellow like you get caught in the web of a charlatan like him?'

Before Kuldeep can recover from this unexpected attack, the man adds, 'Why don't you go up and see the man's misdeeds for yourself. I am sure you can hear it already. Like the Mahabharata, this battle has been raging for days now.' Muttering curses under his breath, the stranger walks off.

Nonplussed, Kuldeep gingerly makes his way up the stairs leading to the apartment on the first floor. The sounds of the argument are clearly audible as he approaches the door bolted from inside. He stands outside for a while, eavesdropping in stunned disbelief. There is no doubt now that the male voice is his guru's. But a tone so harsh, and words so abusive...it is the language of the gutter, not the dulcet tones he was accustomed to listening with such rapt attention in the gurudwara. There is also a female voice saying something in protest.

'You low-caste bitch!' the guru thunders. 'You were starving when I met you. I was the one who fed you and placed you in this luxurious comfort.'

'Let the comfort and luxury burn in hell!' the female responds. 'Had I known of your evil ways, I would have stayed miles away...'

Kuldeep hears the echo of a crisp slap, followed by a shriek and more curses by the woman. From the sounds of the ensuing scuffle, he can make out that the woman is trying to extricate herself from the man's grasp, hurling abuse at him even as she tries to fight off his advances.

Unable to take it any more, Kuldeep hurries down the steps. 'Pick up the baggage and take me to some hotel,' he tells the porter. The porter hoists the holdall on to his head and starts walking. Kuldeep follows, his mind swirling in a flurry of thoughts.

Suppress your passion. Control your desires. This was the relentless message of the guru. But those who chant this mantra to leave their families must be fools or charlatans. If the artificial suppression of hunger, thirst or sleep is unnatural, the same logic must apply to the suppression of passion. To leave your home, your family in the name of curbing your desires is surely unnatural. And if this is the message being delivered by organizations in the name of social reform, we must question their motives.

Spouting high philosophy and delivering moral sermons is one thing, and living a normal life is another. Let's set aside the theoretical precepts taught in the books for a while and undertake a critical examination of our own personal lives. And then place your hand on your heart and ask yourself if you have succeeded in curbing your own desires. You can build a citadel of morality around yourself but you must ask if it has withstood the test. How often does it crack and how many holes have you tried to plug with the clay of suppression? Pose these questions in your own mind and reflect on the answers that you get. You may be surprised to learn that moral standards in your society aren't as low as they are made out to be. Most families lead normal lives and aren't particularly agitated by this issue. The ones most worried about growing immorality, curiously, are the ones who make a career out of advocating this 'suppression of passion'.

Our society tends to apply fairly tough standards on you if you want to detach yourself from the material world and live the life of a hermit. You are expected to abstain from good food and from the company of women. Marriage, of course, becomes a very distant prospect. Yet, the one who accepts such abstinence is always surrounded by attractive women...women who will serve him the finest foods, who are ready to submit to every commandment. And he is expected to be immune to such pleasures? Our epics tell us that passion didn't spare even the legendary sages who performed hard penance, who suspended themselves upside down from a tree for twelve years. Yet, we expect an ordinary mortal to resist the charms of women who have employed each of the sixteen classical modes to adorn themselves before coming to him? They sit at his feet, fawn over him, feed him rare delicacies and massage him with their delicate hands. And nothing should happen to him?

Of course it does! Sooner or later, the dormant spirits of passion awaken and take control of the hermit. Unable to resist, he violates the honour of some innocent woman and flees from the scene. Our society is outraged by his act and soon a posse of sturdy young men grabs their swords and sticks and goes after him. Strange, isn't it? First you tell the hawk that it should desist from eating flesh and that it should get used to a diet of grass and weeds. Poor hawk...just as he is getting used to the new state, you tempt him with some juicy morsels of meat. The famished hawk swoops on it and the bystanders, offended by his action, pounce upon him with sticks and stones. What an extraordinary notion of justice!

Kuldeep's mind is in turmoil. How would he have reacted in a similar situation? He, too, could have been reciting his guru's message about the 'suppression of passion' and convinced himself about its righteousness. But would he have passed the test if he had been surrounded by a bevy of beautiful women? It is easy to prescribe a test but much harder to take it yourself. Who is innocent and who is guilty? Can you really pronounce on this if you haven't experienced the dangers of an arduous trek?

All things considered, Kuldeep decides that he is done with Sant Prem Singh and his dera. The guru's uncouth behaviour is, quite simply, unworthy of a holy man, and Kuldeep has lost all respect for him. His mind dwells over the events of the last few months and the influence that the guru's sermons had on his own actions. Hadn't he vowed to renounce everything and walk away from his home, from his parents? He had turned a deaf ear to the pleadings of his mother. He had even turned down the last wishes of his dying father. And how long did those vows last?

Kuldeep had left Peshawar with the idea of spending a week or two away from home. He had thought that after finishing his work in Amritsar, he would visit Delhi and a couple of other places. But the incident at the guru's dera has shaken him. He spends two days in Amritsar's famous textiles bazaar, completes his purchases and returns to Peshawar.

30

Prakash had no clue that her husband would return so quickly from his trip. He had left for Amritsar on Saturday evening. On Sunday morning, she goes with the servant to Joga Singh gurudwara, leaving the child with his grandmother.

They return well after lunch time but a worried Gian Kaur doesn't have the courage to ask why it took her so long. She waits until Prakash has gone to her room before posing the question to the servant. But the young fellow is beholden only to the mistress. Instead of replying to Gian Kaur's queries, he goes upstairs and informs Prakash that the old woman was trying to probe into her whereabouts.

This triggers the mother of all tantrums and without waiting to come down from her room, Prakash starts to hurl the choicest of abuses at her mother-in-law. The latter, too, has reached the end of her tether and there is no holding back. Insult is matched with insult, abuse with abuse. The battle rages into the night, making it difficult for neighbours to sleep. They are accustomed to Gian Kaur's temper and her frequent slanging matches with Radhia but the venom with which Prakash abuses her is hard for anyone to stomach. So foul is her language that some women have to cover the ears of their young children.

A tense truce prevails when Kuldeep reaches home around ten the following night. Keeping his baggage in the kitchen, he goes up the stairs. The servant is asleep in the kitchen but hearing the door open he wakes up to attend to the bags. Gian Kaur is awake in her room and waits for her son to come to her, touch her feet and take her blessings before proceeding upstairs. The wait is in vain. She is tempted to get up to remonstrate but decides otherwise. She hears Kuldeep's footsteps ascend the stairs, his knock on the door and the harsh tone inquiring, 'Who is it?'

'It's me,' Kuldeep replies impatiently. He can barely wait for the door to open, expecting to be greeted with open arms and taken into a passionate embrace. She opens the door, smiles and retreats to the far corner of the room.

Kuldeep enters the room and pauses in shock. There is a strange kind of smell in the room. 'Where is this smell of cigarettes coming from?' he asks, wrinkling his nose.

Picking up his jacket to hang it properly, she replies, 'I think it is smoke from the naan bai's tandoor in the street. You often get this smell in the room. It's quite unpleasant.'

Kuldeep's eyes sweep over the room. The window facing the street is firmly closed, as indeed it would be in the midst of winter. Besides, he has spent many years in this room without being bothered by smoke from the tandoor. A doubt surfaces in his mind.

Prakash is still standing in the corner, asking him about his visit to Amritsar, his journey, his purchases and so on. Kuldeep offers some vague replies, his mind still distracted by the offensive smell. He sits on the bed and beckons to Prakash to do the same. She does so, but sits on the edge farthest from him. He moves closer to her. Putting his arm around her, he pulls her towards him. His face moves towards her, as if to kiss. She responds, her lips a mere inch away from his. Stunned, he recoils and stands up. The smell of liquor on her breath is too strong to be dismissed.

'Oh my god!' he thinks. 'Not merely one vice but two!'

He reaches out for her hand and holds it to his nose. There is no doubt. Her fingers reek of tobacco.

Prakash has turned pale. Kuldeep glowers at her, his eyes looking straight into hers. She lowers her eyes.

Kuldeep's legs shake with rage. He hears someone from deep inside him shout, 'So Waryam Singh was right about you, wasn't he? Whatever he told Bey ji about you was true!'

She sits still as a statue.

'Prakash!' he thunders. 'Look at me, Prakash!'

One can almost hear Prakash's heartbeat. Her eyes are dug firmly into a spot near her feet.

'What kind of a family are you from, Prakash? Tell me right now!'

Still not getting a word out of her, he places his hand on her shoulder and tugs at her. 'So it's true, isn't it? Everything that Waryam Singh said about you?'

'Please forgive me,' she whispers, falling at his feet.

'Forgive you?' He jerks his feet away in disgust. 'Actually, I am the one who should seek your forgiveness, Prakash. Such unkindness! You could have done what you wanted to me and I would have taken it in my stride. But how could you....how could you defile a Sikh home with something that is taboo in our faith? How could you bring tobacco into this home?'

'I will never do such a thing again. Forgive me this one time,' she whimpers.

'There is absolutely no need to ask for forgiveness,' Kuldeep says, his arms crossed across his chest, trying perhaps to restrain his heart from leaping out. 'I am grateful to the Lord that your true colours have been exposed so soon. Who knows what else might have happened. At least there's no harm done yet. It is by the grace of the Waheguru that I've been saved.'

He continues to pepper her with questions but her lips are sealed and he can neither cajole nor threaten her into breaking that seal. In the midst of his umpteenth effort to prise the truth out of her, he realizes that she must have had an accomplice. He steps out of the door and calls for the servant.

The lad comes upstairs and stands at the edge of the steps, refusing to look up at Kuldeep. Several questions are posed, and each encounters an evasive response. Without warning, Kuldeep steps out of the door and delivers a stinging slap on the fellow's left cheek, followed by another back-handed one on his right. Shaken out of his wits, the boy starts, 'Bibi ji asked me to fetch her two packets of cigarettes. I got her a pack today and another the day before yesterday...I also got her a bottle of liquor...she told me where to go to buy these things...She gave me one rupee as reward...Some of the stuff is inside that small trunk...'

The picture is crystal clear. No further explanations are needed.

Kuldeep opens the smaller of the two trunks and stares at a half-empty bottle of liquor and an open pack of cigarettes. He asks the servant to help him carry the two trunks into his mother's room. Briefly pausing to touch her feet, he quickly returns to his room.

Prakash is lying on the bed, her face buried in the pillow. Standing a short distance away, Kuldeep asks, 'So where would you like to go, Prakash? I will make the arrangements accordingly. I don't blame you for anything. What happened is entirely my fault. I am the one who defied the advice of my elders and now have to pay the price for my actions. But you do realize that it is now impossible for you to stay on in this house.'

She cries, pleads and makes fervent promises of turning a new leaf. What happened was an aberration and will never be repeated, she assures. Kuldeep is unmoved.

'Listen to me, Prakash. I don't seek any revenge, nor do I have the slightest desire to punish you. You are free to stay in this town if you like. Or you can go somewhere else. Until you find another place for yourself, I am willing to provide you some financial support.'

Reaching into his pocket, he takes out some money and places it on her bed. He goes down to his mother's room and sleeps on the bed next to her.

Gian Kaur sits up when she hears him come in. She realizes that he is tense and tries to probe him. He parries all her questions with the same response: 'I am really sleepy now. I'll tell you everything in the morning.'

He gets up early the following morning and quietly goes upstairs. There is no one. Prakash has left the place in the dark of the night.

31

Saroj is a transformed person. The Saroj of yore would have found it impossible to cope with Kuldeep's unwarranted allegations. The gravity of his charges would have been unbearable and might even have crushed her fragile spirit. But this does not happen. Waryam Singh's nobility is like a shining beacon that shows her the path around each blind turn and in every dark alley. The person who just a few weeks back felt so unloved and unwanted that she was losing her will to live now has a strong sense of purpose. She has a renewed sense of self-esteem, a confidence that she is second to none in her will to serve her community.

No doubt, she has gone through a tough time. The slander spread by Kuldeep and the barbed comments of people in the neighbourhood were bad enough. Her grief was compounded by having to witness Kuldeep's second marriage, and she had wept for days on end. But she has since delved deep within her soul and rediscovered the steel in it. She has also found a support that provides her with stability. A new voice echoes in her heart, asking, 'Are you pure of spirit? Of course! I dare anyone to challenge that. And if the spirit is pure, why worry about what people will say? If I believe in myself, I'll do what I think is right!'

She has nothing to fear. Her spirit is pure and her mind is at peace. Yes, there are dogs barking in the street. Some are even snapping at her heels. But she is not afraid. The strength of her spirit is like a baton that she wields to keep them at bay. She has decided to stick by Waryam Singh even if the dogs accuse her of being his mistress. She will work with him as he goes about his noble purpose.

Thoughts like these have frequently crossed her mind as Waryam has stopped dropping in at her house. She can, of course, fathom the reason. He is more concerned about her honour than his own and he has no intention of adding to her travails.

Tempered in the furnace of logic, her mind acquires the strength of steel. Having considered the matter from every perspective, she takes the firm and unalterable decision to marry Waryam Singh, no matter how steep the hurdles. She will resist all opposition and will not be dissuaded. Her resolve will make her union with Waryam so sacred that it would be the envy of the world. She will combine her own interest in literature with Waryam Singh's passion for service to bring about a social revolution. Waryam Singh will continue to help the most wretched members of their society and provide them whatever solace he can, while she will write about their plight and awaken the somnolent conscience of the public. Together, they will help the cause of the poorest and change the world.

She spends the entire day in these thoughts, her determination increasing by the hour.

Ganga Vishan's condition is deteriorating by the day. Years of alcoholism have taken their toll. His enlarged spleen has played havoc with his appetite and disrupted his digestive system. He has a persistent ache in his chest and stomach; his tongue is frequently dry and his arthritis has aggravated. Obesity and arthritis can be a lethal combination and he finds it hard to move around, spending most of his days in bed, lethargic and listless until he gets a fresh shot of alcohol-fuelled energy. And when he can't get it, his throat goes dry and his tongue becomes hard as a piece of wood. 'Oh god! I am dying. I am dying,' he whines.

Saroj finds his condition unbearable. Having spent much of her life trying to dissuade him from drinking, she now sends Mangtu to fetch some liquor that would keep him going. She knows it is a matter of time now.

Having completed her daily chores, she goes to her bed. She has taken a big decision but how should she convey it to Waryam Singh? Reflecting for a few minutes, she gets up to pick up a pad and starts to write.

It is late at night and the moon is spreading its glow all around her. As she watches from her doorstep, Mangtu makes his way down the street. Envelope in hand, he is headed for the house near Maakhnia's Centre.

32

You see fire in a neighbour's house and rush to get buckets of water to douse it. But the water turns into oil, adding fuel to the fire. Soon, the flames, leaping before you, are destroying the very house that you tried to save and are on the verge of consuming you as well. Is there anything more unfortunate than this?

It has been a bit like this with Waryam Singh. His noble deeds threaten to become the cause of his downfall. Tortured by his own dilemmas, he tosses and turns in his bed. It is unusual for him to be at home and in bed at mid-day.

A dog, they say, is a dog's worst enemy. You may be seeing a normal, good-natured dog but place some food before another canine and see how this one turns into a monster. But the dog is still an animal. Think of human beings, the joy they derive from the suffering of others. You could narrate a story, enact a play or even produce a novel. It will remain of limited interest unless you can inject an element of tragedy...the groaning of an unhappy soul, tears streaming down the eyes, blood flowing from assorted cuts...that's what makes it a success. The audience sees the rape of a helpless woman or the hanging of an innocent man in a play and applauds. Now, that's a tragedy, they say.

Waryam Singh finds himself an actor in a similar sort of tragedy, one that involves an innocent and helpless damsel. The scales of justice are in balance. One side has the substantial weight of all his good deeds, the other has the weight of all the allegations that Kuldeep has made against him. This side, too, is growing in substance and even seems to be tilting the scales in its favour. Evil appears to be ready to triumph over virtue.

The streets are agog with stories about Waryam Singh and Saroj. They are described as lovers and comparisons are often made with the classical tales of the undying romance of Heer and Ranjha, of Sassi and Punnu.

The afternoon gives way to evening and the evening to night. Waryam Singh, though, is trapped in an unending cycle of thoughts. His uncomplicated life has entered a complex maze. Each time he looks for a way out, he finds himself staring at a dead end. He has to turn back and start the journey afresh.

His room is dark but a sliver of moonlight enters through cracks in the door to light up his open cupboard. Lying in his bed, he can see the array of medicines, bandages and syrups that comprise the sum total of his fortune. While his eyes are fixed on the cupboard, his train of thought chugs along its own track, stopping at some stations and steaming past others. The halts were at stations like...that old man suffering from gout and crying for medicine; Attiya, whom he hasn't visited since her husband's demise; Jassi's child, who has developed some mysterious ailment; Karam Illahi's mother, whose eyesight is deteriorating by the day; Ghulam, the waterman; Chandu, the washerman; Shahbaaz; Deena...

There comes a time when you are forced to introspect, to delve into those nooks and crannies of your being that you have never felt the need to visit. Waryam Singh is in that kind of state. His eyes are still focused on the same shelf in the cupboard but the train of his thoughts has switched tracks and is moving within him. Am I shameless, do I have no sense of dignity or is it that I simply don't care? Why is it that I continue on my path without being affected by the slander? When did I discover this reservoir of forbearance that has become my strength? How is it that individuals like Kuldeep can attack me time and again and I remain unperturbed? Where did I find such fortitude that I make no distinction between the one who sprinkles salt on my wounds and the one who applies balm on them? Friend or foe, my arms yearn to embrace them. How did this come about?

As he explores unknown recesses within himself, his eyes stray briefly from their vigil on the cupboard and come to rest on a white object lying carelessly on a shelf. It was a kerchief, the one that Saroj had pulled out to wipe her face when she had come in from the rain that evening. The soaked kerchief had been left on the cupboard.

Gazing at it, Waryam Singh blinks his eyes. Why am I concentrating on it? It is nothing but a small piece of cloth. Nothing! But he cannot tear his eyes away from it. And before his eyes, it starts to turn into an apparition, one that bears an eerie resemblance to a young woman at the doorway, shivering and drenched by the downpour. The sliver of moonshine coming through the doorway takes the form of a pair of shining eyes, and the kerchief gradually starts to bear a distinct likeness to Saroj. Reaching out for it, he feels the kerchief nestling in his own hands, radiating warmth into his palms.

Waryam Singh has been alone for as long as he can remember. Lending a helping hand to scores of people, performing the role of a messiah to countless others, he has never been bothered by his own loneliness. It is only during the last few weeks that this has begun to irk him. Unknown to him, his heart has started to yearn for some company, long for the warmth of a feminine touch. New emotions surge through his consciousness.

But the journey on the new track is short-lived and it soon links up with the earlier track...the old man with the gout...Jassi's son...Karam Illahi's mother...Ghulam... Chandu...Shahbaaz...

He places the kerchief back on the shelf and turns his eyes away from the cupboard. They are now focused on the door, soaking in the rays of moonshine as though they are drops of nectar pouring straight into his soul. Could it really be her eyes emitting these beams? he wonders. Engrossed in his reverie, he gets up from the bed and walks up to the door. He opens it to look up and down the street but there is not a soul in sight. The moon is shining bright, casting faint shadows in the street.

He stands at his doorstep for a long while, his eyes transfixed on the lunar splendour. Is it always so gorgeous or is there something special about it tonight, he wonders. He revels in its beauty, admiring every shade on its surface. A cloud wafts across the sky, drifting towards the object of his attention. Waryam Singh frets as it approaches the moon, fearing that it might obliterate it. He watches with disappointment as the cloud gradually covers the moon, leaving the street in darkness.

Bringing his eyes back to earth, he sees a young fellow standing a few feet away. His heart starts to pound as he realizes that it is Saroj's servant. Mangtu hands an envelope to him and leaves without saying a word. Waryam Singh goes inside, sits on the bed and starts to read the letter.

> *You may be surprised to read this, for it is the first time I am not addressing you as Bhapa ji. Why, you may like to know. It is because I have suddenly developed a desire to live my life. I have never felt this way before. But having seen you in action twice, observing the way you tend to sick patients has made me want to live. I should clarify that I have no worldly ambitions, no material goals. Like you, I only want to spend my life serving the poorest, the most wretched. And so, I have gathered all of myself and wrapped it up in this letter. Like this letter, I entrust myself to you.*
>
> *Seeing you at work has kindled a new desire in me which I must satisfy. Instead of a fine silk sari, I seek the coarse bandage soaked in blood as it tries to relieve the pain of an unfortunate soul. I would rather be a medicine than a mere perfume - that's the philosophy I have learnt from you. A perfume will only give a pleasant fragrance, while a medicine can give the gift of life. You told me that 'to live your life within the realm of a vow is a lot harder than merely taking a vow'. I am now ready to enter that realm, to not just live the life of my vow but to cherish it. Will you take me with you into that realm?*
>
> *I know that the nests of birds are made of nothing more than straws and I want to be the*

branch on which you build your nest. When you return to your nest after a long and arduous day, I want to sway gently, sing you a lullaby and help you sleep with the sweetest of dreams.

Please don't misunderstand me. I don't want to be your life partner just because I find it hard to carry the burden of my life and want to transfer the load on to you. Instead, I want to be the inn where you can rest each time you stop en route to your destination. I want to be the bridge when you have to cross a ravine. I want to be the balm when you get injured. Remember, I am Saroj, the lotus. I may have taken birth in the mud but I need calm and clear waters to bloom.

Will you drop in soon to give me your reply in person?

Saroj

Waryam Singh has heard of miracles where dreams and wishes can turn into reality but he has never thought that it could also happen to him. Like the lantern in front of him, he feels a new light illuminate his heart as he reads and rereads the letter. His mind starts to create a wonderful new world where this angel would walk by his side, healing countless patients by the mere reflection of her blessed shadow. Her loving glance would light thousands of dejected eyes, her tender touch would enable scores of hunchbacks to stand erect, her gentle words would turn the wailing of the miserable into lilting melodies. Would she really walk by my side? he wonders.

He spends the night immersed in these thoughts, getting up at the crack of dawn to get ready. For a change, he decides to look into the mirror as he ties his turban, making sure that every roll is properly in place. He brushes his jacket to tidy it up and steps out. Barely ten yards down the street, he is accosted by his old friend Munshi Ram hurrying towards him with a strangely excited expression on his face.

'Where are you off to so early in the morning, Bhapa ji?' Munshi Ram asks affectionately. 'I was coming to your place with some good news.'

'What is it?' he asks impatiently.

'But we must sit down and talk about it. This is no small matter. You are going to be delighted when you hear the whole story.'

Waryam Singh turns back towards the house and opens the door so that they can sit on the bed. Munshi Ram is a reservations clerk at the railway station. He is around thirty years of age, has a wiry built and a face that readily breaks into a smile. Over the years, he has become genuinely fond of Waryam Singh.

'How true is it, Bhapa ji, that if you sin against the pure, the good Lord will not let you go unpunished.'

'Fine! But do come to the point. What is the good news that you want to tell me?'

'What can be better than the fact that god has punished your sworn enemy?'

'My enemy? But there is none that I consider my enemy.'

'Wrong! There is one, at least.'

'And who would that be?'

'Kuldeep.'

'You are wrong, Munshi Ram. I don't even consider him an enemy. Anyway, what's happened to him?'

'Well, you may not consider him an enemy but I certainly do. How can I forgive the one who has cast aspersions on my brother's character? I shall light lamps of ghee to celebrate today.'

'But what has happened to him?'

'The one whom he considered the angel, the goddess, the epitome of all virtue has fled.'

'Who? Prakash?'

'Who else? I heard that there was a major altercation last night. And after that, she disappeared.'

Lines of worry crease Waryam Singh's face. 'Did she go away on her own or was she thrown out by Kuldeep?'

'I have no idea. All I heard was that she had bought a train ticket for Lahore.'

Waryam Singh sits on his bed and ponders for a long while after Munshi Ram has left. After an hour or so, he takes out some papers and writes two letters. One is an application for a week's leave. The other is addressed to Saroj.

Dear Saroj
I received your letter. I had no idea that emotions of love can be transmitted so quickly. It must be telepathy. Your words expressed feelings that I have been trying to hide for so long. It is like a dream come true. I still can't believe it fully.

I left my place this morning to come to you and to place my heart at the feet of my angel. But something entirely unexpected has cropped up, forcing me to leave immediately for Lahore. You will surely wonder why I have to leave in such a rush. I'll explain everything when I get back. You will also be able to read the reply to your letter in the yearning in my eyes.

Yours
Waryam Singh

He rolls up a light bedding and hurries towards the station, hoping that he will be in time to catch the train. As he reaches the station, he explores his pockets to ensure that he has enough money for a return fare to Lahore. He does. Having bought the ticket, his mind moves towards Prakash. I hope I can find her in time, he prays. I just hope that she doesn't fall into the den of prostitution again. All my efforts will have gone in vain if that were to happen.

33

Poor Gian Kaur is unable to bear the cascading effect of setbacks. First, it was the demise of her husband that had reduced her to a shadow of her former self. Then, it was the thoughtlessness of Kuldeep's actions that pushed her to the edge of the abyss. And to top it all, the neighbourhood in which she had spent much of her life is extremely conservative in its outlook. Their constant chatter about Prakash and the contempt with which they speak of Gian Kaur's household are simply intolerable. It erodes her self-esteem, and once that is gone, Gian Kaur's days are numbered. The raging battle with Prakash during Kuldeep's absence, and the knowledge that their private matters are now a public spectacle, is the last straw. A few days after Prakash's unceremonious departure, Gian Kaur suffers from heart failure and passes away in her sleep.

Within a matter of weeks, Kuldeep's life has been turned upside down. A pervasive emptiness envelops his heart, his home and indeed his entire universe. There is no one that he can turn to for support, for himself or even for his child who is barely eight months old. Who will tend to the child now? he frets. The house itself is as barren as the desert, bereft of the succour that the shade of even a single mature tree might have provided.

There is, in the distance, one sliver of hope – a tiny oasis in the midst of a vast desert. Or is it only a mirage? He aspires for it but will he actually get there? How can he face Saroj after all that has transpired? How can he seek the shade of the very tree that he had tried to uproot?

Oh what a sorry pass I have come to, he bemoans. Look at where I was headed and where I've actually landed up! What have I done to myself? Thoughts like these overwhelm him. They occupy his mind night and day, not allowing him a moment's peace. He feels himself sinking under swift currents of recrimination and hopelessness. It won't be long before I go completely mad, he thinks.

Apart from a sister of his mother's, he has no close relatives anywhere in the vicinity of Peshawar. She comes for a few days and takes charge of the child but he realizes that she has a large family of her own. He thinks of Satwant's parents but there is nobody there either. Her mother had died some time back and her father had gone to some foreign land. No one seems particularly sure about his whereabouts.

What's the point of living a life like this? Kuldeep reasons. He wants to die but that, too, is easier said than done. Maybe he can hand the child over to an orphanage and return to his earlier path! Forsake the material world and become a hermit. This seems like a serious possibility and he mulls over the practicalities as he lies in his bed. Which orphanage would be the most convenient, and what train would he take to arrive at some faraway destination?

His reverie is interrupted by a somewhat familiar voice that wafts up the stairs from the kitchen. A few moments later, the boy comes up to inform him that a Muslim fellow accompanied by a veiled woman wants to see him. It must be Ahmed Khan, he thinks, rushing down the steps.

So much has happened. There is so much to talk, so much to share. Within a few minutes of their arrival, Kuldeep has his head on his friend's shoulder and is pouring his heart out. Husband and wife have tears in their eyes as they try to comfort him. The air around them is heavy with a blend of pain and affection.

Ahmed Khan and Zubeida are moved by their friend's plight, by the multiple tragedies that have befallen upon him in quick succession. They had planned their visit to Peshawar to catch up with him. It was almost a year since their tearful parting in Lahore and they were keen to meet Satwant and spend some time with his family. Zubeida had even bought an attractive salwar-kameez for Satwant along with a fancy-looking 'English' soap and some other gifts for the family. She is devastated to learn that Satwant had passed away even before Kuldeep had set foot in his house. How clearly did she recall his emotions, his dreams on the eve of his departure from Lahore!

Zubeida picks up the child and holds him tightly against her bosom. What a beautiful baby, she sighs. Looking at him, you can imagine how beautiful the mother must have been.

To Kuldeep, the arrival of Ahmed Khan and Zubeida is like a boat that had appeared from nowhere to rescue him just as he was on the verge of drowning in the middle of a raging river. He tells them how Satwant had pined for him right until her last breath, waiting for him to return home from jail. He speaks of his own grief after her demise, his decision to renounce his home and family and everything else that has happened. They spend the night talking about the curious twists and turns that life had taken, expressing their horror and sympathy and agonizing over what they can do to pull Kuldeep out of the quicksand that threatens to swallow him.

Three days pass and Kuldeep realizes he cannot detain them indefinitely. Summoning all his courage, he says, 'Ahmed Khan, you have your own home and family to think of. You should say goodbye and leave me to my fate.'

'And what kind of savages do you take us to be?' Zubeida flares even before Ahmed Khan can say a word. 'How can we think of leaving you and your child in this state?'

Moved beyond words, Kuldeep takes her hand and places it on his forehead. 'Bhabhi,' he says, 'from this day you are not just my brother's wife. You are my own sister. I shudder to think what might have happened if the two of you had not turned up. Another three or four days and I would have taken this child to an orphanage.'

Her throat choked with emotion, Zubeida places her hands on Kuldeep's shoulders and kisses the top of his head.

'Please take this child with you,' Kuldeep sobs. 'I want you to adopt him. He will be your child, not mine, from today.' Tears stream down his cheeks as he picks up the child from the cradle and places him in Zubeida's lap.

The ways of nature are truly mysterious. You can cut a branch from a fruit-bearing tree and graft it on to one that is barren. And so it is decided that they would return the following day with the child. They want Kuldeep to come along with them but he resists, arguing that he needs some more time to figure things out and that he might travel around a bit to get a grip on himself. He also has to do something about the textile stocks on which he had spent close to two thousand rupees. He decides that he will hand the stocks over to one of the larger textile merchants in town and recoup whatever he can from the transaction.

Getting ready to leave the next morning, Ahmed Khan puts one hand on his wife's shoulder and the other on Kuldeep's. 'I want a solemn promise from both of you before we leave,' he says.

'Zubeida, now that you have adopted this child, I want you to swear by the name of Allah and his Messenger that you will respect the traditions of this house and that neither beef nor tobacco will enter your home from today.'

Turning her thoughts to Allah and his Messenger, Zubeida closes her eyes, bows her head in deference and takes a silent vow.

Facing Kuldeep, Ahmed Khan looks into his eyes and says, 'And you, my brother, must promise that no matter where you plan to travel, you will first come to Lahore. You will spend some time with us and then go with the blessings of Allah in whichever direction you choose.'

Kuldeep nods in agreement, his eyes focused on Zubeida. Not having experienced the joys of motherhood, she is already at one with the child and together, the two appeared to have entered a world of their own.

Their departure with the child lifts a major responsibility off Kuldeep's shoulders. He heaves a sigh of relief and starts to think about his life and where it is headed. The emptiness of the house returns to haunt him. Now it is just him and the boy, who makes him a chapatti or two along with some tasteless gruel that passes for a meal. Not that he would have been inclined to eat properly if it had tasted better. His appetite has deserted him and he is buried under the collective burden of grief, repentance and remorse. His grief stems from recognition of his own foolishness which has cast a pall of gloom over a bright future. He repents that he had allowed himself to be swayed by flimsy logic to accuse Saroj and Waryam Singh of misconduct. His remorse emerges from the realization that he has lost everything that he valued. If only Saroj were around! She would have kept her promise to save him from drowning in the currents and brought him ashore.

The superficial lustre of Prakash is wearing off Kuldeep's heart, revealing the more lasting colour that is his love for Saroj. He finds it difficult to shut out the events of the last few months and particularly her words that night, 'Whenever you call me, dear Kuldeep...'

Am I even worthy of calling her? he wonders. I can go through seven cycles of birth and rebirth and I still won't measure up to her. Why would she pay any heed to my call now? She extended her hand to save me and I brushed it away. She melted her own heart to make a balm that would heal my wounds and I rebuffed her by saying that even the softest cotton will hurt when it touches me. And yet, she might have forgiven me. She might have set aside all my flaws if I hadn't committed that one transgression. How could I have said what I did about Waryam Singh, a person who helps even his foes, one who devotes every breath to serving humanity! How could I lose my head the way I did?

His mind's eye sweeps across the horizon searching for someone who might stand by him. He can see no one other than Ahmed Khan and Zubeida. But he has already loaded them with a heavy burden. Thanks to them, he has the freedom to leave town and go wherever he wants, to renounce the world if he wishes. He decides to rid himself of all his possessions and start his life afresh.

It takes him a couple of days to free himself of all encumbrances. He now has about twelve thousand rupees in cash, of which he places ten thousand in a fixed deposit in the bank and keeps the remaining with him. He has moved so quickly that nobody in the neighbourhood has got the wind of his intentions. He is ready to leave but hasn't yet picked a destination. Not that it matters. All he wants is to go to a place where nobody knows him and he doesn't know anyone so that he can erase his dismal past.

It is around eight in the evening. He sends the boy to fetch the local junk dealer. Retaining just one trunk and a bedding, he sells off everything else and asks the dealer to cart it away. Having already settled the rent with the landlord, he pays the month's salary to the servant and hails a tonga from the street.

The boy helps him load the trunk and bedding on to the tonga. Kuldeep wears his jacket, wishes the servant well and sits in the tonga. He looks back at the first-floor window one last time to see if Satwant is still standing there, waving at him like she did whenever he left the house.

As the tonga proceeds towards the railway station, his thoughts drift towards Saroj and her words 'Whenever you call me, dear Kuldeep...'

It is a dark, moonless night that magnifies the smallest of lights and makes glow worms appear like brightly shining candles. Saroj's words twinkle like a glow worm in his consciousness. Shouldn't he meet her one last time? Who knows? She has a heart of gold. She just might forgive me. And if she doesn't, I have nothing to lose.

By the time the tonga reaches the railway station, the twinkling light has intensified in radiance and is beckoning him towards it. Brushing aside the porters who come forth to carry his baggage, he tells the tongawallah to turn back. I've forgotten something important, he says.

The tonga turns around and makes its way up the same street.

34

Several days have passed and there is no sign of Waryam Singh. Saroj is getting anxious, counting the days and hours as she waits for the one who has become such a precious part of her life.

After many days, she receives a letter from Delhi. Every sentence of the letter reflects Waryam Singh's acute sense of disappointment. He has searched high and low for Prakash, but to no avail. He intends to spend another two days and if he fails to locate her, he would return to Peshawar. He promises that he would come straight to her home to offer his life and all his devotion at the feet of his goddess.

Saroj has already learned of Prakash's disappearance. She knows that the twin blows of Prakash's departure and his mother's demise would have had a devastating effect on Kuldeep. She feels his pain from the bottom of her heart, and for a brief moment, the empathy overshadows the anger that she has nursed against him for several weeks. However, the memory of his callous behaviour is hard to ignore. His accusations against her and Waryam Singh resonate in her ears.

The three days she spends after receiving Waryam Singh's letter seem like a lifetime to Saroj. Each moment is like an eternity and she searches for ways to pass the time. Radhia has moved to another house and there is nobody at home that she can talk to. It is late in the evening and Babu Ganga Vishan has already retired for the night. She walks across to her cupboard and searches for something interesting to read. She leafs through one book after another but none of them excite her. Why not write something instead, she thinks. There was a time when she used to write short stories and poems on a regular basis. Many readers had appreciated her writing. And yet, she had drifted away from the habit. Reprimanding herself for her sloth, she decides that she would work on writing a short story.

She looks for her old notebook and as she pulls it out from its hiding place under a couple of books, a small photo falls out. Picking it up, she is drawn into it. She is holding the photo and becoming a part of it. It is one of Kuldeep in his early teens; he had presented to her years ago. The bottom part of the photo has a dedication: 'To my Saroj'. Her mind goes back to her childhood, to those simple times when she and Kuldeep used to play with such abandon. She used to sing:

Mohina, that glint in your eye
Went straight through my heart
Like the arrow of love

She remembers the times when she would play the violin and they would sing this song, over and over again. Holding the photo in her hand, she goes back in time and sings '*Mohina, the glint in your eye...*'

She closes her eyes as she sings, her mind taking her into that heavenly stage of their childhood. Just as clouds bearing the tidings of love gently drift into her blue skies, she is awakened by the rumbling sounds of thunder that carry bolts of hatred in their midst. Opening her eyes with a start, she glares at the photo before tearing it up into small pieces and flinging it out of the window.

She picks up her notebook and sits in her chair, her back to the door. She wracks her head for a suitable plot for a story but her thoughts keep going towards Kuldeep. Unconsciously, she starts to hum the same song:

Mohina, I wait at your door
Begging for your time
Spare me a moment
I promise, I want no more

Once again, her eyes close involuntarily and she can hear Kuldeep sing in unison. But it is too real. She can actually hear his voice sing at the door behind her:

Mohina, I wait at your door
Begging for your time
Spare me a moment
I promise, I want no more

She turns her head around and gazes in disbelief. It is indeed Kuldeep singing their childhood song, somewhat off-key but with most of the notes in place. She feels a rising tide of anger within her. But is it just anger or is there something else too? The human eye is capable of observing the smallest of objects but emotions fall in a different category. There are times when even the mind's eye fails to discern them.

She glares at Kuldeep, her eyes going over his form from head to toe as he stands in the doorway. Her limbs shake with anger but words fail her. Why have you come, she wants to know. But instead of posing the question, she continues to examine his face minutely, looking for the answer. His eyes appear moist.

She gets up abruptly from her chair and takes a step towards him. 'Kul...,' she starts to say but the words are caught in her throat. She takes another step and says, 'Kuldeep ji!'

This time she manages to say his name but receives no response. 'Kuldeep ji!' she repeats.

'I am very sorry, Saroj ji. I have come to seek your forgiveness. My mistakes...' Overwhelmed by his own emotions, he breaks down, lowers his head and bends towards Saroj's feet to apologize.

Unable to see him crying, she catches hold of his arms to lift him up and walks him to a chair. Sitting down in the other chair, she looks at him in wonder. A few words and some tears have swept the slate clean, erasing all her misgivings about him. But the reprieve is short-lived. No sooner does her mind move to Waryam Singh than she again feels the familiar burst of anger.

'I know, Saroj ji, that I have behaved so badly with you and Waryam Singh ji that I have no claim to your forgiveness. If I have summoned all my courage to show up at your doorstep, it is because of your promise that...'

Ever the epitome of kindness, Saroj defences threaten to crumble under the onslaught of his tears. 'Promise?' she interjects.

His voice still cracking with emotion, Kuldeep says, 'You were sitting beside me in the park when you made the promise. Kuldeep ji, you had said, whenever you call me, I will come and pull you out of the abyss.'

Like a film running in slow motion, the events of that evening unfold before her eyes. It is all so vivid that it seems like yesterday.

'I'm sorry, Kuldeep ji,' she braces herself as she speaks. 'You have gone so deep under the waves that Saroj's hand cannot reach you there.'

'In that case, I really have no hope left,' he says in a voice laced with disappointment.

'Hope for what?'

'Love,' he says and lowers his eyes.

'You can expect the same amount of love from me that I would have for any other person on this planet.'

'I understand, of course, that I've lost the right to claim any special affection from you. I can only blame myself for that loss. But still, my good Saroj...'

Making a determined effort to keep her emotions in check, she interrupts sternly, 'Before you say anything else, may I ask you to withdraw the prefix "my" that you attached to my name. Please take it back because Saroj now belongs to someone else.'

Kuldeep recoils as though a double-barrelled gun has been fired straight at his forehead. Stepping back, he looks questioningly at her.

'Yes, you should not be surprised. I am with the one you had associated me with.' Her eyes shine with anger.

Kuldeep listens in stunned silence. He doesn't have the courage to say anything in response. What can he say anyway? Her words are like the affirmation of a sentence by the Privy Council itself. There is no higher court of appeal available.

Getting up from the chair, he walks towards the door. He wishes he were invisible, so that neither his footsteps nor the rustle of his clothes would be audible to Saroj.

Saroj stands like a statue as Kuldeep's outline vanishes in the distance. It is true that she neither hears his footsteps nor the rustle of his clothes. All she hears is a deep sigh from the doorstep and a voice that says, 'Goodbye, Saroj ji. My good wishes will always be with you. Though you may not see me again in this lifetime, I will continue to pray that you and Bhapa ji will be able to forgive my sins...'

An equally deep sigh emerges from Saroj as she leaps towards the door. Has she actually seen Kuldeep or is it all a dream? Looking down the street, she wonders if he had really come and left. She opens her mouth to shout, to call him back but fails to muster the energy. Kuldeep has gone out of reach.

Saroj feels her heart sink.

She goes outside the house and, in the light emanating from her room, bends under the window to collect the torn pieces of the photograph. Having gathered them in her hands, she slowly trudges back into the house.

35

When a person tumbles down a steep mountainside, he desperately tries to clutch at any branch or root that can break his fall. But imagine his fate when he latches on to a branch, only to discover that it too has broken off the tree. He has little hope of survival.

Kuldeep is in a similar sort of state. He didn't have too much hope when he had gone to Saroj's place. Deep down, he knew perhaps that redemption was only a remote possibility. And yet, he had gone. Hoping against hope...trying to gauge the pulse of one who is already dead.

His life, now, is devoid of any purpose or meaning. He hasn't decided where he wants to go but that is hardly an immediate concern. To keep his promise to Ahmed Khan and Zubeida, he knows that he will have to go to Lahore before making any other plans.

Having spent the previous night and day in the empty house that he had always called his home, Kuldeep locks the door and hands the key to the naan bai. Once again, a tonga is summoned and the trunk and bedding are hoisted on it.

Accepting the key, the naan bai looks quizzically at him. 'So you didn't leave last night? You came back?'

'Yes...I had forgotten that there was something important to be done.'

'And where are you going?'

'To Lahore. I am visiting a friend,' he replies and clambers on to the tonga. A little later, he has boarded the train to Lahore.

As the train steams out of the station, Kuldeep realizes that this may be the last time he was seeing the city of his birth, the place where he had spent most of his adult life. But he feels no sadness, no sense of loss. If at all he feels anything, it is a numbness that has spread throughout his body. Through the window, he observes the countryside, mottled with farms, trees, shrubs, ponds, all hurtling past at breakneck speed. His own memories move back in time at a similar pace. It wasn't that long ago that he had taken the very same train on his way to Borstal Jail in Lahore. That journey had taken him away from Satwant, this one from Saroj. In between the two, like a flash of lightning, he sees images of Prakash.

He feels something simmering inside him but fails to identify the source. His mind frequently strays in the direction of Waryam Singh and the encounter invariably produces a twinge of jealousy. But that is wrong, he reasons. He is clearly worthy of Saroj, unlike a pauper like me who has no great merit. How I wish my eyes had been open that evening when Saroj extended her arms towards me. However, it took last night's humiliation to bring me to my senses. Surely, I have received the treatment I deserved.

And if there is one bit of silver lining in the dark clouds dominating his horizon, that is the unconditional affection and support that he has received from his erstwhile jailor. When all else seems to be crumbling around him, the burly Pathan and his wife have been a source of infinite comfort.

The train reaches Lahore. As he hurries behind the porter on the narrow footbridge that loops over the railway tracks, his eyes fall on the adjacent platform. He cannot believe his eyes. Ahmed Khan is getting ready to board the Frontier Mail to Peshawar.

Kuldeep asks the porter to leave the baggage with him and, pointing towards Ahmed Khan, dispatches the young fellow to fetch the Pathan. A few minutes later, Ahmed Khan strides towards him, his face beaming with a mix of surprise and unadulterated pleasure. Unable to restrain himself, Kuldeep runs towards his friend and embraces him in a bear hug.

'Ya Allah! Your ways are truly a marvel,' Ahmed Khan exclaims as he virtually lifts Kuldeep off his feet.

Time stands still as Kuldeep revels in the embrace of his friend, tears streaming down his face. Left alone in the world, he can feel a father's affection, a mother's care and a friend's loyalty rolled into one as he claspes his arms around the Pathan.

Catching his breath, he asks, 'And where were you headed, my brother?'

'In your direction! To Peshawar, where else?'

'That's a lie!'

'Here, take a look at this if you must have proof.' Ahmed Khan takes the ticket out of his pocket and hands it to Kuldeep.

'But...why? Is everything all right?'

'Of course! Everything is fine, but...'

'And pray what is this "but"? Come, now. You must tell me all. You've got me worried.'

'There is nothing to worry about, believe me. But I can't reveal the subject yet.'

'Oh! In that case, you must.'

'And if I refuse?'

'Then I will refuse to move another step,' Kuldeep protests and comes to an abrupt halt near the steps of the footbridge.

'All right, all right. I'll tell you everything. But let's get out of the station first.' Ahmed Khan tugs at Kuldeep's arm to take him to the ticket counter where he returns his ticket and obtains a refund. Hiring a tonga, they load their baggage before setting forth in the direction of Borstal Jail.

'All right! Out with it now,' Kuldeep implores.

'Wait! I need to clarify a couple of things before that.'

'What?'

'What are your plans now?'

'I am planning to go on a longish trip. I'll spend a day or two with you, and then I'll be on my way,' Kuldeep replies. Fishing inside his jacket, he pulls out a cheque for ten thousand rupees and places it in Ahmed Khan's hand.

'What is this for?' Ahmed Khan looks in consternation at the four zeroes after the digit '1'.

'I will let you know later. First, I am waiting to hear from you. Why the sudden trip to Peshawar...?'

'No, first explain this cheque.'

Kuldeep explains that he has sold all his assets and he wants this amount to be available to Khan.

'I see,' he snorts. Without a further glance at the cheque, he tears it into tiny bits, rolls them into a tight little wad and places it back in Kuldeep's palm. 'Here! I have stopped taking bribes.'

His action sends a thrill down Kuldeep's spine. Such a big heart! To refuse such a large sum of money so nonchalantly! What can he say after that?

For a while, both remain silent. The clatter of hooves sounds louder than usual.

Turning towards Khan, Kuldeep continues, 'Okay, forget about the cheque and come back to the point. What do you have in mind?'

'It's a major issue, Kuldeep. Not a minor matter that can be revealed so casually.'

'So how do you plan to reveal it?'

'Only after I have extracted a pledge from you.'

'And what kind of pledge would that be?'

'Whatever appeals to me.'

'Fine, then. I am ready for it.'

'Okay. Let me hold your hand first.'

Kuldeep extends his right hand to Khan. Holding it in his own, Khan says, 'You have to swear that you will do as I ask you to. Do you swear?'

'I swear. But what if you ask me to do something I can't?'

'You will still have to do it.'

'Ahmed Khan! That's quite a complicated matter you are drawing me into.'

'Think carefully. I will ask you to do something that you will not want to do. But if you commit, you will have to do it. If you have the courage, stand up like a man and swear that you will. Or else, do what you like!'

Khan's last few words sound like a direct challenge to their friendship. The shock lends clarity to his thoughts and he speaks firmly, 'I swear that I will do whatever you ask me to do. I will gladly enter the jaws of death if that's what you want me to do.'

'Kuldeep! Do you really think that your friend will take you anywhere near the jaws of death? Heavens forbid! But should such an eventuality arise, rest assured that Ahmed Khan will be ready to enter the jaws of death before you.'

'Fine, my brother! Are you ready to tell me now?' Kuldeep enquires impatiently.

'Not yet. You have to take your vow properly.'

'Does that mean you don't trust me?'

'Not until you have sworn.'

'And you want me to swear by...?'

'By me.'

'No, Ahmed Khan. Don't make me do that. I will not swear by you even if I have to give up my own life. I am ready to swear by anyone else.'

'I guess that's the end of the matter, then,' Ahmed Khan sighs.

'No! How can you be so inconsiderate? I am ready to swear by my son.'

Closing Kuldeep's mouth with his hand, Ahmed Khan rebukes, 'Mind your words, will you! That child is no longer yours. He is mine and you have no right to swear by one who is not yours.'

He tugs at Kuldeep's hand and forces him to place it on his head. 'Swear now that you will do as I ask you to.'

'I swear that I will do as you say,' Kuldeep repeats after him.

The tonga is making leisurely progress along Ferozepur Road.

'What I want, Kuldeep, is difficult but not impossible. I feel that you cannot spend the rest of your life as a single man.'

'And what does that mean?'

'Well, your bhabhi feels that it is not very appropriate for a single person like you to be staying with a family like ours.'

'Get to the point, Ahmed Khan. What are you trying to say?'

'What we want to say is that you should get married.'

'And is that all?'

'That's all.'

'Why did you have to make me swear on you for something like this?'

'I had to. Trust me.'

'But... but...?'

'Now that you have agreed to do as I say, just leave everything to me. I'll manage it.'

'Ahmed Khan! I really don't want to stick my head into that noose once again,' he protests.

'Maybe you don't want to. And neither do I. But your bhabhi refuses to budge.'

Kuldeep is silent.

'So it's settled, then?' Ahmed Khan continues.

'Do I have any choice?' he counters. 'After the way you've made me swear upon you?'

'I made you take the pledge so that you remain firm in your commitment.'

'But who...? How...?'

'Just hold your breath! I'll tie up everything. You will have to marry my sister.'

'What?' Kuldeep exclaims in shock.

'Yes,' Khan replies firmly. 'My sister! And you don't have to worry about the issue of religion. I am not an idiot that I will mess around with your religion. If you want, she will be more than ready to embrace the Sikh faith. Is that acceptable to you?'

There is no response from Kuldeep. Ahmed Khan repeats his question.

The tonga is approaching the jail. As it slows down on a turn, the tongawallah lights up a cigarette and Kuldeep gets a whiff of the smoke as it drifts in his direction. He closes his eyes as his mind goes back to the sight of a redolent Prakash, her eyes languorous under the spell of liquor. Hatred and infatuation. He feels a struggle of conflicting emotions arise within him.

'Ahmed Khan,' Kuldeep starts hesitantly. 'You put me in a...'

'You have sworn on my head, Kuldeep. Please keep that in mind,' Khan interjects.

The tonga comes to a halt in front of the house and they alight from it. Kuldeep is the first to enter while Ahmed Khan pays off the tongawallah. As he crosses the doorstep, Kuldeep stops in his tracks. His eyes fall on his child who is clinging to a woman strolling in the courtyard. It is Prakash.

36

'What happened? Did the sight of my sister upset you?' Ahmed Khan asks, following Kuldeep into the house.

What is going on, Kuldeep wonders. Am I watching a scene from a play in a theatre? What is this woman doing here? And how is she Ahmed Khan's sister?

It is five in the evening and Zubeida is sitting at her sewing machine, stitching a dress for little Baljit. Kuldeep has still not recovered from the shock of seeing Prakash. And Prakash has vanished into an adjacent room.

'I had to go to Peshawar to fetch him. You think he's come on his own?' Ahmed Khan says in an attempt to lighten the atmosphere.

'Come on now,' Zubeida counters. 'Even an airplane couldn't have brought you back in two hours.'

Ahmed Khan tells her about their encounter at the station before turning his attention towards Kuldeep.

'Why do you look so disturbed?' he asks.

'Nothing. I am fine.'

'Ever since you saw Prakash, you seem to have...' he teases.

'But...how come...she...?'

'Don't let this bother you, Bhara ji,' Zubeida says. 'It is for her sake that your brother was prepared to go all the way to Peshawar to fetch you.'

'This is not fair, my dear Bhabhi. I am afraid I'll have to leave Lahore today itself.'

'What? How dare you think of such a thing?' Ahmed Khan glowers at him. 'Have you already forgotten the pledge that you took?'

'Ahmed Khan! Ahmed Bhai!' Kuldeep sighs. 'You can get me to do anything for you but don't bind me to this. Please.'

Seeing Kuldeep grow tense by the minute, Ahmed Khan turns to his wife and says, 'Why don't you prepare dinner. The two of us will go out for a stroll.'

They walk along the street for a while. A brick kiln stands a short distance away, spewing a cloud of white smoke from its chimney.

'Please don't get upset, Kuldeep. Trust me. I am your friend and I only have your interest at heart. I will never do anything that would hurt you.'

Kuldeep's eyes are focused on the chimney. It looks like a giant cigarette blowing smoke in his direction.

Ahmed Khan can see that Kuldeep continues to nurse a strong hostility towards Prakash. He is concerned that his elaborate plan may come unstuck. He realizes he needs to try a different tack.

'Kuldeep, we know how badly Prakash behaved with you. She has revealed everything to your bhabhi. Believe me, she genuinely regrets her actions. She also realizes that what she did is not easy to forgive. But this shock has opened her eyes. The bad company in which she spent so many years had cast a spell on her. However, I am sure that the blood of a good family flows through her veins. Otherwise, after she left your home and returned to Lahore, she could easily have gone back to her old place in the brothel. But the important thing is that she did not do so.'

The compassion in Ahmed Khan's voice, the lines of concern on his face start to have their effect on Kuldeep. His frayed nerves are calmed by his tone and he begins to relax a bit. 'But how did she find her way to your house?' he enquires.

'I want to tell you all that and some more. That's why I suggested that we come out of the house,' Ahmed Khan starts. 'The day I returned home from my vacation, our neighbours told us that a comely young woman with sharp features and a fair complexion had come several times to see me. They told her that I was away and also informed her of the day I was expected to return. She was back at our place the day we returned home. Your bhabhi and I were both surprised because we had never met her earlier. We offered her a cup of tea but I could see that she was not comfortable saying anything in my presence. So I went out for a while, leaving her alone in the company of your bhabhi.'

'But how did she manage to find your house? How did she get the address?' Kuldeep wants to know.

'From you, of course.'

It dawns on Kuldeep that he had often spoken to Prakash about the time he had spent in jail and the special bond of friendship he had developed with Ahmed Khan. He had also referred to his visit to their home.

'Listen to me, Kuldeep,' the Pathan continues. 'To err is human. Even the best of us make mistakes. And in her case, it is the legacy of the company that she was forced to keep over all those years. Also, who is this Waryam Singh? Prakash was all praise for him, saying if ever god sent an angel to this earth, it is him.'

'She is right about that,' Kuldeep acknowledges. 'Waryam Singh is nothing less than an angel.'

'She kept saying that it was Waryam Singh who saved her life, who helped her get a job in your house, who gave her advice about changing her life.'

'Well, I must say that I didn't know that much about her past. She had woven a different yarn for me,' Kuldeep mutters.

'I know. She told us that she did so out of sheer necessity. Who would have given her a job after knowing about her background? It was on Waryam Singh's advice that she created a false story about her past.'

'So Waryam Singh wanted to destroy us, did he?'

'Far from it, Kuldeep. How could he have known that you would fall so quickly for her? In fact, when he learnt that you were trying to woo her, he tried whatever he could to dissuade you. He felt that Prakash wasn't yet worthy of your trust, of being a member of your household.'

'You are right, Ahmed Khan. He did try all kinds of means to distract me and keep me away from her. The fault was mine. I'd lost my head and thought of him as my sworn enemy.'

'But you lost your head even more when she committed a blunder and you threw her out of your house. Had you shown a bit of patience, she might have mended her ways within a few days and you would have spared yourself the catastrophe that followed. I consider myself a pretty good judge of character, Kuldeep. And I can see that she is not a bad person at heart. It is just that years of bad company have overshadowed her virtues. But I can see her good side emerging by the day. How can I forget the moment when she saw little Baljit? She picked him up and held him close to her chest, crying so bitterly that it was difficult for your bhabhi and me to restrain ourselves.

'I believe that she has been quite honest in narrating her whole tale to your bhabhi. That's what prompts me to say that she is good at heart. She told us that when she returned to Lahore, she had every intention of going back to her attic in the infamous Heera Mandi. But once she arrived in the city, she changed her mind. She remembered your conversations with her about a friend who is a constable in Borstal Jail. So she made it her mission to find us and to see if we might be able to persuade you to give her a second chance.

'I decided that she could stay in our house and I made her my sister. I also promised her that I would do whatever I could to bring her husband back to her. So I took leave for another three days and was ready to leave for Peshawar. And that's also the reason I made you take the pledge that you did.'

Ahmed Khan's passionate explanation and the utter selflessness of his action have their effect on Kuldeep. In the mirror of his mind, Prakash's image is a little cleaner than before.

It is fairly dark in the evening when they return home. As they enter, Kuldeep sees Prakash sobbing uncontrollably and Zubeida, arms around her, trying her best to console her.

'Bhara ji, she's going to die crying like this if she doesn't get your love,' Zubeida pleads.

Kuldeep's heart melts as Prakash falls at his feet, sobbing in penitence. Ahmed Khan and Zubeida discreetly leave the room as Kuldeep lifts Prakash up and embraces her. Having experienced the grim emptiness of his life over the last few weeks, he feels a new energy traverse his veins, a feeling of completeness that he had lost.

The child, sleeping peacefully till now, wakes up and starts to cry. Prakash picks him up and unexpectedly passes him over to Kuldeep. He realizes that this is probably the first time that he has held the child properly. He bends his head and starts to kiss the baby's face. Zubeida looks up from her perch in the adjacent kitchen where she is giving the finishing touches to some rice biryani and smiles. 'Be careful, Bhara ji. Don't spoil the child – he doesn't belong to you, remember!'

'Oh let him be.' Ahmed Khan grins. 'Let him console himself that the child is his own.'

There is a new kind of bonhomie in the house, a

playfulness that suggests they have known each other for years. A delightful aroma wafts from the biryani and Zubeida pronounces the food ready.

'Bhabhi, I am going to eat from your plate tonight,' Kuldeep tells Zubeida with childlike glee.

'Certainly,' she laughs. 'Let us do that.'

'And what about me?' Ahmed Khan complains.

'Oh you can eat with your sister!' Zubeida replies.

'But why don't we all eat from the same plate,' Prakash suggests.

Everyone agrees. Caste, religion and social status go out of the window as they sit down to enjoy their repast.

Kuldeep observes Zubeida as the banter continues. He notices that each time there is a reference to the child, she lowers her eyes or looks away. It doesn't take him long to figure out the reason. Long denied the joy of having a child of her own, she has finally tasted the pleasure but is concerned that it is destined to be short-lived. Turning towards her, he says, 'Bhabhi, I want to strike a deal would you. Are you up for it?'

'Deal? What might that be?'

'Look! You've given my Prakash back to me. So you keep your Baljit. Isn't that fair?'

A wave of joy sweeps through the Pathan's wife as she smiles. 'But that's already done.'

'But there's a difference. I had earlier handed him over to you so that you could look after him. Now, I am giving him to you by way of gratitude.'

Her worries addressed, Zubeida gets up to embrace Kuldeep and kiss him on the head, holding him as though he was baby Baljit and not Kuldeep. Gently caressing his back, she says, 'Bhara ji, may the good Lord fulfil all your desires. You have blessed me with a son! May Allah bless you with seven sons!'

They are getting ready to go to bed when Ahmed Khan suggests, 'You know, Kuldeep, I had taken three days' leave to go to Peshawar. Now that we've sorted everything out, why don't we all take a break for a couple of days?'

'Well, I'd left Peshawar for a trip that might have lasted my lifetime but I am ready to compromise and limit it to a couple of days if that's what suits you,' Kuldeep jokes.

They debate for a while before deciding to go across to Amritsar. Kuldeep goes to bed with the feeling that it wasn't late at night but the dawn of a new day in his life.

As the sun rises the next morning, its warm rays are like a balm over the bruised hearts of Kuldeep and Prakash. They have a leisurely morning and soon after lunch, the group is ready for its excursion to Amritsar.

37

Saroj feels strangely dispirited after Kuldeep's departure. She has been trying to deny Kuldeep even the tiniest corner in her heart and yet, this incident has again ignited some dormant embers. It has created a fresh surge of affection and sympathy that is undoing her resolve. Images of his tearful face standing in her doorway refuse to leave her. She is annoyed with herself for treating him so harshly.

She feels deeply uneasy with each passing hour, unable to banish the sinking feeling that she has pushed him towards some kind of disaster.

I hope he doesn't do anything dire, she prays. Pacing furiously up and down her room, she wants her feet to fly her towards him, to save his life, each time she remembers his parting words, 'You may not see me again in this lifetime...' What did he mean when he said that? Did he want to end his life or merely go off to some faraway place?

She takes out the notebook from her bookshelf, the one in which Kuldeep's photo lay all these years, and starts to leaf through its pages. They are replete with memories old and new. Picking up her pencil, she scribbles something on the inside cover, a note perhaps that would jog her memory at some later date. She then turns her attention to a bottle of glue and starts to painstakingly assemble the pieces of the photo on a piece of paper. After an hour's effort, the photo is largely complete but there are still a couple of missing pieces. Their absence leaves a gap in the picture.

Putting the pieces together, she wonders if she has also broken Kuldeep's heart into small parts resembling these little bits of paper. What's the point of trying to join these lifeless pieces of paper together if I can't do anything to fix his broken heart? Oh God! Kuldeep!

The following day, Babu Ganga Vishan calls his lawyer so that he can prepare his will.

It is nine in the evening and images of a depressed Kuldeep heading towards his death continue their macabre dance before Saroj's eyes. She turns around in her bed and buries her head in her pillow to shake the thoughts away. It works for a while but she can now hear her heart cursing her. What you did was nothing less than pushing a man from the top of a cliff, she accuses herself. So why should you be surprised if he ends up dead? Did he deserve to die just because he made some mistakes? Anyone can make a mistake but you don't hang him for it. You try to reason things out, to resolve matters with love and empathy. Why didn't you do that, Saroj?

Unable to stay still, she gets up and calls her servant. 'I need to go out for a while, Mangtu. Come with me.'

Accompanied by the lad, she starts to walk briskly towards Kuldeep's house. The road seems longer than usual, or maybe she senses that she is running against time. She hails a tonga. Stopping in front of his house, she asks Mangtu to knock at the door and call him. He returns within moments. 'It's locked,' he reports.

'Locked?' she exclaims. Alighting from the tonga, she walks across to the naan bai's shop. Kuldeep had left for the railway station a little while ago, she learns. He had a trunk and some bedding with him. Some more questions reveal that he had cleared out of the house, sold all his stuff and left the key in the naan bai's custody. The naan bai had been asked to hand it over to the landlord the following day.

Saroj knows that the Calcutta Mail was the main train leaving Peshawar at night. There are still a few minutes left before the scheduled departure time of ten. She clambers back into the tonga. 'Quickly! Take me to the station. I have a train to catch and there is very little time. You'll get a bonus if I make it in time.'

Spurred by the lure of a bonus, the tongawallah makes liberal use of his whip as the tonga clatters through the empty streets. It seems ready to fly off the road but that still isn't quick enough for Saroj. Hurry up please, she urges even as she hangs on to the sidebar for dear life.

The tonga is at the gate of the station when she hears the departure whistle of the train. 'Wait here for me,' she instructs Mangtu, dashing towards the platform, ignoring the gatekeeper's queries about her ticket.

Once inside the station, she dodges past piles of baggage, crates of fruit, and people returning after seeing off their friends and relatives. Alas! As she reaches the platform, she can see the back of the last coach receding in the distance. She stands rooted to her spot near a tea stall, her eyes gazing down the railway tracks long after the train has disappeared. She feels that a piece of her had detached itself and left her forever. Her head spins as she keeps peering into the distance, trying to focus at the point where the two tracks seem to converge.

Forcing herself to return to the world around her, she notices a railway official looking closely at her as he goes past with a red lantern. Further down the platform, a couple of porters are pulling a heavy handcart, its frail wooden wheels protesting at every turn. Across the tracks, a lonely engine chugs desultorily towards the railway sheds behind the station. The platform itself has emptied out, making her feel strangely alone in a place that was packed with hordes of passengers and their friends and relatives only a few minutes back.

Her feet feel like lead as she drags herself back towards the tonga. She settles on the back seat and lets out a deep sigh of despair.

She remains forlorn and restless for a long time after returning home. The night appears endless and she pulls herself out of her bed well before the sun is ready to make its appearance on the horizon. Years of participation in religious service have taught her that when dark clouds of gloom stretch across the sky, when you see nothing but despair, an honest prayer is your only hope for solace. She knows, too, that not only is she the principal accused in the case but has also pronounced herself guilty. The only court of appeal still open is that of the Almighty.

Heading straight for the gurudwara, she stands for a long while, praying silently.

38

Waryam Singh gets off the train at Peshawar, dejected that his journey has been such a complete failure. He hasn't been able to find a single clue that might lead him to Prakash. He had spent days on end in Lahore, visiting all the popular haunts that Prakash had spoken about, methodically combing each street, talking to hundreds of persons but without a shred of luck. He knows that she isn't in Peshawar because he had confirmed that she had bought a ticket for Lahore and had, in fact, boarded the train. But Lahore is hardly a village or even a small town where you can enquire about the whereabouts of a missing person on the streets. Trying to look for an individual in a sprawling metropolis is no less than searching for a needle in a haystack.

Recalling that Prakash had also spent some time in Delhi where she was known as Putlibai, he decided to extend his search there. Once there, he trawled the streets and alleys of the historic city, going around the fabled mosques and forts, hurrying past bustling markets and sprawling havelis until he meandered into areas so disreputable that a visitor was surely putting his standing and honour at risk. And for someone like Waryam Singh, whose reputation had already been called into question, this was a positively hazardous undertaking no matter how noble his intent.

He knows that the only remaining hope for tracking Prakash is Kuldeep himself. The prospect of going across to meet Kuldeep on this fraught subject is not a pleasant one. The conversation is bound to be difficult and maybe unpleasant too. But this is the last resort and Waryam Singh is hardly one to be deterred by such obstacles. Leaving the station, he heads straight for Kuldeep's house. Finding the door locked, he goes across to the neighbour's and learns that he had vacated the place and left for the station the previous night. Further inquiries with the naan bai reveal that he was planning to visit his friend in Lahore, possibly the same Pathan couple who had come a few days back and had left with his son.

Waryam Singh's head reels under the onslaught of bad news. At the end of his interrogation of the naan bai, he concludes that Kuldeep has left Peshawar for good. What is the boy up to now, he frets. Is he off to become a hermit or something, having left his home and given away his child? But then, why has he gone to Lahore?

He recalls a conversation that he had several months ago with Gian Kaur about a friend of Kuldeep's who is a constable in the jail in Lahore. But where will that trail lead? Preoccupied with thoughts of both Prakash and Kuldeep, he slowly makes his way towards Babu Mohalla.

He had promised Saroj that he would come to see her as soon as he returned to Peshawar. During his depressing odyssey in Lahore and Delhi, he had often cheered himself up with thoughts of their imminent encounter, their first since that exchange of letters. And yet, now he finds his joy buried under a mountain of worry. As he approaches Saroj's doorstep, he knows that lines of concern on his face overshadowed the excitement that he has so eagerly anticipated. He is overcome by a profound sense of fatigue as he enters the house and learns from the servant that Saroj had gone to the gurudwara. As Mangtu sets off to inform her about his arrival, Waryam Singh goes towards Babu Ganga Vishan's room.

He is reclining in his overstuffed chair, gazing pensively at the ceiling. 'Sat Sri Akal,' Waryam Singh greets as he enters the room.

Ganga Vishan's eyes light up. 'So you are back, Waryam Singh? You are going to live a thousand years. It's barely an hour since I asked Saroj about you. I was wondering that I haven't seen you since ages. Are you well? Come, make yourself comfortable and tell me.'

Waryam Singh pulls up a chair close to him and replies vaguely about various preoccupations.

Looking affectionately at him, Ganga Vishan says, 'Waryam Singh, from this day I want to call you my own son.'

'But Babu ji, I've always been like your son, haven't I?'

'True, but today I am giving a legal shape to our relationship,' he says, reaching towards the cabinet to pick up a rolled-up sheet of paper and pass it on to Waryam Singh.

'What is this, Babu ji?' Waryam Singh takes the paper and glances at it casually.

'It's my will.'

'Your will?' he asks without reading the paper.

'Yes, my son.' Ganga Vishan's eyes shine with fondness. 'Saroj has spoken at length about herself and about you. Listen to me, son! Along with this house and everything else that I own, I am also handing over to you the most precious piece of my heart. Saroj has been the anchor of my life. I've lasted all these years simply by looking at her and admiring her virtues. Her mother, too, was a true angel. Devastated by her untimely demise, I sought to comfort myself with the help of liquor. Poor Saroj! You might consider her the daughter of an alcoholic but she is also the offspring of a goddess.'

Pausing for a moment to wipe his eyes, he continues, 'Waryam Singh, Saroj is truly a very precious treasure. I know that I don't need to say this because you are one who already appreciates her qualities. As for me, all I want is that the two of you should enjoy a long and happy life together. I will be delighted if the Anand Karaj can be performed this week itself. You know, Waryam Singh, that I have always been fairly conservative and rigid in my views about issues like caste, community, status and marriage. But I've realized that I can't mortgage my daughter's future and sacrifice her happiness at the altar of my orthodoxy.'

Tears well up in his eyes again as he speaks of his daughter. 'As per the terms of this will, you will be the rightful owner of this house and everything in it. I also have around nine thousand rupees in the bank. Together, this should amount to a sum of about twenty-five thousand rupees. I hope that it will carry you through your lifetimes. As for me, who can predict anything about this life of ours? I am pretty sure that my tenure on this planet is going to end fairly soon.'

Waryam Singh bows respectfully before Ganga Vishan to signal his consent. Before he can say anything, the old man indicates that he is tired and wants to rest. Waryam Singh helps him get up from the chair and leads him to his bed.

Stepping out, he goes into Saroj's room. She isn't back yet and he starts looking at the books on her bookshelf. His eyes fall on a notebook with a blue cover. As he opens it, he comes across the carefully pasted pieces of a photograph on the inside cover. Two or three empty spaces suggest that some pieces are still missing. He can make out that it is a childhood photo of Kuldeep. The pot of glue on the table and the dampness on the cover of the book are evidence that the photo has been freshly pasted on it.

Unable to resist himself, he turns the pages of the notebook. They are the pages of a personal diary, each entry clearly marked with the date on which it had been written. Long paragraphs of prose are occasionally interspersed with poems. Much of the notebook is dedicated to memories and incidents pertaining to Kuldeep, but Waryam Singh also begins to make a frequent appearance in the latter pages. Several of the recent incidents involving him and Saroj are recounted in pleasant detail. His eyes glisten as he reads one of the last entries:

> ... *I dedicate my life, my very existence to that noble soul, that angel. The purity of his life has transformed me from mere glass into gold. I have set aside any notion of fear or hesitation and boldly discussed everything with Bauji. How wonderful, that he has overcome his orthodox views and blessed my proposed marriage. He also plans to call the lawyer soon to prepare his will so that he can bequeath all his assets to my future husband.*

Waryam Singh is about to return the notebook to the bookshelf when he notices a more recent entry scribbled on the inside of the back cover. After making sure that Saroj isn't back, he starts to read:

> *Kuldeep showed up so unexpectedly today, the same Kuldeep that I had banished from my thoughts. My perception that the love that I had*

once nurtured for him had turned into hatred also proved to be wrong. Crushed by the burden of misfortunes and the angst over his own follies, the poor fellow looked utterly miserable as he stood at my doorstep and wept. He begged forgiveness and pleaded for my love. But how could I forgive the man who had trampled all over the honour of that purest of souls? I wouldn't forgive anyone who did that! So I turned him down. He wept some more, swallowed the humiliation I inflicted upon him and left. And as he walked away in despair, he took all my peace of mind with him. I was so sure that I had managed to expel him from my heart, not knowing that this thief had managed to hide away in some remote corner from where he appeared today and...

There isn't an inch of space left on the cardboard cover of the notebook and as the words trail off into nothingness, it is clear that the narrative has remained incomplete.

Waryam Singh puts the notebook back and sits down to wait for Saroj.

39

Saroj is deep in meditation at the gurudwara when Mangtu taps her shoulder to inform her that Waryam Singh was waiting at home. Her mind is in turmoil, all her prayers focused on one objective. Please, my Waheguru, please save Kuldeep. Save my Kuldeep, please.

Getting up from her prayers, she walks home with Mangtu. The absence of any sleep the previous night, combined with the relentless build-up of fear and anxiety, has taken its toll. She doesn't want Waryam Singh to see any of this. She had prepared herself to greet him with unbridled joy but worry about Kuldeep had cast a pall of gloom on her countenance.

Despite her efforts to force a cheerful smile on her face as she approaches her home, Waryam Singh greets her with the query, 'What's wrong, Saroj? Are you unwell? Your face looks so pale!'

'Nothing major,' she replies. 'I've been a bit under the weather for the last couple of days.' Pulling up a chair beside him, she asks, 'When did you get back?'

Waryam Singh recounts the details of his trip, his futile search of countless streets, alleys and by-lanes and his misgivings about Prakash's fate. Turning towards her, he says, 'My apologies, Saroj, I couldn't come to you as soon as I received your letter...'

'No need for any apology,' she interjects. 'Your absence has doubled my respect for you. I understand even more clearly that you don't live for yourself but for the well-being of others. That's why I have surrendered my heart to you. Have you seen Bau ji yet?'

'I did,' Waryam Singh replies in a tone that reflects his appreciation of the older man. 'I had assumed that Babu ji would balk upon receiving your request. I am simply bowled over by the readiness with which he agreed, and by his generosity. But Saroj, I need to sit down and have a long chat with you. I must share with you details about my life that neither you nor anyone else knows.'

'Please tell me, Bhapa...' Saroj checks herself from addressing him as an older brother.

'So listen, Saroj. I come from such a lowly position that it may be unreasonable for me to aspire for a flower that is perched on a lofty branch.'

'You? And lowly?' Saroj flares up. 'No matter where you come from, you will always be on a high pedestal for me. And remember that Saroj, the lotus flower, is also born in fetid waters, not on lofty branches.'

'That is the stuff of poetry, Saroj. I am a person of extremely limited means.'

'Enough!' Saroj protests. 'I don't want to hear this. Please be candid and tell me that, like Kuldeep, you also want to reject me.'

Persisting with his efforts to find a way that would ease him out of Saroj's heart, Waryam Singh continues, 'You are not being realistic, Saroj. My parents belonged to that lowest of castes that are regarded as untouchables. Giani ji, who was my godfather and mentor, told me that we come from some backward village in the province of UP. Our village was decimated by an attack of plague that claimed virtually every household in the area. It consumed every member of our family. I was lucky to come out alive because of Giani ji, who arrived like an angel to administer medicines to the wretched. He took me under his wing and brought me up like his own son from the time I was barely a year and a half old.

'But I had this strange wanderlust in me. Instead of staying put to assist him in his pious tasks, I drifted away on my own, moving from one place to another. I returned to discover that Giani ji had passed away in my absence. I've always been assailed by the remorse that I wasn't around to serve him when he needed me.

'You accuse me of rejecting you...like Kuldeep had done?

For god's sake, don't be so unfair. Look at the state to which Kuldeep has been condemned. Even though he wronged us and hurt us through his actions, my heart cries for him. As soon as I got off the train today, I went straight to his house but the poor fellow had already left the place.'

His words stir her emotions and he can see her agitation as she speaks. 'He came here yesterday.'

'He came here?' Waryam Singh feigns ignorance. 'To meet you?'

'He said he wanted to seek forgiveness – from you and from me.'

'Really? And what did you say?'

'I told him off and turned him away.'

'What? You turned him away?'

'Yes! That's what I did.' Sensing a surge of emotion, she hurries into the kitchen. 'Let me call Mangtu and ask him to fix some dinner.' When she returns, her eyes are dry but red, revealing they had been rubbed hastily with her dupatta.

'Saroj,' Waryam Singh remarks caustically. 'Didn't you feel any sympathy for the hapless fellow? If he had come before me in that kind of state, I would have gladly embraced him even if I knew that he wanted to kill me.'

Listening to him, Saroj wonders, Is this man a human being from our own planet? Or is he some kind of a messiah who has descended from the heavens.

'Try to understand his condition, Saroj,' Waryam Singh continues. 'He lost both his parents within the space of a few months. His wife has disappeared and his home has fallen apart. He has a small child to care for. He feels lost, clueless, looking for some straw that he can clutch. And yet, you ticked him off and spurned him? He must have been devastated by your attitude. But anyway, go on. What happened after that?'

'He left,' she whispers despairingly.

'You didn't try to stop him?'

'No.'

'And he didn't say anything?'

'He did...he said that I might never see him again. Please ask Waryam Singh to forgive me, he said.'

'Oh! What have you done, Saroj!' Waryam Singh springs from his chair. 'Don't you know his tempestuous nature? He is capable of going to any extreme. I wish you had reflected upon his reason for coming to you.'

Tears again surface in her eyes and this time she makes no effort to hide them, 'He came to remind me of a promise that I had made to him some time ago.'

'What promise?'

'I had promised that if ever he needed help, he could call me and I would be there for him.'

'So what did you say?'

'I...I told him that he should no longer have any such expectation from me. That I was now... that I...'

'That you are now with Waryam Singh?'

Saroj is silent.

'And how did he react?'

'I've already told you what he said.'

'And he left? Oh! The poor soul! I am afraid he might have gone forever,' Waryam Singh exclaims, pacing up and down the room. He is trying to discern her feelings, looking for evidence that might support the sentiments that she had expressed in that final note in her diary. After a while, he sits down and looks closely at Saroj. Her face is ashen.

'Saroj!' He places his hand on her shoulder.

'Yes, Bhapa ji!' Embarrassed that she has again used the

same expression, she brings her palm across her mouth and turns her face away.

'There is no need to feel shy about this,' Waryam Singh says, pulling her hand away from her face. 'Your addressing me as Bhapa ji sounds perfectly normal to me. Perhaps that is the relationship we are destined to have, Saroj. What can be more sacred than the relationship between a brother and a sister?'

Saroj directs a probing glance at him before lowering her face.

'Look at me, Saroj.' Waryam Singh lifts her chin. He has a spiritual, almost mystic look in his eyes. 'Do you know why we are meeting today?'

Saroj looks at him with a question in her eyes.

'We are here because Babu ji's will seeks to bind us into a relationship.'

'That is true,' Saroj acknowledges.

'Well, I want to make this relationship so sacred that it rises above the level of normal worldly ties.'

'How?'

'By declaring ourselves brother and sister.' Waryam Singh's face glows as though lit up by the first rays of the morning sun.

'And don't worry about the will, Saroj.' He pats her head affectionately. 'I will transfer all the property rights to Kuldeep. I hope my sister will agree with this.'

Saroj feels her head bow involuntarily towards his feet as she looks at him with renewed reverence. He holds her to lift her up and plants a brotherly kiss on her forehead. Saroj feels elated, experiencing the warmth of a brother's protective embrace. They stand still for a long time, soaking in the beauty of an entirely new feeling.

Stepping back to break the embrace, Waryam Singh says, 'But first we must try to save Kuldeep.'

'But...but...' Saroj is unable to complete her thoughts.

'If we can take the train tonight, we may be able to catch up with him in Lahore. I have a gut feeling that he has gone to that constable friend of his. After all, he is the one who took the responsibility to bring up the child. Will you accompany me on this mission, Saroj?'

'I'll do as you say, Bhapa ji.'

'So will you join me, Saroj?' he asks again. 'It gives you an opportunity to save two lives at one go – both Kuldeep and his child. Please don't think that this is going to impede our progress on the path of idealism that you outlined in your letter. I feel that we'll be even more effective if we have Kuldeep by our side.'

Saroj marvels once again at the man's seemingly boundless ability to sacrifice himself for others. Her voice revealing the hint of a nervous tremor, she asks softly, 'I am not too sure about anything right now, Bhapa ji. All I know is that I've found my guide in you and in your soul. I've decided to firmly attach myself to you so that I can follow you wherever you go, do whatever you say.'

'All right, then. Please go and seek your father's permission so that we can leave for Lahore tonight,' Waryam Singh says, getting up to leave. He takes her hand in his own and smiles at the look of affection in her eyes. 'Take care, dear sister,' he says.

'You too, Bhapa ji,' she replies, gripping his hand.

Waryam Singh leaves the house as Saroj goes into her father's room. Is there any comparison, he asks himself, between the purity of this spiritual love and its more worldly counterpart? Who can say but the one who has seen the reflection of his own love in the eyes of another.

40

It is, perhaps, a natural human desire to see the other bank of the stream of life. Some are able to see it through their naked eyes while others have to embellish their vision with the colours of their imagination. Our two passengers are headed for the same bank but the price each is required to pay is quite different. One has to pay the price of life, while the other has to sacrifice the very aspirations of life. You can give up your life for someone and still end up with a feeling of complete satisfaction. But what happens when you have to give up all your aspirations for someone? What will life be if it is bereft of aspirations? You could say that your sense of contentment comes from within and that you need nothing more. Nevertheless, this is a price that can only be paid by one who has already dedicated every particle of his self to others.

Is whatever Waryam Singh gets in lieu of surrendering his own aspirations worth the price? Perhaps! He has tried to build his life around the principle that the satisfaction derived from giving is greater than that derived from receiving. Is that what sustains the radiance on his face, that keeps the forces of darkness at bay?

Saroj's eyes, too, shine with an intense hope and also a prayer. A part of her heart is full of devotion and the other overflows with a sense of longing. The scales between the two are evenly balanced, although they seem to be tilting in favour of longing. A feeling of love, growing out of longing, occupies the vacant space in her heart. Longing is emboldened, perhaps, by the fact that it has obtained the blessings of devotion. Occupied with their own objectives, the two travellers head towards the other bank of their lives.

Saroj is trying to absorb the newest twists in her eventful life. Barely forty-eight hours ago, she was looking at Waryam Singh as her soon-to-be husband. And now, the same person has become the object of a profound sort of devotion that borders on the sacred. Kuldeep, meanwhile, is no more exiled from her thoughts – he now occupies her mind and body, almost becoming a part of every breath she takes.

Why do I have this uneasy feeling? Saroj wonders, looking out of the train's window. Is it the excitement that stems from an imminent encounter with your loved one, or is it a sense of foreboding that things may not turn out as we expect them to.? What if we are unable to find Kuldeep? Or if he has already taken some extreme step? Or if we arrive too late and he has already left for some unknown destination?

The fortress of her resolve begins to crumble under repeated onslaughts mounted by negative thoughts. Tales like Sassi-Punnu and Sohni-Mahiwal that embodied great romance but ended in tragedy race through her mind. She sees Sassi, the princess, trudging through the parched desert in search of Punnu, and Sohni, the potter, trying to cross a raging river on her earthen pot to meet her Mahiwal who waits on the other bank. A tremor of fear goes through her body.

She rubs her eyes and pulls herself up in her seat to climb out of her melancholic reverie. She wants her mind to look at a brighter picture. I can't lose Kuldeep now, she tells herself. If my love is true and firm, there is no reason to think that I won't find him. And won't Kuldeep be besides himself with joy when he hears Bhapa ji tell him, 'Here, Kuldeep. I offer my sister's hand to you. And you can also have her property and financial assets.' Oh, what a moment it will be when Bhapa ji embraces Kuldeep and lifts him off his feet. Kuldeep will then be mine forever. And that little child, Satwant's only remaining symbol, will cling lovingly to my bosom. I would have kept my promise to the dying woman and, who knows, she might even smile at me from the heavens as her soul finally gets to rest in peace. But will such an auspicious time actually come? What if...?

That 'what if?' brings her back to reality with a thud. She feels the world of her dreams shatter around her. It is replaced by desolate images of blood and of imminent death. Her mind swirling, she turns towards her fellow passenger for comfort.

Waryam Singh, meanwhile, has stuck his turbaned head out of the window to observe the rapidly changing vista outside, or maybe to get a better view inside his own world. Saroj's hand is shaking with fear as she clutches his arm and asks, 'How much longer to go, Bhapa ji?'

Coming out of his trance, Waryam Singh smiles. 'What's wrong, Saroj? Are you tired already? We've just left Gujranwala, which means that we should be in Lahore in about an hour and a half. It is two right now, so I guess we should reach there around three thirty or so.'

Saroj is silent.

'But Saroj, what if we don't find Kuldeep in Lahore?'

Saroj recoils at the unexpected reappearance of the dreaded 'what if?' Unable to hide her uneasiness, she turns her face away.

'Don't get upset, Saroj,' he reassures her as if he has read her mind. 'A voice inside me says that he is definitely with that constable friend of his at Borstal Jail.'

Saroj doesn't say anything but her eyes ask, 'And what if he isn't there either?'

The remaining ninety minutes of the journey seem an eternity but the train finally chugs into Lahore station. Within seconds, the coaches are swarming with porters, dressed in their typical blue shirts and red turbans as they offer to help the passengers unload their baggage. Waryam Singh entrusts his bedding to an elderly porter and follows him down the platform, with Saroj walking a few steps behind him. They have barely gone a few yards when Waryam Singh stops in his tracks and turns towards Saroj. 'Look over there! That's Kuldeep, and Prakash is with him.'

She follows his glance and lets out a shriek. Four passengers are boarding the coach adjacent to the one from which they had just alighted. Kuldeep goes in first and holds out his hand to assist Prakash. They are followed by a Muslim couple, the veiled lady carrying Kuldeep's child on her shoulder.

Waryam Singh keeps looking at the door of the coach long after they have disappeared from view, his mind reeling under a flood of unanswered questions. The sight is all too much for Saroj to bear. Physical exhaustion and frayed nerves are unable to ward off the latest shock, and as she faints, her head crashes into the wrought-iron railing on the platform. She falls near Waryam's feet, blood gushing out of an ugly wound above her temple.

Waryam stands paralysed. The sight of an unconscious Saroj sprawling on the platform, a pool of blood rapidly accumulating around her head, is too much even for his sturdy constitution. A crowd of bystanders soon gather around them, some offering to help and others merely looking and commenting on the tragic condition of the victim. Take her to the waiting room, one of them suggests, coming forth to help Waryam. Together, they take her to the spacious hall where the porter spreads out his bedding so that she can be placed on it. The porter is dispatched to fetch a doctor.

While waiting for the doctor to arrive, Waryam Singh does whatever he can to stop the bleeding. He dabs a towel in cold water and presses it against her wound while others try to fan her with a newspaper. But she remains unconscious, bleeding.

By the time the doctor arrives, the train has left the platform for Amritsar and the crowds have started to dissipate. The bleeding has slowed to a trickle but Saroj is still unconscious. Waryam Singh narrates the circumstances of her situation to the doctor, who takes her pulse, examines the gash above her temple and the blood that has soaked into the bedding before turning towards Waryam Singh.

'Sardar ji, the patient is in serious condition. It is possible that she suffered a heart attack as a result of the shock. The situation is complicated by the excessive loss of blood. I think it is vital that we take her immediately to a good hospital.'

Waryam Singh pauses for a while to think clearly. Saroj is his priority but he cannot ignore the fact that Ganga Vishan, too, is on his last legs and cannot be left alone for any length of time. The best scenario would be to get Saroj to Peshawar so that he can tend to both father and daughter. He discusses the dilemma with the doctor.

'If you can get the patient to Peshawar within the next fifteen to twenty hours and admit her to a hospital where she will get good care, she might survive. But there is no train to Peshawar till eight tonight and I don't think you can afford to wait that long at this station. The delay could be...'

'Doctor Sahib, I don't know if we can impose so much on you,' Waryam Singh addresses him with folded hands. 'But if we can get a taxi and you can accompany us to Peshawar, I will be eternally indebted to you. Please don't worry about your charges. We will readily take care of that.'

The doctor agrees immediately, saying that he would rush to his clinic to pick up some essential medicines and would be back at the station with a taxi within half an hour.

Waryam Singh sits beside Saroj, checking her pulse, calling her name, holding her hand and caressing her forehead. Unable to elicit a response, he feels his own heart sinking. He curses his fate and laments at the way his well-intentioned plans have so suddenly gone awry.

The taxi speeds along the Grand Trunk Road. Saroj is curled up on the rear seat, her head nestling on Waryam Singh's lap. The doctor is on the front seat next to the driver, his head swivelling around time and again to keep a watchful eye on the patient. He has administered several injections but the patient remains unconscious.

The light has started to fade as the sun, winding up its business for the day, makes a gentle descent over the horizon. Saroj stirs briefly. Her face is contorted with pain as she whispers, 'Kuldeep! My Kuldeep!'

Waryam Singh tries to comfort her. He checks her temperature. The bar of mercury has crossed the 105-degree mark. He knows her life is ebbing away. His eyes are drenched and he has given up all pretence of trying to restrain his tears. The doctor takes out his syringe to administer another injection but Waryam Singh tells him, sobbing, 'Let her be, Doctor Sahib.'

Saroj opens her eyes and gazes at him. 'Saroj! My dear Saroj!' he cries, embracing her.

'Where am I?'

'In your brother's lap, dear Saroj. Look at me.'

She tries to focus her eyes on his face. 'Bhapa ji,' she says.

'Yes, my dear.' Waryam Singh removes a few strands of hair from her burning forehead. 'What's happened to my little sister? Wake up, Saroj.'

'Bhapa ji! Dear Bhapa ji! You have given me so much love!' She puts all her strength into raising her arms so that they can go around his neck.

'Are you feeling a little better now?' Waryam Singh feels her red-hot forehead.

'Better?' She gives him a strange smile. 'I am feeling better, Bhapa ji. But why am I crammed into this tight little corner? And Bhapa ji...I think I am going now...This house...This house is going to collapse, Bhapa ji...Ah...'

The doctor admonishes Waryam Singh, 'Let her lie down properly and don't make her talk.'

'Doctor Sahib,' Waryam Singh croaks, 'please don't separate her from me now.' His throat is choked with the pain rising from his heart.

Saroj's eyes are closed but she makes another effort to speak. 'Kuldeep...I must save him, Bhapa ji...Kuldeep...that evil man...that devil...that heartless stone...that Kuldeep. Bhapa ji...I am going...save me, Bhapa ji!'

Tears stream down Waryam's face. He looks at the doctor,

who rubs his hands helplessly and rolls his eyes towards the heavens.

The driver honks incessantly to persuade bullock carts, cyclists and other slow-moving vehicles to give way. Waryam Singh feels her cries subside and her body become still. Her head stops moving in his lap and he feels the warmth ebb out of her body. His tears stop and his hand ceases caressing her forehead. The doctor takes a long while to check her pulse before silently shaking his head.

The taxi speeds through the dark, lonely night, its silence punctured every now and then by the angry blaring of the vehicle's horn. It sounds like the roar of death, sending birds into a scared huddle in the safety of their nests, their heads buried under their wings until the taxi is out of earshot.

Translator's Note

List of Books

P.S.

Insights
Interviews &
More ...

Translator's Note

He was an unusually gifted man, my grandfather Sardar Nanak Singh. Affectionately called Bauji by friends and family, his prodigious literary output over half a century won him the status of 'Father of the Punjabi Novel' from literary critics. To his millions of fans, he was simply Nanak Singh – the 'novelist' who enthralled them with his tales of romance and tragedy, of noble heroes and rapacious villains.

All these and more are revealed in the undulations of *Adh Khidya Phul*, in characters that draw the reader into their lives. But what sets this book apart from the two score others that he wrote is the presence of several incidents and characters that are drawn from the first twenty-five or thirty years of Bauji's own life. We get an inkling of this when we read the foreword, not that it is always a reliable guide to reality. Bauji often used the foreword as a device to lure the reader into his web. But in this one, he does seem to go that extra yard to suggest

BOOKS

Novels

Matraiyee Maa
(1924)

Kaal Chakkar
(1924)

Mitha Mohra
(1926)

Prem Sangeet
(1929)

Phauladi Phul
(1931)

Chitta Lahu
(1932)

that the first few pages are more fact than fiction.

Kagtaan di Bedhi *(1935)*

Paap Di Khatti *(1936)*

Pyar Di Duniya *(1938)*

Garib Di Duniya *(1939)*

Adh Khidya Phul *(1940)*

I was intrigued by this declaration. Did characters of the purity of Waryam Singh, the duplicity of Sant Prem Singh, the virtuosity of Saroj, the fickleness of Kuldeep actually exist? I did know from family folklore that Bauji had gone to Borstal Jail as part of the freedom struggle, that he had also been present at the Jallianwala Bagh massacre. There were, in fact, some in the family who complained that we never secured the material benefits of being a 'freedom fighter's family' because Bauji simply didn't believe in any of that.

Questions about *Adh Khidya Phul* took me into conversations with family elders and into a serious rereading of *Meri Duniya*, the autobiography that Bauji first wrote in 1949. On Waryam Singh, the answer was ambiguous but illuminating. Bauji explains this in the context of his own early days and a digression at this juncture might be worthwhile.

Nanak Singh was born into a modest Hindu family in the small hamlet of Chak Hamid in Daadan Khan tehsil of Jhelum district (now in Pakistan) in 1897. The oldest of four siblings, he was named Hans Raj and spent his first eight years in the village before accompanying his father to Peshawar to help him in his shop. His mother and two younger brothers joined them a few months later but the joy of a family reunion was short-lived. His father was consumed by a bout of pneumonia even while his mother was on the verge of delivering her fourth child. The responsibility of running the family store fell on young Hans Raj at an early age, taking him out of school before he had completed fifth grade.

He was barely an adolescent when he came into contact with Savitri, who lived a couple of houses down the street from him in the Sadar area of Peshawar. As youngsters, they would spend hours together and Bauji describes her as his first and only romance. He saw her get married while she was still in her early teens, and return home as a child widow a few months later. She was fond of literature and music and he had a gift for crafting poetry and songs with a simple rhyme and metre. To make an impression on her, he also took to learning music from a Bengali friend and soon reached a level of proficiency that allowed him to be her tutor. They spent hours together, he on the harmonium with a new melody each day, she the doting student singing along in her lilting voice. But it was not to be. She was struck by a strange malady – tuberculosis, perhaps. None of the medicines worked, and while a last-ditch effort to take her into the clean mountain air of the hills near Peshawar

***Pavitar Paapi* (1942)**

***Jeewan Sangram* (1942)**

***Dhundle Parchhaven* (1944)**

***Door Kinara* (1945)**

***Tuttee Veena* (1946)**

seemed to induce a miraculous recovery for a while, it turned out to be a false dawn. Not yet twenty, Bauji saw her life ebb away before his eyes.

He speaks about this in his autobiography, sharing his pain with his readers. 'What was Savitri like?' he poses the rhetorical question. In response, he quotes his own description of Saroj in *Adh Khidya Phul* – a quiet, elegant, self-confident young woman who retains her dignity even after suffering the ignominy of being a child widow.

Love Marriage* *(1947)

Gangajali Vich Sharab* *(1947)

Agg di Khed* *(1948)

Khoon De Sohile* *(1948)

Manjhdhar* *(1949)

Chittarkar* *(1950)

Savitri's death left the young poet adrift. His mother, who anchored his early years, also passed away and he found himself in the company of an aimless group of youth who were happy to wine and dine him while he entertained them with his poems and couplets. He took to smoking, drinking and even the occasional theft of cash from his uncle's store. But he was fortunate to find a mentor in Giani Bagh Singh, an erudite Sikh scholar who encouraged him to use his skills as a musician and start his own kirtan jatha to sing hymns at the local Singh Sabha Gurudwara.

The gurudwara congregations and the discipline of practice sessions and performances with his newly formed kirtan jatha of hymn singers restored a sense of order to young Hans Raj's life and it is around this time that he ran into Giani Sher

Singh, a fiery preacher and ardent nationalist. Still in search of his moorings, the combined influence of Giani Bagh Singh and Giani Sher Singh led him to convert to Sikhism with the name Nanak Singh. With all the zeal of the recent convert, he plunged headlong into the communal politics of the day, writing diatribes against the Arya Samaj movement and turning his poetic skills towards writing verses in praise of the Sikh gurus. *Satguru Mahima*, a small booklet of such poems, became an instant hit, selling over one hundred thousand copies and becoming the source of his financial sustenance for the next several years.

He also fell in love with the atmosphere of the gurudwara – the melodious singing of hymns, the sermons by religious leaders on the virtues and rewards of leading a pious life and the joys of entering a world that is infused by spirituality and stands at a distance from mundane material concerns. He also came under the influence of a preacher who bears an eerie resemblance to Sant Prem Singh. In the chapter 'From Peshawar to Amritsar' of *Meri Duniya*, Bauji describes his infatuation with the magnetic personality of the preacher and the power of his words. Barely twenty years old, Nanak Singh wound up the printing press that he was running with a partner and moved into the preacher's dera to spend his days in

***Aadam Khor* (1951)**

***Katti Hoi Patang* (1952)**

***Suman Kanta* (1952)**

***Nasoor* (1953)**

***Banjar* (1956)**

***Aastak Nastak* (1956)**

Sangam (1957)

Pujari (1958)

Chhalava (1959)

Anseetey Zakham (1959)

Ik Mian Do Talwaraan (1960)

Pathar De Khamb (1960)

close proximity to his spiritual master. He wanted to live the life of detachment from the material world that the preacher advocated so lucidly in his sermons. But the affair was short-lived. It wasn't long before he discovered that the preacher enjoyed all the good things of life, maintained a healthy bank balance and was probably engaged in a sexual relationship with the woman who was believed to be his most ardent devotee. Unable to accept the hypocrisy, a disillusioned Nanak Singh made a hasty exit from the dera. He was chastened by the experience and remained a lifelong sceptic about religious charlatans that often show up in his novels in the form of characters like Sant Prem Singh of *Adh Khidya Phul*.

Reading the autobiography, in fact, makes it quite clear that Bauji's quest for his own identity during his teens and early twenties finds a reflection in the fickle character of Kuldeep. He is a decent fellow, means no harm to anyone but lacks the strength of conviction that can guide his own destiny.

This discovery came as something of a shock to me. Although Bauji died in 1971 when I was all of twelve years old, I have vivid memories of him as this saintly figure in his simple white kurta-pyjama with a plain white turban and flowing grey beard. True, during our summer vacations in Preet Nagar, he would often regale my cousins and me with some impromptu stories that provided us a glimpse into his literary genius. But it was his simplicity, his idealism and his deep-seated commitment to social reform that gave him a kind of other-worldly, almost ethereal quality. We knew, as we were growing up, that we were privileged to be in the family of a truly exceptional individual. To read so many years later that he indulged in smoking and drinking and admitted to other aberrations gave me a completely new insight into his character.

Which brings us back to our original question about Waryam Singh. If Saroj is Savitri from real life, Sant Prem Singh takes after the preacher in Amritsar and Kuldeep bears resemblance to the early phase of the author himself, who is Waryam Singh? Was he a real person too? Where was that cottage of his located in the hills? Bauji acknowledges in *Meri Duniya* that the character of Waryam Singh has shades of a real person. As does the character of Baba Rode in his novel *Chitta Lahu*, of Sant Som Prakash in *Kaal Chakkar*, of Sunder Das in *Love Marriage*, of the editor in *Gangajali vich Sharab*...and so on. Each of these characters represents a facet of the idealism of Giani Bagh Singh, the mentor to whom Bauji proclaims his own undying gratitude.

In what looks like a curious epiphany, it was Giani Bagh Singh who advised the young

***Var Nahi Sarap* (1962)**

***Koi Harya Boot Rahio Ree* (1964)**

***Sarapian Roohan* (1965)**

***Gagan Damama Bajia* (1967)**

SHORT STORIES

Hanjhuan De Haar (1935)

Sadhran De Haar (1935)

Midhey Hoye Phul (1938)

Thandiyaan Chhawaan (1940)

Nanak Singh to go to jail to discover his true calling in life. And so he signed up for the Guru ka Bagh campaign aimed at wresting control of major Sikh gurudwaras from priests who were British loyalists. The British government had declared the campaign illegal and protestors were marched off for varying spells at Lahore's infamous Borstal Jail, where Bauji was interned for over nine months.

True to the epiphany, the months spent in jail in 1922 gave him the time to reflect, to overcome the loss of Savitri, to introspect on his own fickleness and to look for solutions to his dilemmas within himself. He was also fortunate to meet several unusual individuals, one of whom was an activist of the Congress party named Pandit Jagan Nath. Clearly a man of some influence, Pandit Jagan Nath had been able to get permission for bringing a trunk-load of books including an extensive selection of Hindi novels by Munshi Premchand into his cell. Undeterred by the minor constraint that he had a barely passing acquaintance with Hindi, Bauji proceeded to borrow and read each one of the novels before coming to the momentous conclusion that this was what he really wanted to do – to write novels that would move the hearts and minds of people, that would bring social reform, that would transform society and perhaps even help in bringing independence to the country. And so it was that he managed to lay his hands on some paper and started to write his first novel. Tentatively titled *Adh Khidi Kali* or *A Half-blossomed Bud*, it looked at the problems in contemporary society through the travails of his beloved Savitri. But an untimely search of his cell led the jailors to confiscate his still incomplete novel, leaving the budding novelist despondent and loathe to take up another novel for several more years. But write he did, and by the time he resumed the tale of Savitri as Saroj in *Adh Khidya Phul* a good eighteen years later in 1940, he had already established a formidable reputation as one of the pre-eminent writers of his generation. Had it not been for the intervention of the jailor, it could have been his first novel, written when he was all of twenty-five years old.

But my digression has taken me away from an important milestone. Even before his participation in the Guru ka Bagh campaign, it is believed that Bauji was present in Jallianwala Bagh in Amritsar when General Dyer's troops unleashed a hail of bullets on a group of peaceful protestors. It was the popular Baisakhi festival, 13 April 1919, and he had gone to the venue with two of his friends. Both died in the firing and family folklore has it that Bauji fainted and was piled up amongst the dead bodies.

PLAYS

***B.A. Pass* (1944)**

***Paap Da Fal* (1972)**

***Chaur Chaanan* (1973)**

***Dhobi Da Kutta* (1981)**

***Saarh Sati* (1981)**

Meri Duniya
(1949)

He also lost partial hearing during the firing. Having started off in his teens as a writer of songs and religious poems, he expressed himself through a long poem called 'Khooni Visakhi'.

Published in May 1920, *Khooni Visakhi* traces the run-up to the infamous Rowlatt Act, promulgated on 18 March 1919 to suppress the growing tide of protests against the excesses of colonial rule. It speaks of the call for nationwide strike or 'hartal' given by Mahatma Gandhi on 6 April and the impact of the hartal in Punjab and, in particular, in Amritsar. There is a particularly moving reference to the Hindu–Muslim unity forged by prominent local Congress leaders Dr Satya Pal and Dr Saifuddin Kitchlew who led a public rally on the occasion of the Ram Navami festival on 9 April. Both leaders were arrested and a wave of popular anger swept the city when they were taken away to an undisclosed location on 10 April. A group of protestors went to the office of Deputy Commissioner Michael Irving to seek the release of their leaders but police firing on them exacerbated tensions, leading to rioting in several parts of the city. Brigadier General R.E.H. Dyer was summoned from the Jallandhar Cantonment to come with a military contingent and establish order.

The poem recounts the resolve of the people of Amritsar to assemble at Jallianwala

Bagh on Baisakhi day to express their anger and to map their future course of action. The firing on the unarmed, peaceful congregation, the deaths of many hundreds and the bullet injuries suffered by thousands of others cast a pall of gloom over the city. *Khooni Visakhi* captures the pathos in verse, mocking at British rule and celebrating the stoic resistance of the ordinary people of Amritsar. The colonial administration banned the book and confiscated and destroyed virtually all copies. And it remained unavailable to the public for another six decades until a copy was located and the book was republished in 1980.

Charhdi Kala* *(1972)

At a very different level, *Adh Khidya Phul* also provides an insight into Nanak Singh, the writer who saw his novels as catalysts for social change. It was written in 1940 at a time of rising tension between the Sikh and Muslim communities. But the friendship between Kuldeep and Ahmed Khan, the adoption of Kuldeep's child by Zubeida, and Ahmed's promise that the Muslim household will ban beef and tobacco from their home in deference to Sikh sensibilities are a strong testament for religious tolerance.

The character of Saroj underlines another of the author's favourite themes – the empowerment of woman. He presents Saroj as a strong, talented and educated woman. She has suffered the social ignominy of being a child widow and could easily have gone into a shell. Yet, she is prepared to live life on her terms and to contribute to society through her own idealism.

Sant Prem Singh, too, is used to highlight one of the author's recurrent themes. Beware of superstitious beliefs and of religious charlatans who claim to show you the true path. There is no virtue in renouncing the material world, in abdicating your obligations to your family. The true path is more likely to be found through honest toil and dedication.

Waryam Singh, too, bears a similar message. He refers to himself as one from a very low caste, possibly even an untouchable. And yet, his virtues persuade even a conservative like Babu Ganga Vishan to accept him as a son-in-law and to bequeath his property to him.

Although commonplace today, these ideas were fairly revolutionary at the time and ran counter to prevailing social mores in the Punjab of the 1920s and '30s. Nanak Singh's abiding commitment to rational thought, social egalitarianism and religious tolerance were key elements in making him an important driver of social change for an entire generation of Punjabis.

As a writer, he hit a golden patch between 1930 and 1960, producing at least one substantive novel each year that goes beyond

POETRY

***Satgur Mahima* (1918)**

***Gur Kirat* (1919)**

***Khooni Visakhi* (1920)**

***Zakhmi Dil* (1922)**

fiction to provide a glimpse into the contemporary social history of that period. His novel *Ik Mian Do Talwaraan* – based on the life of Kartar Singh Sarabha and the Ghadar movement of the early twentieth century – won him the prestigious Sahitya Akademi Award in 1962. By the time he passed away in December 1971, he had left behind a formidable body of work – a total of fifty-nine books including thirty-eight novels. Forty years after his death, several of those have entered the realm of 'classics' of Punjabi literature. They are prescribed texts in high school and college courses and dozens of doctoral dissertations have been completed on the works of a man who had virtually no formal education. Many of his books are in their twentieth or thirtieth imprints and his position at the pinnacle of Punjabi literature as the 'Father of the Punjabi Novel' remains uncontested and secure.

From a grandson who is a diplomat trying to masquerade as an amateur translator, this book is an effort to bring his work out of the narrow confines of Punjabi and into the larger literary public.

TRANSLATION

***Soolan Di Sej* (1936)**

***Pathar De Panchhi* (1937)**

***Rajni* (1939)**

***Tasveer De Doven Passey* (1941)**

***Pathar Kamba* (1942)**

***France Da Dakoo* (1942)**

***Praschit* (1943)**

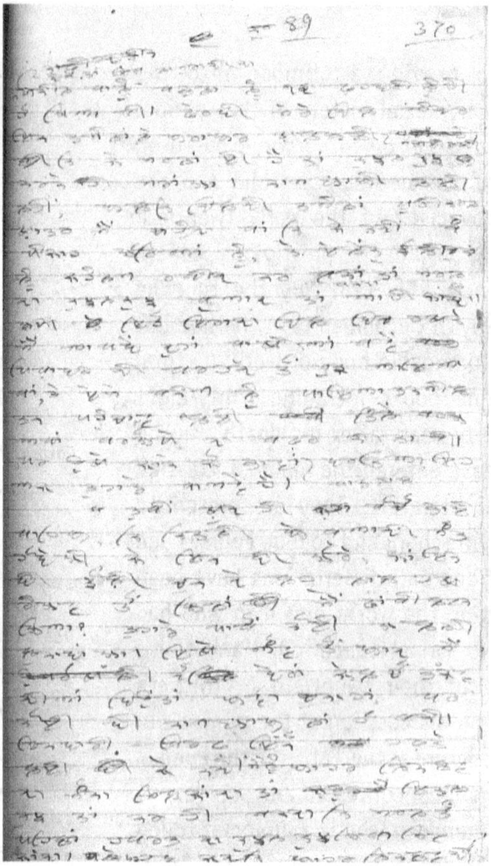

Pages from the handwritten manuscript of Nanak Singh's novel *Ik Mian Do Talwaraan* which won the Sahitya Akademi Award. The novel captures the nationalist zeal and revolutionary spirit of the Ghadar movement of the early twentieth century through the life of Kartar Singh Sarabha. The Ghadar Party was founded by a cross-section of Indians in California in April 1913 with the simple motto 'Stake everything for the freedom of the country'. Like many other Ghadarites, Sarabha returned to India from California to fight for India's independence from British rule. However, a police informer revealed their plans; the campaign was unsuccessful and many of the aspiring revolutionaries were arrested. Sarabha was one of sixty-three Ghadarites who were tried and sentenced at the Lahore Central Jail in 1915. Describing him as the most dangerous of all the rebels because 'he is very proud of the crimes committed by him' the court sentenced Sarabha to death. Barely nineteen years old, he was hanged in Lahore on 16 November 1915 and became an inspiration for other young revolutionaries like Bhagat Singh and Udham Singh.

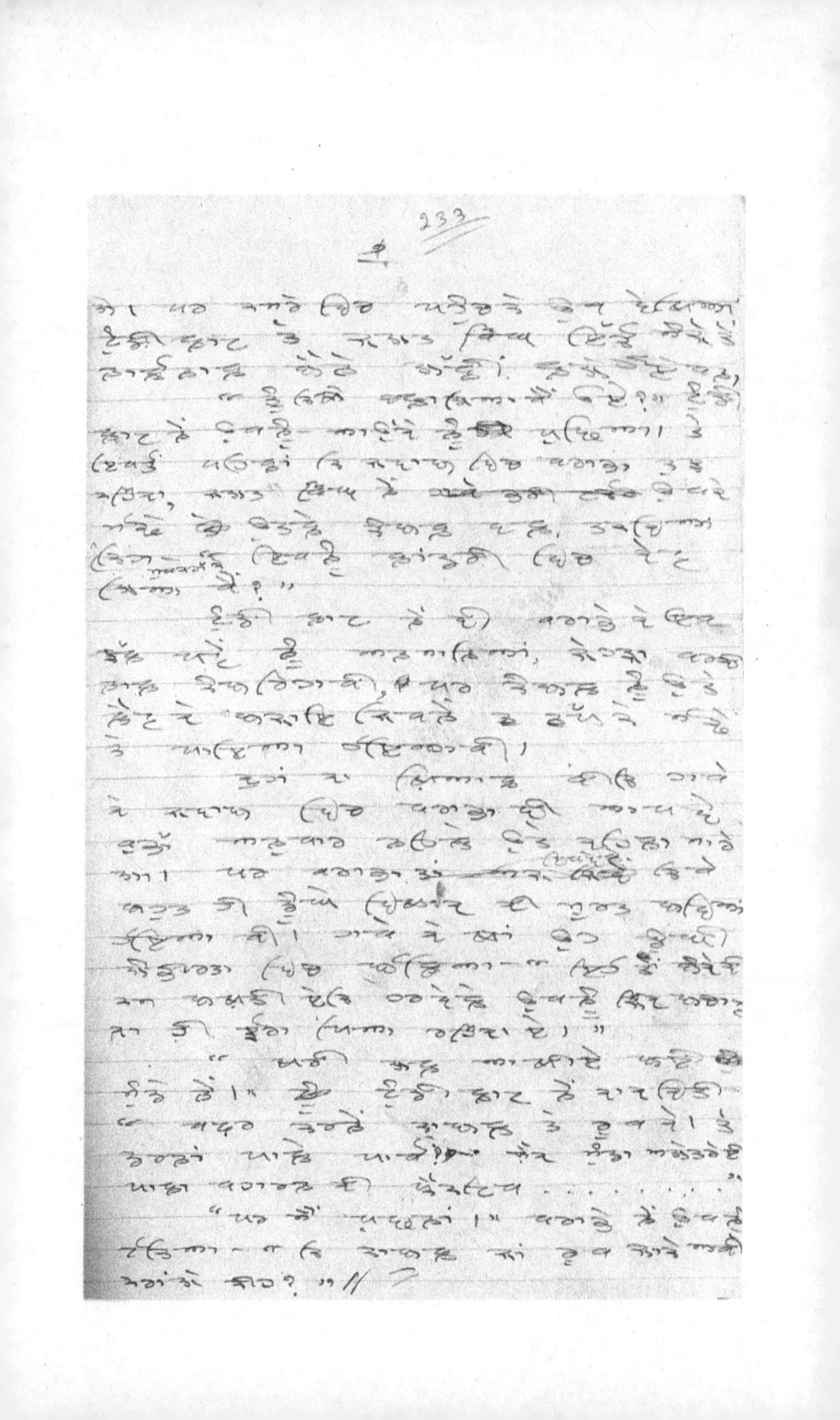

ACKNOWLEDGEMENTS

This book wouldn't have been possible without the constant motivation and encouragement from my parents who insisted that my grandfather's works deserve a wider audience and believed that I am the one who can make this happen. My wife Mani, who always wants me to do more, took additional burdens on herself and made sure that I could spend quality time on the translation. I am also deeply grateful to Dr Rajinder Singh for his valuable assistance on many facets of translation. Shantanu's editing ironed out the rough edges and Karthika's positive energy is infectious.

HARPER**PERENNIAL**

Harper Perennial presents special editions of its finest books in translation

Age of Frenzy
Mahabaleshwar Sail
Translated from the Konkani by Vidya Pai

A Life Incomplete
Nanak Singh
Translated from the Punjabi by Navdeep Suri

Mohanaswamy
Vasudhendra
Translated from the Kannada by Rashmi Terdal

The Music of Solitude
Krishna Sobti
Translated from the Hindi by Vasudha Dalmia

No Presents Please: Mumbai Stories
Jayant Kaikini
Translated from the Kannada by Tejaswini Niranjana

A Preface to Man
Subhash Chandran
Translated from the Malayalam by Fathima E.V.

The Secret Garland
Andal
Translated from the Tamil by Archana Venkatesan

Shala
Milind Bokil
Translated from the Marathi by Vikrant Pande

The Weary Generations
Abdullah Hussein
Translated from the Urdu by the author

Written in Tears
Arupa Patangia Kalita
Translated from the Assamese by Ranjita Biswas

HARPERPERENNIAL

Bhima: Lone Warrior
M.T. Vasudevan Nair
Translated from the Malayalam by Gita Krishnankutty

Chemmeen
Thakazhi Sivasankara Pillai
Translated from the Malayalam by Anita Nair

Ghachar Ghochar
Vivek Shanbhag
Translated from the Kannada by Srinath Perur

Hindutva or Hind Swaraj
U.R. Ananthamurthy
Translated from the Kannada by Keerti Ramachandra & Vivek Shanbhag

The Liberation of Sita
Volga
Translated from the Telugu by T. Vijay Kumar & C. Vijayasree

A Life Misspent
Suryakant Tripathi Nirala
Translated from the Hindi by Satti Khanna

The Sea Lies Ahead
Intizar Husain
Translated from the Urdu by Rakhshanda Jalil

Selected Poems
Joy Goswami
Translated from the Bengali by Sampurna Chattarji

Wild Animals Prohibited: Stories/Anti-stories
Subimal Misra
Translated from the Bengali by V. Ramaswamy

Wild Words: Four Tamil Poets
Malathi Maithri, Salma, Kutti Revathi and Sukirtharani
Translated from the Tamil by Lakshmi Holmström